COLD WAR
– 2395 –

NEF HOUSE PUBLISHING

ISBN: 978-1-948374-43-9 (paperback)

Cover by Thea Magerand

www.rcarnevale.com
www.nefhousepublishing.com

COLD WAR
– 2395 –

ROBERT CARNEVALE

NEF HOUSE PUBLISHING

CHAPTER 1

Wesley

Earth-003: District of Columbia, the White House

"A cure for the communist cold," the Americans had cheered, as though voting for Roseanne Faust and her archaic platform of Cold War fearmongering was something to be proud of. Sitting across from the unmanageable woman in question, my mood as gray as her wiry hair and the cloudy sky peering through the Oval Office's windows behind her, I think the American people got it wrong.

"There's no business left to discuss, Madam President."

"How long do you think you can avoid picking sides, Wesley? Even if the Russians haven't exhausted your limited usefulness yet, we can all see the end from here." She rises out of her chair in a fit of barely tempered rage. She's a touch more aggressive than I'd anticipated.

"Neutrality suits me quite well, thank you very much," I reply. "And wiping away a transaction that's all but set in stone would gravely harm my reputation as an unbiased busi-nessman." I let out a huff and prepare to stand.

"Ha. You know what would gravely harm you even more?" she asks, not giving me time to respond. "A Russian OSV-12 laser rifle. Nice suit, by the way." She pauses to take a sip of water, then sits down. Her brow furrows as she scowls at me.

"You've put me in a very tough position and show no signs of cracking," she says, scraping her nails against the Resolute desk's flawless resin finish. "I have one final offer."

Although I can't fathom what could possibly make her so interested in the Nebulus sector—a patch of barren, resource-less planets that have long been my least attractive piece of interstellar real estate—I also don't care. I just need to know how much she wants it, and her desperation is evident.

"I'm listening," I say, relaxing into my seat again.

"Wesley, in exchange for the entirety of the Nebulus sector, including but not limited to any sections already agreed upon by a Russian party, I am prepared to pay a bill of two hundred trillion dollars. Whatever that converts to in pounds."

"Pound sterling."

"Look, I'll pay it in teatime biscuits if that's what your prime minister wants. Point is, that's twice the original offer, a sum I can't increase any further without robbing our na-tional treasury."

"Music to my ears. Now, I'm almost prepared to—"

"Madam President," interrupts one of the two Secret Service agents who've been silently stationed at the back of the room. "We've detected a security breach."

Though the room is incredibly quiet, I can make out a distinct hiss. The agents each have a finger pressed firmly against their earpieces. Their eyes narrow as they receive audio feedback until, in unison, they dash toward us.

"Get back!" one yells, his next words muffled by a blast of white noise that drowns out all other sound in the room.

One of the agents loops a massive arm around my upper torso and whisks me out of my chair, as if I'm nothing more than a child under his control. He sidesteps the desk the other agent has just flipped over and tosses me to the ground behind it, scrunching his bulky frame in beside me. I pick myself up off all fours and crouch, my breath quickening. I try to make sense of what's happening. Within the timespan of a few unhealthily fast heartbeats, Faust and I are hunkered down behind her keeled-over presidential desk, agents peeking out on either side of us with weapons drawn.

The white noise doesn't let up, meaning I still can't hear a thing. To compensate, I abandon my self-preservation instincts and rise above the side of the desk, just enough to see what's going on at the other end of the room.

Puncturing the pristine white paint of the Oval Office's northern wall, a single bottle-cap-sized scorch mark appears. It begins moving, singeing the wall as it travels, making perfect right angles until it has formed the burnt outline of a door. The agent to my right grabs my neck and slams me down to the floor, yelling at me. The white noise is dissipating, and I can hear the tail end of his sentence.

". . . *your head down!*" he shouts, pistol drawn as he braces his recoil shoulder against the desk. It's quite good advice—a fact I come to realize when a massive detonation deafens the room again and sends burnt plaster hurling across the Oval Office with such force that pieces rocket overhead and smash against the windows behind us, coating us in dust and residue.

In a desperate attempt to bottleneck whatever lies waiting outside, the agents unload suppressive fire through the breach in the wall. As sound returns to the room in the form of nonstop gunfire, I wonder if we might be able to stave off the attack by simply waiting until backup arrives. It's a very thick desk, after all. But my hope disappears when I turn my head back toward the Oval's rear windows, where three glowing green eyes stare back at me.

On the other side of the glass, a figure clad in jet-black dragon skin armor and luminescent trifocal goggles finishes planting some sort of charge, then rappels upward as soon as they notice I'm watching. Before I can warn the preoccupied agents, the intruder detonates their explosive, swings through the shattering window panes, and plants bullets in both my protectors' skulls. Beside me, my last means of safety slump over, dead.

The rappelling assailant lands directly behind the last two of us alive, flanked by a second armored soldier who has followed them through the breached window. With their rifles aimed at us, they tell us not to move. Their English is broken, their accents unmistakably Eastern European, and I find myself regretting that I wasn't a little more amicable to Faust during our negotiations a few minutes ago.

Faust and I comply with the soldiers' demands and remain frozen as more intruders filter through the hole in the wall across from us. Seconds later, we're surrounded by a full squad of troops. They waste no time binding our wrists, gagging us, and mobilizing us.

We pass through the smoking hole in the office wall and are met by a marching party of other captured civilians. The soldiers shove us in line with them. Our hostage parade then begins its trek through the West Wing's halls.

We make it a few dozen meters before we're stopped in front of the press briefing room. I see remnants of a scene similar to the one I had witnessed firsthand just a few minutes ago: a smoldering hole in the wall and a lot of dead Secret Service agents and civilians. As far as I can tell, the only living occupant remaining is a downed staffer who looks critically injured. Her body is covered in burn marks, and her legs are crushed and pulpy, riddled with debris from the attack. The soldiers don't allow me time to vomit. They shove me forward, not happy with my wide-eyed, quivering-lipped dawdling. I get one last glimpse of that poor woman as a bullet is put through her head, shot by our escorts so our parade doesn't lose its pace.

For every act of horror along our thorough sweep of the White House, one question echoes inside my head: Where is the military, the police, or any other defense? So far, the only people who've given these intruders any resistance are a few stray Secret Service agents and a handful of stupid, or perhaps immeasurably brave, civilians. Oddly, the president herself isn't one of those individuals. It's not like I'm expecting her to spit the gag out of her mouth through sheer willpower, but still, seeing nothing more than her head hung low enrages me. She's taking the situation like a coward.

The moment I have that thought, I want to punch myself, as it's clear I'm no better. People are dying around me, and what am I doing? Watching and trying not to process it. The thought haunts me right up until our party is herded outside through the front doors of the White House. Awaiting us are three small, civilian-class shuttles, stationed right on the front lawn.

Though it's too little, too late, I finally hear them: the distant sounds of sirens wailing and people shouting. None of it matters, though; the troops are already corralling us aboard the shuttles. The first five of us in line, including myself and the president, are rushed up the boarding ramp of the closest craft, accompanied by four emotionless soldiers. They bark at us in Russian, but my body is on autopilot and I barely hear it. My head is turned, looking back at the civilians still stranded on the lawn. I watch them for as long as I can until the rising boarding ramp blocks out everything but the American flag waving despairingly atop a defiled White House, the last sight I see before I'm trapped in darkness.

Our shuttle's engines roar to life, and a soldier smashes something against the back of my head. Unable to fight the bells ringing inside my skull, I pass out, certain that death won't be far behind.

CHAPTER 2

Gourd

"**S**pace," they used to say. "The final frontier." They wondered what it would be like to drift lazily through the Milky Way, marveling at its vastness and the wonders it held. They were stupid. There's nothing out here but floating rocks and wasted time.

I wish I could travel back a few hundred years to tell people how shitty space is, because here I am, sitting in a tiny one-man fighter with a pilot's seat tighter than a damn toaster slot, waiting for something, *anything*, to happen. No supernovas, no meteor showers, no sudden appearances by the commies who kidnapped our president, nada. Speaking of which, when are those fellas gonna show up?

"Three civilian shuttles coming in from the northwest sector. Twenty cloaked signatures right behind them," Bravo Squad's Sergeant Toufexis announces, right on cue.

"Alpha Squad is good to go," Sergeant Barton replies as his Marines finalize their ambush formation right above us. Yankee Squad's Sergeant Marx and Delta Squad's Sergeant

McGregor follow suit, ordering their ships to assemble overhead.

Through the dome of my cockpit, I peer up at the United States Cosmo Marine fleet hovering in tactical formation. Against the backdrop of Earth-003's sun, our dozens of armored fighters' scaly silhouettes resemble a dragon—the kind getting ready to snack on some wily Reds.

"Remember, scalpel strike," Captain Grimm tells his sergeants while drifting his fighter into the middle of the fleet's formation. "Take out the escort ships, secure the civilian shuttles, and shut down the enemy. Give them no time for whatever contingency plans they have for Madam President."

While he preps the others for the first phase of attack, I glance at my ship's biometric scanner, which is tracking the president's unique exothermic heat signature. Little blips appear across the radar—a damn good sign. Madam President is close by.

"Ready . . ." Grimm says as time slows to a crawl around us.

Overhead, the full force of Romeo Company lies in wait. All fighters' thrusters are engaged, and every pilot's trigger finger is ready.

"Now!" Grimm barks as the Russians rocket into our intercept range.

McGregor's squad swoops in overhead, making it look like they're beelining for the shuttles. Since fighter-class craft can't utilize blaster weaponry while cloaking shields are engaged, Delta's ballsy divebomb scores them a response of twenty instantly uncloaked Russian ships, all clustered tightly around our trio of targets.

With their cloaking shields down, I get a better look at the opposition, and something ain't right. These Reds are moving faster than any other Russian fighters I've ever seen—hell, faster than *any* fighters I've ever seen. They're hitting parsecs-per-hour counts that shouldn't be possible.

The sergeants curse up a storm over open comms as they try to keep up with the lightning-fast enemy forces. I wanna jump in and help out, but I can't; I just have to sit here and wait while everyone else gets all the action. Alpha, Bravo, and Yankee charge after Delta to keep the heat on our foes, and even as our forces start taking hits, I don't get the word from my captain to intervene. Only once our guys have thoroughly distracted each and every Russkie craft does Captain Grimm finally give my partner and me the signal to begin phase two of the strike.

"Time to save the day and take all the credit," says First Lieutenant James Beecher, my lone Sierra squadmate and lifelong battle brother. Rescuing the president is a pretty tall order, and I'm glad as hell Beecher's the guy I get to share that responsibility with.

"Punch it," I shout, and Sierra Squad finally enters the game. My rear thrusters kick into gear and blast my fighter forward alongside Beecher's as we dive into the fray. I sink into my chair, absorbing the g-forces of rapid acceleration—it's the sort of rush that never gets old.

The scene in front of me is dense, at least by space-combat standards. I can just barely make out the three crimson shuttles behind the flurry of laser fire and cluster missile spray, but they're needles in a space-sized haystack. Around me, fellow Marines whip past at top speed, either tailing or being tailed by the commie bastards I'm proud to call my enemy.

The Russian fighters blur across my field of view so quickly I can barely keep track of their silver jet streams as they perform janky zero-g corkscrew spins, high yo-yos, and a whole load of other fancy horseshit I don't have time for.

"Something's seriously off about these ships, Gourd. I don't understand," Beecher shouts over comms as we get a closer look at the Reds' incredible speed, an ally below us narrowly avoiding a hostile fighter's ramming attempt.

"We don't have to understand 'em, we just have to fry 'em," I shout back. Now's not the time to get cold feet—now's the time to make our mamas proud.

I follow Beecher's craft as it shoots into the center of the conflict with laser rifles pounding, totaling any Russian ship dumb enough to set off my buddy's hair-trigger reflexes. Yankee, Bravo, Delta, and Alpha keep the Reds off our flanks, giving us a straight shot at our target. Beecher and I pivot left and right, alternating sides while I stay slightly above him for overhead coverage. Our pattern is good and we're in sync like two dancing beagles as we zero in on our target; the civilian shuttles get closer and closer with each passing second. Then the monkey wrench hits.

"Sierra Squad, do you read?" It's Alpha Squad's Sergeant Barton. He sounds worried.

"We read you. What's the matter?" Beecher responds.

"They're gaining on us—we've got to split up. Your six is going to be exposed for about fifteen seconds." Fifteen seconds is about twelve more than the Reds need to mow down a lone pair of unprotected fighters like ours. Not good.

"Jesus Christ. All right, do what you have to do," Beecher grumbles.

Just as we're about to dart backward to cover our own tails, my cockpit's monitor flashes red, displaying the text: "enemy lock in progress." Shit. I shoot my ship downward, abandoning Beecher as I try to shake off whoever has their sights aimed up my ass.

"Gourd, what's going on?" he shouts after my break from formation.

"They got a lock on me, man! Watch my six!"

"Our six, your six, my six, everyone's six! Fuck!" he responds as his fighter flies in the direction of my jet stream.

"Bogey spotted," Beecher tells me. "Going in for the shot . . ."

Seconds pass as my partner goes to work, but the preliminary lock warning on my display remains active.

"Jesus, Gourd, they're too fast!" he says, not used to being outmaneuvered by the Reds.

I feel his frustration; they're giving me a pretty good run for my money too.

I start whipping out the textbook tricks. I flat-scissor the enemy then corkscrew away, hastily changing my orientation in hopes of throwing off the fucker. For a split second, the lock breaks as I'm in a barrel roll, but it comes back immediately when I stop spinning. There goes that plan.

Out of time and ideas, I strain to think up a new trick in the seconds I have left. Thankfully, my thought process is interrupted by my comms light blinking to life. Beecher has a plan of his own in mind.

"Fly toward me and boost up before impact; I'll take your guy head on," Beecher says.

It's risky as hell—even if I don't accidentally kill him,

there's a good chance the Russian will. But at the rate the enemy's closing in, it's the best option I have.

I rip around until I'm on a collision course with Beecher. I burst up, down, and to the sides to make sure the Russian doesn't get in a cheap shot while Beecher and I set up the maneuver, my buddy now directly aligned with the nose of my ship.

I kick my four-ton fighter's underbelly thrusters into high-gear and blast upward with just seconds to spare. Now above Beecher, I tilt down to see the scene below with my own eyes, and it's perfect. Beecher nails the bogey head on, tearing our surprised foe to shreds with a volley of cluster missile shots. The enemy ship bursts over the front of Beecher's fighter in a shower of badass wreckage, bits and baubles of the smoldering opposition sliding off his spotless craft as he glides through the newly cleared line of sight.

"Whew!" he yells.

"That was insane," I shoot back.

"You bet! Now—"

Before he can finish, Alpha Squad's leader announces they've returned to help. Better late than never, I guess.

"All right, we're good now," Barton says. "Got you 'til the finish line, Sierras."

"Did you see that shit?" Beecher asks him.

"No, what ha—" Barton starts, but Beecher's disappointment is evident as he cuts the sergeant off.

"Never mind. Let's get the job done," he says.

I fall back into my left-right pivot pattern with him. The battle led by Yankee, Bravo, and Delta lights up our backsides as we drift away from the main pack and close in on the shuttles. For only twenty fighters, these Reds are putting up a hell of a fight.

Beecher hits me up on squad comms amidst our preparations for the final push.

"You good to go? We both seeing the president's exothermics on the left shuttle?" he asks as I work on unbuckling every restraint holding me down inside my tight little cockpit. Wish they'd make these things a little bigger for someone my size—ah, what am I saying. If it's good enough for my military, it's good enough for me.

"I'm good. And yeah, left," I respond, giving him the green light to give the Alphas the word.

"Barton," Beecher says. "Gourd and I are gonna pull up underneath them. You ready to drop the low-intensity EMP so we can get inside without any headaches?"

"I'm sending an officer to make the drop. The rest of us will cover you."

The trio of target shuttles blast ahead as Beecher, me, and our Alpha escort all dash to keep up. Slowly but surely, the leftmost shuttle's exterior airlock gets closer and closer until the crimson hull of that speedy bugger casts a shadow over our fighters. A few seconds more and we're directly underneath the target.

"All right, Alpha ranger, we're in position. Drop the EMP," Beecher orders.

I pull the switch by my seat that unfurls the EMP-diffusion cage around the interior of my cockpit so that when everything else goes dark I'll still have a suit that can browse the internet.

The lone Alpha pilot does as he's told. The blue brick exits his fighter, hurtles toward the shuttle's tail fin, and detonates, bringing both it and us offline. Our ships' thrusters die instantly, leaving us to coast on pure momentum.

With our fighters now useless tin cans speeding through space, I uncage myself and slide on my suit's helmet until its airtight seal locks. Immediately, I get a notification from my helmet's radio line. Beecher's trying to reach me via suit comms. In the silence of space, connect calls are the only option.

"Ready?" he asks, his voice echoing inside my helmet.

"As ever."

Knowing I can't initiate a standard cockpit dome ejection since the blast would push my fighter away from its perfect parallel with the shuttle, I instead rely on my suit's mechanical strength and punch a man-sized hole through the dome myself. A spray of shattered micrometeorite-proof glass hits me as I rocket my fist upward, though my suit's nanogel coating repels it without issue. I rise from the shattered cockpit, my armored knuckles spitting out the shards of glass they've just broken through and swallowed.

I float up into the gap between my fighter and the enemy's shuttle. Once I'm no longer touching my craft, I kick on my suit's rocket boots. Beecher executes the same strategy on his end and appears alongside me as we blast toward the shuttle above in unison.

We boost along until we're in a position to grip the edge of the exterior airlock panel, our anticipated point of entry. Beecher swings over to the left side of the panel while I bear-hug the right, our backs pressed against nothing but the emptiness of space. Our boots' magnets cling to the shuttle, securing us to our target and freeing us to proceed.

Since the lock's exterior manual override is closer to his side than mine, Beecher works a little magic with his hands and cracks that bad boy open, enabling us to slip inside. Once we've officially boarded the shuttle, we close the panel behind us so no stray space cats can get in. As expected, the EMP knocked the shuttle's primary antigravity systems offline, so we rely on our magnetic boots to keep us attached to the floor while we deal with the shuttle's second airlock. It's also equipped with a handy-dandy manual override. Since the EMP took down virtually all security measures, nothing stops us from opening the second panel just like the first. As we make our way through, we hear the shuttle's backup gravity systems hum to life.

Now past two panels, both of which have been safely re-sealed to prevent the vacuum of space from fucking up everyone in the shuttle who's not us, it's clear we've almost reached our target. Beecher takes a moment to scan the ceiling of the small room we occupy with his helmet. "Multiple emergency airlocks. Not electronic, so they're still in working order. Looks like they're set to deploy in response to changes in pressure and door integrity."

After glancing at the next doorway standing between us and our mission, Beecher and I look at each other.

"No override here," I say, cracking my knuckles. "We damage it even a little and those emergency panels come down. Zero risk. So let's slice the fucker open and be done with it." Between the two perfectly intact airlocks from our entry as well as the emergency ones, a little damage here won't affect the people on the other side. Speaking of which . . .

I look at the doorway blocking our entry to the main cabin

and scan it with my helmet. "I can't make out the president's exothermics with so many heat signatures fuzzing up visuals. There's a lot of action going on in there . . ."

Beecher scans the door as well. "Then we take our chances. The unmoving heat signatures must be hostages, probably including the president. Avoid those," he says, giving me the A-okay to make an entrance.

I shoot him a thumbs-up, and out from my suit's wrist mounts come the laser sabers. If open sesame ain't gonna do the trick, these flashy butter knives will—because one way or the other, we're gonna save the president trapped on the opposite side of that door.

CHAPTER 3

Wesley

When I wake up, I wish I hadn't. Good Lord, my head hurts. And what's that dreadful chafing sensation on my wrists—oh, I'm tied up. Wonderful.

A little ways away from me there's a fellow hostage whose dress shirt is stained with blood. There's a gash on his cheek. He looks every bit as afraid as I am, and I wish with all my might I could say something, anything, to ease his worries. Sadly, good intentions don't dissolve the thick rag in my mouth.

My other fellow captives look no better off. I, however, am uninjured since I didn't bother fighting. In retrospect, maybe it would have been nobler to have gone down swinging than live to be an expendable body for terrorists to use. It's strange that the president, who's restrained in fewer bonds than the rest of us, doesn't share my sentiment. She's not resisting in the slightest.

One of the soldiers piloting our craft barks something in Russian at his comrades. Even without the usual benefit of having a translator by my side, my elementary knowledge of the language acquired from years of business dealings allows me to understand two words: *get* and *her*. Are they no longer interested in hostages?

The two soldiers who've just been called to action march over and kneel beside Faust. They undo her bonds, wire by wire, until she's no longer on her knees and tied to the floor like the rest of us. Once she's standing, they remove her gag, slicing the cloth in half before ripping it out of her mouth. She coughs a little, then mutters something under her breath. In Russian.

She shoots a glare at the men who've just freed her as she follows them to the front of the shuttle. *My God*, I think. I lock eyes with the other hostages. The fear we share is briefly overshadowed by mortification. Then one of the Russians says something and tosses a gun into Faust's hands, causing my stomach to lurch.

She argues with the soldiers for a brief moment before forfeiting the debate and heading toward us. She can't be about to do what I think she's about to do. Can she?

For a second, she pauses her march, seeming to ponder that question herself. Uncertainty flashes in her eyes. She nervously grips the gun in her hand, her knuckles white as bone. Can she stomach being not only a traitor but a murderer? At first, it seems the answer is no. She's frozen in place, unwilling to budge. Then the Russian who gave her the gun adds his two pence. Whatever he says gets her moving again. The struggle in her eyes is gone, replaced by a hollow sadness.

"I'm sorry," she says to the first man in line, the one with the blood-soaked dress shirt. Before he can emit a single gut-tural protest through his gag, she points the gun directly at his forehead, shifts her gaze in the opposite direction, and pulls the trigger.

Unlike her, I don't have the ability to look away. The man's head jerks backward as the bullet drags it toward the shuttle's wall. When the deed is done, the interior plating behind him sparkles crimson and pink.

I seem to have a tougher stomach than the second person in line, because the girl who's one hostage away from me violently retches as much as she can manage within the tight confines of her restraints. The look of fear in her eyes is enough to make the president pause once more. Faust's moment of indecision means nothing, however. After a beat of silence, the president manages to rein in her conscience and resume business.

"I'm sorry."

With that, one more head rockets toward the shuttle wall, the blast of blood spraying far and wide enough to make contact with my face. It's the worst thing I've ever felt—the hot red liquid that was just giving life to that poor girl smearing across my cheek. It's about to get a lot worse, though. The president approaches the man directly next to me, the last hostage before my number is up.

Faust plants her feet firmly, shoulder-width apart, as she raises her pistol a third time. Her index finger squeezes the trigger, the gun recoils, and the bullet exits the chamber, racing directly toward another innocent person's skull.

It doesn't meet its mark.

Suddenly, our ship's interior lights die, and a

weightlessness overtakes everyone in the cabin, lifting the president and all four Russian soldiers off their feet. As for myself and the poor sod next to me, we float up a centimeter or two, but our wire restraints stop us from going anywhere worthwhile. The president, clearly confused, lets the gun slip out of her hand. The Russians are far less clumsy and quickly adapt to the loss of gravity. They speak to each other for a short while then bounce toward the cabin's exit. After listening to whatever's happening on the other side, they float back to their previous posts and begin bickering. Their voices are panicked. Meanwhile, the president tries to shimmy alongside the cabin walls to retrieve her gun, but it's drifted out of reach. No one but me seems to notice or care about a dull rumble sounding from beneath us, which I hope indicates backup life support and gravity systems kicking into gear; the last thing I need right now is to start turning blue or have the disgusting fluids lining the ship's walls floating toward me in zero-g.

Thankfully, not long after said liquids begin to swim through the air, they fall.

The president crashes to the floor, letting out a pained grunt as her face collides with the cold metal plates. She doesn't get up right away, and neither do the Russians. The two pilots who'd been hovering by the front windshield lie on the floor, dizzily rubbing their balaclava-covered heads, and the other pair of soldiers remain sprawled out next to the president. She doesn't seem to be doing so well, struggling to lift herself up off the floor. Before any of them can get back on their feet, a thudding noise—almost like heavy footsteps—makes its way toward us from the back of the ship. The sound stirs the president into action, prompting her to forego recovery as she crawls toward the pistol that's now on the other side of the shuttle.

More thuds echo from behind the cabin doorway, followed by what sounds like the sharp clinks of emergency airlock panels sliding into place to contain whatever's happening outside. Then there's a mysterious humming, accompanied by two white laser blades piercing through the top of the cabin door. The president's scuttle hastens as she claws at the pistol, gripping it by the time the searing hot lasers have cut through half of the door's outer frame just a few feet away. The incoming threat doesn't distract Faust—far from it. Without any hesitation she aims the pistol at the man next to me and pulls the trigger, blasting his skull wide open.

The lasers have almost finished cutting their rectangular hole as her sights turn to me. Pistol pointed, she's about to pull the trigger just as—WHAM—the door hatch, completely melted from its frame, comes rocketing forward, the bottom edge of it slamming into her and knocking the pistol out of her hand once more.

Even after hitting Faust, the hatch continues to hurtle forward, barreling into the first pair of Russians before thudding to a halt directly in front of the two pilots. They barely have time to reach for their rifles before my rescuers burst through the opening they've just created.

Two incredibly bulky, blue-armored individuals charge forward with pistols drawn, shoulders pressed against one another as they unload a pair of unbelievably synchronized shots, their bullets curving in midair to pierce the pilots' skulls.

One of these newly arrived warriors notices me amidst

the slushy, vile pool of liquids on the floor and leans down. He seems to acknowledge that I'm hardly a threat and, with nothing more than his blue-plated thumb, snaps all of my wire restraints in half.

"Next part might hurt a little," the man says, his real voice hidden behind his helmet's speech modifier. Then that same thumb slips up the backside of my neck, sliding between it and the knot of my cloth gag. Not giving me time to protest, he yanks forward, his motion precise but aggressive. The gag slams against the front of my mouth until the fabric tears and the cloth finally falls off. It lands on the floor, sliced clean in half, and I'm free from the last of my bondage.

I immediately start coughing and sputtering as I relearn how to operate my mouth, spit and a light spray of bile flying out in the interim. The armored man seems to understand and just looks toward his even bigger, bulkier comrade, who's busy putting bullets in both remaining Russians' heads. It's good to know that those bastards aren't coming back. But how are my rescuers going to handle—

As if on cue, her eyelids flick open. Before I can alert either of the two newcomers, Faust has the pistol in her hand for the third time in the past five minutes. I do the only thing I can think of and roll quickly to the left, directly behind the shin of the man who freed me. I tumble into the shadow of his glistening armor just in time for the bullet to hit him—Faust's shot narrowly missing me as the man's leg eats the blast instead. He marches toward her and slams the pistol out of her hand, not showing an inkling of pain in the process. Then I see the shiny coating on his suit's surface literally spit the flattened bullet back out. Who are these guys?

"Madam President, what the hell are you thinking?" my bullet-spitting human shield asks, standing over her.

Now's my chance. Through the gross soup of liquids still floating in my mouth, I manage to spit out the only words that matter.

"She's a traitor!" I shout, my voice hoarse and desperate. "S-she, she killed the others!"

The leaner blue-armored man plants his boot on top of the president's pistol and looks at his partner, then back down at Faust.

"Care to explain, Madam President?" he asks.

She has no case whatsoever, and she knows it. She stares at me coldly but neglects to protest, prompting the two soldiers to exchange glances.

"One second," the trim soldier says, standing between myself and the president. He presses a finger against his helmet—presumably sending a message to his superior—while his silent partner stays beside Faust, boxing her in.

"Captain, we're gonna need you in here, ASAP. Don't bring anyone else. We've got one hell of a code red on our hands." He then focuses his attention on me. "Tell us everything."

CHAPTER 4

Beecher

While Captain Grimm hears Wesley's story for the first time, I get to work on verifying his claims. I lean toward the deceased hostages, ordering my helmet to start scanning the bodies for links between their bullet wounds and the gun the president was holding when Gourd and I seized the shuttle. Within seconds the results are on my HUD, showing direct matches between the bullets' deformities and victims' impact wounds—not to mention fragments of the bullets are still detectable inside the deceased bodies. My helmet scans a bit more and reveals an extensive fingerprint trail detailing the president's movement patterns, which clears up any missing links in Wesley's narrative. I give Captain Grimm the signal that the civilian's version of events checks out.

"Hmph," Captain growls. "Lieutenants, search the piloting area for a black box. Any record of the ship's activity could put a lot of questions to rest about what NURS was up to."

"NURS?" Wesley inquires, unfamiliar with the name.

Grimm's referring to the brand-new terrorist cell we all

just suffered a firsthand run-in with, the organization that made their grand debut today by kidnapping the President of the United States.

"The Russian government made a statement hours ago, Wesley, while you were . . . in here. They're not taking responsibility. They claim these actions are the work of a separatist group calling themselves the New Union of the Red Star."

As Wesley processes, Grimm refocuses the conversation.

"Now, like I said, Lieutenants. Find that black box."

I head over to the flight navigation panels with Gourd. It's not like evidence pointing toward a sinister agenda isn't smothering us from every angle as it is; we're up to our knees in proof of NURS's capabilities, and now we have reason to suspect our own president is involved in their schemes. Still, if there's one person I prefer to have absolute, concrete proof against when I accuse them of treason, it's the president of my country. Fingers crossed these terrorists wanted to monitor employee performance and kept a recording device on board.

I step over the melted rectangle formerly known as the cabin door and walk past the two deceased pilots, working my way toward the navigation system. It looks like it's still offline from the EMP blast.

"Look at all these scribbles, man. Can't read a word," Gourd complains, unable to make sense of the Russian text plastered onto every touchpad, button, and storage unit around us.

"Forgetting something?" I tap my helmet to remind him of the built-in translator on these things.

"Oh, right," he says, futzing with his helmet until he finds the switch he's looking for.

Mine is already in the process of recalibrating itself to read the hieroglyphic-like symbols in front of me. My heads-up display—HUD, for short—clutters itself with a wall of rapidly blurring English characters, one by one becoming unidentifiable scribbles before changing back into the Russian text I'm having so much trouble reading. Then, in a single blink, every word appears in legible, sensible English. People joke that Americans only know one language, but hey, when you've got a super suit, who needs bilingualism?

Now that I've deciphered the text in front of me, I begin working my way from the top down, starting with the overhead storage bins hanging above the navigation module. The first set of containers is packed with foodstuffs: nourishment tablets, water canteens, and assorted vitamin pastes. These in-flight meal substitutes indicate a lengthy journey was planned. Hmm.

I make my way over to the next row of cases. In them I find spare balaclavas, rappelling wires, and a load of other irrelevant equipment. So many pieces of terrorist shit, so few black boxes.

"Anything yet?" I ask Gourd, hoping he's having better luck than I am. I look over my shoulder and see him on the ground, searching through the compartment beneath the flight module's mount.

"No dice, man," he replies.

It's to be expected, I guess. Terrorists aren't exactly known for encouraging audiovisual coverage of their covert operations.

After Gourd and I feel up every nook and cranny a black box could possibly be hiding in, we meet each other in the middle at the primary control panel.

"Well, shit," Gourd says, realizing we've both come up empty-handed.

"Least we can do is get this puppy powered up again. The EMP disruption has to have worn off by now." I hope we can at least salvage some useful intel from the ship's flight data once we get it back online. Gourd and I fire up the activation systems in an attempt to kickstart the bucket of Bolshevik bolts.

"What do you two think you're doing?" Captain barks, responding to the sudden buzz of energy flowing through the shuttle's previously lifeless husk.

"We're just getting systems back online, Cap—ooooh," I say, realizing our error.

"R Company, come in. I repeat, we are in control of the shuttle. Stand down," Grimm shouts into his helmet's audio receiver.

I guess we'll know they got the message if the shuttle doesn't get torn to shreds in the next few seconds.

. . .

. . . any moment now . . .

. . .

Phew.

The lights in the cabin blip to life as the shuttle's power comes back online and energy flows toward the navigation system. Panel by panel, touchpads and buttons begin to glow bright blue, regaining functionality and enabling Gourd and me to begin the next leg of our investigation—

Then it appears. In all its pixelated glory, a complete map

of the ship's navigation plan materializes across the screens in front of us. The EMP did more than just freeze the shuttle, it froze the system's mission data. Never thought I'd see the day when a misbehaving application made my day less stressful, but here it is.

At first, Gourd and I are ecstatic. After all, we got in—something we never thought would be so easy. Our moment of victory is short-lived, however, as the map in front of us raises a lot more questions than it answers.

"Wesley, you know that sector you were talking about? Nebulus, right?"

"Yes."

"Have you found something, Lieutenant?" Grimm interjects.

"It turns out that's where the shuttle was heading."

Silence enters the cabin as the four of us try to wrap our heads around the implications of the flight plan.

"But . . . how? Why? The president and I . . . just earlier today . . ." Wesley says, failing to piece together an explanation for his planetary real estate's involvement in the current quagmire.

"That ain't right," Gourd mumbles, looking down at his feet.

"Yes, something's off, and we're one step behind the enemy," Grimm says, his jaw tense and gaze steely. "Any comment, Madam President?" he asks, mistrust and cynicism radiating from his stoic figure as he turns to face her.

It's only now that I realize how silent she's been the whole time, having sequestered herself to her own little corner of the cabin.

"It's not . . . so obvious," she mumbles, unable to finish her sentence. Taking a pause, she rubs her temples vigorously, her head reddening in response to whatever unseen malady is afflicting her.

Honestly, if she's getting a migraine right now, I feel no sympathy. Thanks to her, we all have a major headache on our hands.

"So, she tries to buy the sector even though she's in bed with terrorists who are already going there? That makes no fucking sense," Gourd says, visibly agitated.

Captain Grimm turns back to the president. "That's not going to cut it. We move forward under my authority, unless you can explain yourself in your next sentence."

"I . . . can't," she responds, massaging her temples even more aggressively than before.

"Right. My authority it is, then."

That was cold, even by Captain's standards. Not wanting to get hung up on the social dynamics of our shuttle's un-happy occupants, I turn back to the navigation system to see if I can dig up anything else of value. I use both hands to blow up the minimized map of the shuttle's target coordinates, un-til it's full screen and displaying the entire flight plan. I see a path from our current location to the precise spot the shuttle is destined for.

The target coordinates of the flight plan are tagged as "E-203 K" in the computer. That specific location isn't actu-ally inside the Nebulus sector but sits directly on the border of it and another obscure outer-edge zone. I relay the new intel to my captain.

"Hmm. Anything else?" he inquires.

I do a quick search but can't find anything worthwhile. These info logs are light as hell on details, something I'm sure is intentional. Worse, it seems the EMP did end up doing a little damage; some of the files are corrupted and inaccessible. Ugh. All we've got is a glowing treasure map.

"Sorry, Captain, that's all there is. Still, a detailed outline of the exact route to the shuttle's mysterious destination isn't the worst find, yeah?"

"He's not wrong," Gourd adds casually, backing me up.

Out of the corner of my eye, I see the president nodding very subtly, unable to speak but trying to get some sort of message across.

"Not to mention it's clear they were planning to bring the president there," I say, in an effort to get Captain to name a plan of action.

"Obviously, there are wheels in motion here that none of us fully understand. I see no reason why I shouldn't just forward these coordinates to command so they can—"

"No," the president interrupts, cutting off Grimm. It looks like she's gotten whatever that headache was under control.

"And why not, Madam President?" Captain asks.

"They'll wipe out every ship command flings at them, with a single button press," she fires back, her voice weak but assertive.

"Hell of a claim."

"It's the truth, Captain. Everything you've seen here today was necessary," Faust says, essentially confirming that she aided and abetted terrorists. She massages her forehead and intermittently clenches her jaw as she speaks.

"If anything besides our shuttle . . . with me on it," she

continues, taking a second to scrunch her face together in pain before resuming her train of thought, "arrives anywhere near that station, it isn't getting in. And if we're gonna stop them, we need to move. Now."

Captain takes off his helmet to look her directly in the eyes, American to American.

"Tell me your name, Marine," she orders from her slumped position on the floor.

He hesitates for a moment before responding.

"Captain Gerard Grimm of Romeo Company."

"Captain Grimm, every allegation against me is true. Those poor souls on the other side of the cabin didn't do a damn thing to deserve . . ." She gestures woefully toward the shuttle's deceased Americans. "I only did it because if I didn't, the enemy would. And I'm not about to sit on the sidelines and watch my own people die by their hand. Not now, not ever."

On one hand, she killed innocent people. On the other, we have enough circumstantial evidence to make the case that she might be telling the truth about having some greater purpose. Right now, only the former is solid enough to hold up in court.

Wesley, over on my left, is fuming. "Or maybe you just didn't want witnesses!" he interjects, cutting off President Faust's solemn speech.

Her response is surprisingly tempered.

"I won't lie, Wesley, you were so close"—she gestures with a pinch of her fingers—"to becoming collateral. Hate me all you want. But as I said in that meeting earlier today and as I'll say now, I have a country to look out for. Witnesses or otherwise, we're all in the same boat now . . . and we need . . . to get . . . moving . . ." she drawls, her face tensing up as she presses her hands against her head, struggling to refocus on Grimm.

"You don't have to trust a thing I say . . . after today, Captain. I wouldn't blame you. But know that if there's . . . any chance of surviving what's coming our way . . . then our shuttle, and our shuttle alone, needs to reach that station . . ." She trails off, her fluttering eyelids slowing and muscles relaxing as she passes out on the floor.

"You know, I'm not a doctor, but something tells me she hasn't been normal these past few minutes," I remark, looking down at her unmoving body.

"Quiet, Lieutenant," Grimm orders, kneeling to examine her. Putting his helmet back on, he engages its medic mode protocol. It emits a blue grid of scanning rays that travel across the president's dormant frame from head to toe, searching for irregularities. As peculiar as her health appears, the scan's three sweeps reveal nothing out of the ordinary. I suppose she really could have had one hell of a migraine . . . but that explanation seems too convenient.

Grimm doesn't say a word. Instead, he starts to walk around the cabin. His pace is slow and indecisive, like he's not entirely confident in where he's going or what he's doing. I've never seen him so uncertain . . . it's a little unsettling.

He moves to the area Gourd and I were inspecting minutes ago and checks the overhead bins, stopping at the one holding food supplies. After counting its contents, he roams over to our post by the navigation system.

"Did you notice a tracking signal, men?"

We shake our heads in response. If there was one, it wasn't readily visible. Grimm doesn't seem to take our word for it, however, and moves behind us to inspect the system himself. Ignoring most of the software displays, he ventures a hand toward the back of the control panel emulator, the black-cased hardware that makes up most of the piloting module's physical size. He fishes around back there for a few seconds before freezing, then forcefully yanks at something entirely out of our view. After a bit more fidgeting, I hear a snap, and he reveals a small light switch scrunched between his blue-plated fingers, its wires completely torn and glass bulb shattered.

"No buzz, no light . . . it wasn't live. That EMP knocked the shuttle off the grid," Captain says, formulating an idea he's yet to share with the rest of our group. His pace slows as he moves back to his starting position, the region of the cabin from where he can fully see and evaluate everyone.

"Do we trust our brothers and sisters to protect our country, men?" Grimm asks. Seems like the wrong time for a trust-fall exercise, but I'll play along.

"Yes, sir," Gourd and I say.

"And are we willing to give our lives in the line of duty?"

"Yes, sir," we say again. Can't really answer no to that question and still have our job, after all.

"Then, if there's even the slightest chance she's telling the truth, is it not worth following? If it's a lie, our fellow Marines will continue to guard and protect the home front. If it's the truth . . . well, is it not our sworn duty to stop the threat or die trying?"

Always the hero, Captain Grimm.

"Beecher, Gourd, and you too, Wesley, listen closely. What I'm about to propose will cross boundaries, most of which our lives may not recover from if we move forward. If you want out, now's the time. We can pass the president's warning to the higher-ups authorized to make these sorts of decisions. All those in favor, say aye."

The room falls silent as Gourd and I give our mute consent to join Captain on whatever he's planning. Then there's Wesley. I look at the blood-soaked, vomit-coated British dandy and I just can't picture him agreeing to whatever the captain's about to propose. He's not the kind of guy built for the chaos of war. He's a suit—the last person I'd expect to sign on for a military op. When I look at him appearing to contemplate the decision seriously, I assume he's just posturing to save face.

Then he says the magic words: "Fuck it, I'm in."

Maybe I should just stop being surprised by things. Wesley's declaration is practically the fifteenth thing to happen to me today that's completely unprecedented.

"Wesley, I've never led a civilian into uncharted enemy territory before, and the mission at hand won't afford any training wheels. You're choosing to come entirely of your own discretion and at your own risk. Are you sure you want in?"

"No, but after what I just went through . . ." He pauses, searching for the right words to describe the emotions bubbling up inside of him. "Hell, there's no way I could opt out and not live to regret it."

I'm glad he feels compelled to help save the free world. It's either that, or he figured that by declining to join us after

seeing what he's seen, he'd be detained by the US government for many months or years, if not the rest of his life.

Regardless of motivation, he's made his choice. Grimm
gives him a pat on the back and a nod of affirmation before
tilting both himself and the new recruit toward Gourd and
me, marking the start of today's second mission briefing.

"It's settled, then. These are your squadmates, First
Lieutenants James Beecher and Thomas Gourd. And as
you've heard, I'm the captain," he says, once again taking off
his helmet. He props it against his hip while extending his
right arm for a handshake. "Gerard Grimm."

Wesley timidly stretches out his arm to meet the handshake. "Wesley Clarke, sir."

"Right, well, one of these two"—he takes a second to gesture toward us—"or myself can give you the abridged version
of how to handle a gun while we're in transit, in case you're
not already acquainted."

Based on the uneasy look Wesley gives in response, I assume he's not, in fact, acquainted with gun usage.

"And we'll be in transit for a while if the station really is
on the fringe of the Nebulus sector. Here's how I see it, men.
Based on what the control module is reading, the shuttle's
cloaking system is back online and fully operational. Plus, the
Russians stocked rations in here to feed a group of at least ten
people. There are five of us, meaning we should be fine getting there and, God willing, getting back. And regarding . . ."
He trails off for a moment as we all look down at the unconscious leader of the free world, mixed emotions clouding the
space between us. "Well, there's only one option."

He breaks away from the briefing to speak into his

comms, lifting the mouthpiece of his helmet toward his lips. "R Company, we've failed. The president didn't make it."

Both Gourd and I take our helmets off to make sure we're seeing and hearing things properly. All our eyes, Wesley's included, grow wide as we hear the captain openly lie about the status of the single most important life in our country. Gourd in particular looks like he just heard that his sister defected to the New Soviet Union. After all, sure, he and I have stretched the rules in the past, but we always reel it in when a mission gets too dicey. Grimm, though? We've never seen him go against the grain. My partner and I stand slack-jawed, staring blankly at the man we thought we understood, as the responses of our fellow Marines flood in through our helmets' speakers, their voices filled with confusion and anger. But the captain doesn't stop there.

"Furthermore," the captain continues, "we've triggered some kind of fail-safe. Our shuttle's cabin has released an unidentified toxin, the likes of which my two lieutenants and I are trapped in. Our ACA suits' breathing filters are minimizing the impact for now, but I'm requesting immediate permission from command to take the shuttle to the nearest biohazard-containment-ready medical station."

Our astonishment increases exponentially as the lie grows larger with every word our captain speaks.

"No, we do not have time for a HAZMAT evacuation and on-site evaluation; we could be dead by the time the cruiser gets here. Those of you in Alpha Squad with ACAs equipped, have you secured the other two shuttles?" There's a pause. "Good, then retrieve your onboard repair kits and patch up our ship's jammed right-side thrusters. That's an order."

After the command is issued, we wait in absolute silence for Alpha Squad to start their work on the shuttle. Wesley slips out of view of the main cockpit windshield while Gourd and I move the president to the opposite side of the cabin so she's just as hidden as our new British ally. Captain Grimm takes the liberty of manning the control panels and killing the lights to further occlude the already muddled view of the ship's interior. All of our helmets are back on, leaving no indication that we've been speaking freely without them for the past twenty minutes.

A massive cloud of tension hangs over each of us. It's only a matter of time until we see our allies outside the window— brave peers who, thanks to us, fully believe they've failed their country. I can't imagine being on the other side of the situation right now. Luckily, I don't have to. Before I overthink our plan to the point of doubting it, the first tremor from up above arrives.

The shuttle gently rocks back and forth as Alpha Squad descends upon us, working to repair the damage we inadvertently inflicted while trying to subdue the craft. We can't see our allies, but their presence is felt when a shower of sparks cascades over the cockpit windshield while we wait for the shuttle's return to full functionality. Bouts of motion rumble through the cabin, shaking us as the work progresses, our shared silence growing more unnerving with every passing second. For the first time in a very, very long time, I don't have the slightest idea what Gourd is thinking.

We all clench up as a shadowy figure blocks out what little light the stars were providing us, but it turns out to be nothing more than an Alpha. Now directly in front of the windshield, he gives us a thumbs-up, communicating that the work is done. Captain, Gourd, and I all give him a salute of gratitude, possibly the last one ever. The weight of that realization grows heavier and heavier by the second. And it doesn't help when that lone Alpha salutes back at us. It only reminds me that we're liars and he, along with the rest of R Company, are unwitting bystanders caught up in something bigger than any of us know. I begin to understand what the president may have been getting at with all the "higher authority and priority" chatter. The greater good is tough shit, if that really is what we're about to go chasing after.

The Alpha drifts out of sight, allowing starlight to pour back into our shuttle's interior. The distant celestial objects, beacons of brightness against our shrouded and clouded walls, give us the cue that it's time to depart.

Captain Grimm reports into his helmet mic that Sierra Squad is going to start making its way toward the nearest biohazard containment bay, located on the other side of Earth-003. Sergeant Barton replies that an escort unit of Alpha fighters will accompany us to ensure safe travel and our personal fighters will be returned to R Company's orbital cruiser. To not attract suspicion, Grimm complies. He then turns to Gourd and me, gesturing that we should man the dual piloting station. We do as we're told and march over to the seats, sitting stiffly in the chairs formerly occupied by the dead men lying on the floor behind us.

"Alphas will be on our sides the whole way, men. I'll give the signal when we're clear to cloak and hit hyperspeed."

I suppress a pained sigh and nod, gripping my flight stick as Gourd gets situated in front of the thruster controls. Left hand on the stick and right on the coordinate panels, I give the verbal confirmation that I'm set. Gourd does the same, and Captain gives us the green to begin our steady chug. The shadows of two escort fighters chip away at our windshield's glow, and I think one last thought about what we're about to leave behind.

We press forward in a standard flight pattern for the first couple of miles, until we're far enough away from the rest of R Company to have a chance at slipping away undetected.

"Beecher, decrease acceleration by half a notch," Captain orders. It's just enough of a decrease to get the escorts ahead of us so we're out of their immediate peripheral vision, and minute enough of a change that they won't notice it.

I slow us down ever so slightly, setting a pace we maintain until we see the frames of the Alpha fighters come into view ahead of us.

"Activate cloak," Captain continues.

Gourd punches in the command, and after a few seconds the system's cloaking indicator turns green, giving us the all-clear. Having only a few seconds before the two escorts realize we're off the grid, I tilt the shuttle ninety degrees so we're in a straight shot for alignment with the original flight path coordinates.

It's time for the final command—the one that'll brand us deserters. Three Marines gone AWOL. The final straw to break the military camel's back.

"Enter hyperspeed."

The thrusters hit full acceleration as the shuttle prepares itself for our forward jump, taking just enough time to rev up that we start to hear worried chatter from our Alpha escorts' comms. I close my eyes, knowing we're one jump away from total abandonment—no help to come and rescue us from whatever lies ahead.

Captain Grimm shares the sober moment with us, slowly taking off his helmet. After a deep breath, he presses his helmet mic's speaker, muting the voices of our allies. I refocus my attention on the infinite sea of open space ahead, still feeling the captain's guiding presence behind me, along with Gourd's unease, and newcomer Wesley's respectful silence somewhere in the back of the cabin.

The stars blur around us as our small crew silently signs away the last chance we have of scrapping our plan. Against our better judgment, we're now four men who've decided to take the fate of the country into our own hands.

CHAPTER 5

Wesley

Did I make the right decision? Is life actually about more than money, or is that just what I told myself when I was hopped up on adrenaline and hastily decided to join three Marines' interstellar goose chase? After all, money is always good, always impartial. I knew that fact earlier today. How could I forget it so quickly? Money would never kill me. Whatever these men are hunting, however, most certainly will. And lest I forget . . .

I glance across the floor at President Faust, who lies unconscious and exposed. Who is she to call me collateral? Conniving bitch. If the captain's made her dead on the record, I don't see much reason to keep her around. However, I doubt the Americans will lay a finger on her. *Sigh.* At least she won't be getting her hands on a gun again.

It looks like I'll be getting one, though. When I stop staring at my feet and lift my head, I'm greeted by the cold, blue-eyed gaze of the captain. His hand is outstretched, gripping a rifle barrel.

"The lieutenants are having a harder time than expected

manually piloting our damaged shuttle through the debris fields that've forced us to exit hyperspeed, so I'll be the one to give you the run-through."

"Yes, sir." The nod I give him is robotic, betraying the forced confidence on my face.

"Hold it."

I take it from him and hold it just like I would a rifle back on the range, with the butt tucked against my right shoulder as my left hand braces the under-barrel.

"Not bad. You ever used holosights before?"

Holosights? Wait, what kind of rifle am I holding, exactly? I look down at the hefty firearm and realize I'm not in possession of just any rifle—I'm in possession of one torn from the cold, dead grip of a terrorist's hand. I try to maintain my composure as much as possible, but even so, my knees lock up and a lump forms in my throat.

"Wesley, deep breaths. That man had his chance to use it effectively. It's a tool. Nothing more," he says, helping steady a slight jitter I've acquired over the past few seconds. "Now, have you ever used one of these kinds of sights before?"

"No, sir."

"Not a big deal. See those notches scaling up and down the side rails? They'll automatically track whoever you're aiming at and guide your shot. No work on your part besides pointing and squeezing."

I relax as he makes it abundantly clear I have nothing to worry about, and after a few more tips and pointers—how to reload, how to use the bipod—he's got me shaped up to be a civilian with a fighting chance. It's a hell of an accomplishment, given who we are likely to be going up against. But Captain still has one more lesson in store.

"I saw the way you looked at her, Wesley. I know what you're thinking, and I don't blame you." He pauses to read my face, his gaze fixing on my scowl, and continues anyway. "She's bound to wake up at some point. And when she does, we'll have to talk to her. No matter what she says, I need you to promise me you won't lay a hand on her."

I can't hide the hungry look in my eyes. He speeds up his speech, denying me a chance to propose that we dump Faust's body into space to reduce the clutter inside the shuttle.

"We're just pawns until we have a better understanding of what's going on. Until then, we need her. She's battered and bruised enough, and she's the only thing we have that'll get you a shot at those Russians. So, do I have a promise?"

Hmph.

"Yes, sir." My words sound every bit as flat and hollow as they feel leaving my lips. It's not like I'm in a position to refuse him, anyway.

"Good, and I'll promise you something in return. If she so much as eyeballs a gun in your vicinity, I'll stop anything before it begins."

With his somewhat reassuring declaration, the captain gets any remaining tensions down to a minimum, paving the way for casual chatter between him, Lieutenant Beecher, and myself. The big one on the left . . . Gourd? . . . hardly says a word, but what do I know. Maybe he's the strong, silent type. In any case, all is well and good on our journey. Until a groan comes from the back of the cabin.

Faust picks herself up off the ground and, realizing she's

in no state to move around, quickly grabs hold of the over-head railing behind her, clutching it with a grip that makes her wrist veins pop out. The woman's frailty doesn't seem to mitigate her ability to make noise.

"What are all these bodies still doing here? If we get pulled over by a border transport at the edge—actually, where are we right now?" She slowly shimmies herself toward the lieu-tenants, still clutching the railing. The captain watches her from across the cabin with a calm demeanor and, more tell-ingly, a hand on his holster.

She finally reaches the cockpit and braces herself on the back of the two pilot seats, leaning in between Lieutenants Beecher and Gourd to monitor flight progress.

"No, no, no. Captain, this won't do."

"What won't do?" he responds, irritated.

"These bodies have to go, stat. And we can't take the main entry port. We're infiltrating, not knocking on the front door," she grouses. "I need to adjust us so we're not DOA—"

"Hold it right there," Captain says, his command freezing Faust in place.

She swivels her head just enough to make eye contact with him.

"You'll do no such thing without my authority," he continues.

"Captain, there are two ways we go about getting inside: Main entrance, they're onto us in seconds and we're fried. Service entrance, there's a good chance we make it inside without a scratch."

"Fry us with what? Nothing's penetrating our armor—" Beecher interjects, only to be swatted down by Faust.

"Ha! You think you're wearing that inside? Do you know what's in there? Of course you don't. You'll all be squashed blueberries on top of our English muffin here," she spits with a glance in my direction, "unless we do a little roleplay."

"Get to the point, Madam President," the captain says, hesitating before adding a "please."

"You all are going to ditch those suits. Toss them out the emergency airlocks. We can't have anything setting off alarms."

"Or we could toss you out," I interrupt. She wants these men to ditch the one tool that'll give us a fighting shot? She's lost the plot. The smell of treachery is strong, and it's growing ever more rancid by the second.

"Oh, Top Gun Wesley's toting a big boy blaster now? I'm on your side, Wes."

"What side *is* that exactly, Roseanne?"

"The side of the survivor. And that goes for all of you," she says. "We're all in grave danger. The least you can do is help me minimize it."

Lieutenant Beecher looks at her, then back to the captain, who also has his eyes locked on Roseanne. Lieutenant Gourd is staring straight ahead, not saying anything. That still leaves three of us and one of her. Every word she says is just another nail in her cof—

"Okay," the captain says, giving in to her suggestions. *What is he thinking?*

"Captain Grimm, if I may—"

"Yeah, Captain, I—"

But, in sequence, Grimm silences both Beecher and me, signaling there will be no debate.

"What do you have in mind," he asks the president.

"You four are going to need to fit yourselves into the Russians' suits, then dump the dead bodies and your armor out the back. Tracker pistols, all of it. If it isn't Russian, it isn't staying."

Repulsed doesn't even begin to explain my reaction.

"You heard her, men. No asteroids left in sight, so set us on cruise control and drop the suits."

Expecting protest, I'm left with nothing but disappointment when the mighty blue armor that saved us all just a few hours ago unlocks from the bodies of my squadmates, plate after plate falling to the ground in a cacophony of clinks and clanks until the Marines' uniform wetsuits are fully exposed. Now, without their helmets, I get a clear look at their moods. Beecher is somewhere between bemused and fuming, while Gourd, Christ, I don't know where he is. Out to lunch would be the best description.

"Gourd, toss these things," Captain orders.

Without question, the giant grabs a heap of armor and marches toward the emergency airlocks, disappearing behind the cabin's entrance frame. Grimm and Beecher drag the two bodies from the piloting area and clump them in a corner alongside the other pair of dead Russians. After pilfering one of the enemy corpse's clothing, the captain turns to Faust.

"Want to give us some assurance things won't get uglier?"

"Tentatively speaking, it only gets better from here," she responds.

The next five minutes of my life are among the most uncomfortable I've ever endured, which is quite a statement coming from a chap still fresh off choking on a gag and struggling against wire restraints. Picking up one man from the pile, I slowly remove his face mask, only to realize the top half of it is still drenched in blood.

"Um . . ." I say, bringing attention to the issue with our disguises.

"There are spares in the upper right-hand drawers," Beecher grumbles as he works to pull the shirt off his selected man.

I guess there's really no getting out of president's . . . er, captain's . . . orders. I discard the soiled face mask, then focus on getting my soldier's armor off his body and onto mine. The first task, removing his ammo belt, is easiest. From there, things get stickier as I have to deal with the direct-contact clothing. I creep my fingers inside the hem of his suit's top, planning to pull it up and over. Two things complicate my objective: the shaking of my hands as they brush against a dead man's skin, and the fact that his clothing is oddly clingy. Since I refuse to ask for help in such a grotesque matter, I rummage around the bulky Russian's deceased carcass for a bit until I find and loosen the fasteners on his shoulder braces, freeing up his dragon skin. From there, it's a simple matter of removing the man's undershirt and pants.

I reduce the dead man to nothing but his briefs so he can join his allies in post-mortem embarrassment, while Beecher, Gourd, and Captain Grimm finish their clothing swaps. With no American super armor left on the ship, I can only hope the captain knows what he's doing.

I turn off my brain as I equip the last few pieces of my new Russian clothing, finishing with a loose, novice-grade fastening of the dragon skin before I sling its accompanying ammo belt over my shoulder. Hopefully the pouched extra magazines aren't needed, but if they are, my cohorts and I will have them draped across our chests.

"Good, now the bodies. Let's get these things out of here. Wesley, you can sit it out," Grimm graciously orders, leaving me to watch in horror as my previous captors and fellow hostages are shipped out of the shuttle through the series of airlocks keeping us safe from the cold vacuum of space. *To think . . . that could've been me.*

After disposal of the bodies and all remaining spare clothing, Beecher comes back into the cabin and tosses us each a fresh new balaclava.

"And one for you . . . and for you. Gourd, hopefully that fits you all right. It's the biggest size in the box."

Gourd puts it on and gives a thumbs-up.

"Now, let's get that flight path adjusted. There's an off-grid route around that moon next to the target coordinates, if we approach from the side." The president then takes the liberty of tampering with the flight control system. It looks like she also accelerates the shuttle's speed while she's there.

Beecher marches back to the piloting area and moves her aside, looking back at Grimm to see if he should restore the previous route. The captain shakes his head, keeping in line with his current slew of leadership-relinquishing decisions.

"All right. Flight path's adjusted and our ETA's accelerated. If my time estimates are correct, that'll give you all a front row seat to the main attraction, gentlemen, without any of the logistical concerns. Now, Captain, is there any food left aboard?"

"There are tablets and water canteens up front. Go light, we're pacing ourselves."

"A good idea."

She's put a gun to my head, ordered her own men to sacrifice their best armor, has all of us wearing dead men's clothing, rearranged our flight path, and now all she can think about is food. How can she even have an appetite right now? We've been flying for over half a day and I haven't had even a passing desire for much more than a sip of water.

. . . Speaking of appetites, how did she know there was food on board? She was unconscious when the captain did his inventory, and the Russians certainly didn't offer her in-flight refreshments during our initial takeoff.

I don't care if the president gets her way with Grimm— and if his two men choose to follow her orders by proxy, so be it. Over the past few hours, I've developed a new personal maxim for what to do when dealing with Roseanne Faust: keep both eyes open.

CHAPTER 6

Beecher

O h. My. God. I get it, it's been a good twenty-something hours of flight and people are tired. Hell, exhausted even. All perfectly understandable. But why does Wesley have to snore so loudly? Even if space wasn't muting the sound of our thrusters, I'm pretty sure that guy would.

And the president, well, shit. She's asleep too, though I still don't know if I can trust her, eyes closed or not. For instance, the flight path we're on: I'm about a minute from announcing to everyone that we're here and it's wake-up time, but looking outside, "here" isn't much of anything. The station we're aiming for is either deceptively well-hidden or it's a trap. Given Faust's track record today, the latter doesn't seem unlikely. I hope Grimm knows what he's doing listening to her.

Actually, what's Grimm's deal? He hasn't spoken a word in hours. It's not like he's asleep, I know that much. Looking back, I see him quietly chewing on a vitamin-paste wafer, thinking. I hope he's using his time to hash out a justifiable rationale for his recent decisions. Not that he's obligated to explain himself to us or anything. I'd just appreciate it if he did.

And speaking of people who need to do a bit more talking, what's going on with Gourd? Big guy hasn't made a peep for . . . well, it's been a while. In fact, I don't think he's said a word since we ditched R Company. We're all a little frazzled given the circumstances, but almost an entire day without a single word? The only time I can remember him even moving his mouth was to munch on some tablets a few hours ago.

I think I'll try to make contact with him while it's still quiet in here. We're far outside the sector, after all. We've got a bit of time.

"Hey, man," I say, turning toward him after a few seconds of no response.

He continues to stare blankly ahead. I give him a tap on the shoulder. He jumps a little, snapping out of his robot-like trance. Then he looks at me.

"You feeling okay?" I ask.

"Fine."

That's all I get, one word. And coming from his mouth right now, it doesn't even sound like one. Words are meant to convey emotions, yet his single-syllable response is empty. It's forced out of him, like it just came off an assembly line and was shipped via expedited mail to shut me up as quickly and efficiently as possible.

Whatever's bothering him isn't impairing his ability to do his job, so Captain won't care. But Gourd's more than a battle-hardened ogre; he's my best friend. I have to try to get through to him and see what's grinding the gears under his hood.

"Man, if you're just saying that to get me to piss off, you can be straight about it."

"Don't worry about me. I can shoot a gun and fly a ship. I'm good."

Hardly, I think, resisting the urge to roll my eyes. "I ain't buying that for two seconds, chief. Tell Papa Beecher what's wrong."

"Piss off."

"I'd be glad to, after you let me help you out."

"There's nothing to help. Now *piss off*."

Sounds like someone's in a salty mood. What a shame on such a fine cosmic afternoon. What's gotten into him? It's not like I even pushed hard. And no one's given him any shit at all inside our shuttle, so I can't imagine anyone else being the issue. I wish he'd communicate. No one solves their problems by being distant. At least, I know Gourd doesn't.

"One last chance to chat it out before I wake up everyone."

"No."

All right, have it your way, pal. Can't help someone who's not in the mood to help himself.

"Rise 'n shine, everyone. We're crossing over the Nebulus sector border in three . . . two . . . one."

The rest of the crew slowly returns to the land of the living. Wesley stretches his arms, letting out a big yawn to signal he's alive and well. The president's already transformed from sleeping, docile old woman to treacherous commander in chief. Captain's awake and alert. Gourd's still quiet and pissed.

"So we came all the way here for what, exactly? What I'm seeing doesn't seem worth freaking out over," I say, looking out at the great big nothingness currently in front of the cockpit window.

Wesley comes over to the piloting area to tour guide for us and make sure the map is telling the truth. "That's exactly what I've been saying: it's nothing. Nothing as far as the eye can see, only broken up by some of the most useless planet clusters and dwarf moons we've ever discovered. Why all the fuss over the place, I can't imagine."

"You won't have to, Wes," the president chimes in, joining us in the cockpit. "Give it a few minutes. And Lieutenants, dial up our speed a notch. By my calculations, the show's about to start."

We do as we're told since Captain doesn't intervene.

"More surprises, I assume?" Wesley asks.

"If you want to call them that," she responds coolly.

The cockpit is claustrophobic as is; doubling the number of conscious hotheads in it might not have been a good idea.

"Why the hell can't you just tell us what's coming instead of playing games, *Madam President?*" Wesley spits, his venom not helping the overall mood in the slightest.

"Because I want us all to keep calm heads. The minute I tell you there's a wasp on the window, you're liable to flip out, Wes."

"I'd have a calm head if you'd just tell us what we're up against!"

"Does it matter? Whatever I tell you, it's going be something you're particularly unprepared for. You're out of your depth here."

"At least I have the guts to stand up for what's right in the face of stiff odds. Unlike you, you despicable harpy—"

The brutal slap of an angry president's palm against a churlish Brit's cheek echoes throughout the cabin.

My head swivels toward the drama. Wesley takes a second to recover—his cheek turning scarlet. The president's eyes narrow, her laser-like gaze scornful and unforgiving. It looks like Wesley believes in equality of outcomes, though, because before she can react, his hand is up in the air and ready to come slamming down for a knockout-grade backhand. It goes soaring toward her, his rebound slap nearly making contact with its target until a large gloved hand stops it no more than an inch from the president's face.

"Wesley," Captain barks, still holding the Brit's wrist in place. Even though Grimm's grip must be crushing Wesley, that doesn't stop the civvy from standing his ground.

"What? I signed on to follow you, not her. And yet she might as well be the captain! She killed her own subordinates before you got here. What makes you think you're any different? She's taken your armor, pointed us toward a trap, and you want me to calm down?"

To be honest, I'm with Wesley. What say you, Captain?

"It's complicated—"

"And another thing!" Wesley says, doing the unthinkable by cutting off Grimm. "How did she know we had food on board, huh? She wasn't awake for that. She couldn't know."

"You don't think the Russians would pack something for a long journey?"

Wesley has no retort. Captain continues, now that he's found a chink in our new recruit's argument.

"Stop stirring the pot. And Beecher, why're you just staring like an idiot? Help out here."

Why's he have to bring me into the mix?

"With all due respect, Captain, you haven't given us a whole lot to go on, and the trend of taking orders from"—I tilt my head in the president's direction—"is unsettling, to say the least."

Grimm's face grows . . . grimmer. The man's early crow's-feet crease in frustration as he narrows his eyes to give me the what's what.

"You've followed my lead all the way here and now you think there's something off? Don't complain about getting wet when you're ten feet under, Lieutenant!" he roars.

"I want assurance! A fucking statement, or something," I shout back, surprising myself.

"You want a statement?" He releases Wesley's hand. "Here's a fucking statement. There's something bigger than us going on right now, and God help me, I have and will continue to do my best to keep you three alive. Everyone aboard shares the same goals right now. Got it?" he says, eliciting huffs from the president and Wesley for very different reasons.

To be frank, I'm not really happy with the response either, but it does soften my aggressive edge.

"All right, now let's everybody just calm the hell down," Captain finishes, signaling that the fight is adjourned.

Considering we were all on the verge of slapping each other sore a few moments ago, any degree calmer than that won't be hard to achieve. There's still a lot of hot air circulating, but it could be worse.

It's only when I turn back around that I realize "worse" can take some surprising forms. I'm not faced with some massive

Russian inspection frigate or swarm of hornet drones. No, the thing I'm faced with is Gourd breaking down. He has his hands around his neck and looks a little too red in the head for comfort. Jesus, he can't breathe.

I burst out of my seat and shove my hands into the nearby food bin, grabbing a water canteen and ripping off its cap. I whip around to Gourd's seat, place one hand against the back of his neck, and guide the canteen toward his mouth with the other.

Gourd's giant paws swing for the water and yank it out of my grip, eager to clear up whatever blocked airway is threatening to asphyxiate him.

After taking a great many sips, he coughs up some of the water, spraying the backwash over the floor beneath his seat. I'm not worried about Gourd's esophageal waterfall, though. Of all the liquids sloshing around the shuttle's interior over the past day, a bit of diluted saliva is the least of our worries.

As he coughs and sputters, head hung low toward the floor, I see the rest of our motley crew has decided to back off. From a distance, Wesley pipes up.

"Is there any way I can—"

"No, I got it," I respond. Once my guy is done hacking up every last drop of H_2O I forced into him, I get to work.

"What the hell is going on with you, man?" I whisper.

"Everything . . . too much . . ." he responds, gibberish filling up the spaces between his heavy breaths as he vacates his seat.

Captain takes the piloting reins alongside Faust, leaving me to handle Gourd. As much as I don't like the idea of Faust being in charge of the shuttle, I still trust Grimm to keep her in check. Plus, Wesley will be there. Feeling cleared to do so, I prop one of Gourd's massive arms around my shoulder and help guide the giant to the back of the shuttle where we sit on the cabin's elevated seats, away from the wish-wash of liquids circulating below. I release him, and his hulking arm slips over the back of my head and into his lap. He sits with his head down and spine slouched.

"All right, well, we made a scene, so if that's what you're afraid of, it's over."

"Shit. Man, I—I dunno, okay? I couldn't breathe."

"That's a dumb way to say 'anxiety attack.'"

Now that he's been called out, Gourd finally spills what's on his mind. "Listen, man, nothing going on right now is right. When I woke up today, there wasn't a goddamn thing I had to worry about. Good was good, bad was bad, and shit would sort itself out, y'know?"

"Yeah, I know."

"And things are going fine and the ships are flying and we're gonna rush the fuck outta some commies, and it's just how it's supposed to be. But then we get in the shuttle and everything"—he gestures with his hands, pointing around the inside of the shuttle—"everything changes! We're supposed to be taking orders and fighting for our country. And I do that damn well," he sputters, his voice walking the fine line between assertive and sobbing.

"You do, buddy. No one's arguing that."

"But everyone has to take orders. The country gives the president orders; she gives orders to the military; our captains give orders to us. But so far two of those are in the fucking garbage, and then when you got in that fight with Cap and everyone, it's like, does any of it even matter? If the chain of command is completely broken, then what chain binds us?"

"If you really didn't like the sound of our current mission, why'd you sign on?" I ask.

"'Cause you did, bro! 'Cause you did," he says, softening up substantially.

I've never seen such an exposed side of him. It's weird. A Gourd who's not emotionally up to smashing your head in is cause for concern. "What?"

"When the president tried to pop that civvy's cap earlier, all that other shit started to come into my brain. Then I was like, if no one has to follow orders, who's gonna stop me from saying 'fuck it' and leaving? But then you signed on. I already lost my understanding of my damn job, I couldn't lose my pal too."

"Haven't lost me yet, man. And if my understanding is correct, our job is still to save the country."

"But what does saving the country even mean now? If we're the ones who save it, that means it wasn't saved by the military, it was saved by some AWOL assholes playing dress-up."

"I guess we are AWOL assholes. But if that's what's best for the country . . . right?"

"But . . ." Gourd leans in, narrowing his eyes. "How can we know if following Captain is best for the country?"

Thank God no one overheard that . . . at least, I hope they didn't. Keeping my voice down as much as possible, I answer him. "We don't. That's why you can only follow your gut, and God knows you got one to follow."

"Ha-ha, you little piece of shit," he responds, a small smile creeping across his face.

The smile wears off, though, as he takes a good long minute to contemplate what I just told him, tossing it over and over in his head until it finds a resting place up there. He looks like he's trying to deduce if I'm making sense, and if so, how. Luckily, he seems to sort it out internally and snaps back into shape, good as new—barring a little puffiness around the eyes.

"Thank you," he says, marking the first time I think he's ever said that to me.

He sticks out his hand. I meet it, and we share a good, firm handshake.

"I'm with you 'til the bitter end," I tell him.

It's a feel-good moment, and I'm enjoying it, damn it. I don't care if we look like a pair of jagoffs; we cleared the air on some shit that needed fumigating. No rest for the weary, though. Within a minute of Gourd's recovery and our return to standing, the president announces something big is going down outside the cockpit window.

"Look alive, boys. It's time to see what we're here for." The dread in her eyes tells me it's a good idea to pay attention to whatever's coming up.

At first, I have no clue what she's talking about. All I see in front of us are stars, asteroids, and some crusty planets that look like raisins. Unable to see what's so special about all these damn rocks, I look a little more closely. Only then does *it* become visible.

The object in question looks like a liquid bullet, one that's staining the starways with its silver trail. It stretches thousands of miles long, warping the purplish hues in the distance into voids of nothingness, creating slivers of darkness blacker than space itself. The bullet keeps pressing forward, visually distorting every atom of matter it touches along the way until it makes contact with the surface of a planet. Instead of flattening out or creating an impact crater, the bullet penetrates the surface and disappears inside. Then the entirety of the planet's outer shell begins to crumble, its crust breaking up with every passing second until it's trillions of little rocks that just happen to resemble a spheroid.

Through the network of cracks, the bright silver light of the needlelike bullet begins to seep through, briefly illuminating the planet's exterior before the entire thing is swallowed from the inside by black light. Where there was a planet just moments ago, there is nothing but residue from the mysterious silver object, matted across an empty void.

"No fucking way," Gourd mumbles.

"What . . . what is that thing?" Wesley asks, his voice sharing the same nervousness that consumes us all.

Faust finally answers a question with total transparency. "That, Wesley . . . that is what we're here to kill."

CHAPTER 7

Gourd

"Earth-068: Grenada," Captain says, his gravelly voice reluctantly referencing the biggest conspiracy in intergalactic-era United States history. Eight years ago, half of a US territory blipped out of existence overnight, and no one knew where it—or the people on it—went. Half of an entire planet just gone. Everyone across the galaxy flipped the fuck out. Some folks, including myself, believed the official statement from the government that the incident was a Soviet attack of unprecedented proportions. Hell, it's why I enlisted.

Of course, there were the usual hardcore tinfoil hatters who claimed Earth-068 had always been a half-eaten apple and that "the men in charge" just wanted us to see it at the right time. But there were also those who whispered about it being an inside job, theorizing that our government nuked half of one of its own planets for . . . "reasons." Eight years later, it looks like we can finally debunk all of those clowns.

Thinking about the situation at hand, something occurs to me: The fighters earlier, the ones giving us so much trouble— what color were their jet streams?

"Guys . . . the bogeys. That's the second silver-colored horseshit we've seen today," I say. I glance over at Captain, and judging by his frown, it seems he's connecting the dots too. It's all forming a big picture now, and we don't like the look of it one bit.

"That's why we're taking the back door," the president says, ending our sightseeing break by slamming her hands back onto the controls. "No demolecularization for us."

Captain swirls around in his chair and readies himself to co-pilot our shuttle all the way to the mystery station. He and Faust dial up the thrusters, and our little intergalactic tug-boat starts to chug again. It doesn't get faster than a chug, though.

"What's with the slowdown, Cap?"

"Radar. Cloaking at Mach 1 isn't an option," he responds, Faust nodding in agreement. Long cruise it is, then.

"Might want to entertain yourself by looking starboard, Lieutenants," the president says as we drift out of view of the self-cannibalizing planet.

Curious guy that I am, I peek starboard, and sure enough, a new sign of the devil is waiting for my virgin eyes. At first, I can't tell what I'm looking at, thanks to the structure's position in relation to the sun. Its shadow-covered exterior conceals most of its details in darkness, but I can still see that it's big, free-floating, and shaped like a canister of potato chips. I'm not impressed. Big whoop, there's a giant rolling pin drifting through space. Pfft. We have spookier things to worry about, like wherever that silver death-goop came from. Unless . . . oh, I get it now.

"But why are they destroying my planets?" Wesley asks, oblivious to the realities of war.

"Testing," Grimm grunts.

"I've been . . . sacrificing them, the whole time . . ." Wesley murmurs. Looks like he's got a little case of seller's remorse. Even if all he gave them were big balls of rock, it must be pretty rough to know he helped the wrong team.

"Next time, don't sell to the Reds, my man," I advise Wesley, giving him a firm slap on the back that knocks him forward.

"Next time? If we get through whatever's coming up, I'm changing professions," he says.

That works too.

Suddenly, the shuttle ride gets a little bumpy as our craft clips some stray space rocks. I knew letting the president pilot our ship wasn't gonna work.

"Rock beats paper *and* shuttle! What's with the chops?" I ask.

"We're preparing to enter an asteroid field behind those moons up ahead," the president replies. It's the dumbest idea I've heard in . . . well, at least in the past few minutes. Asteroid fields are not places we want to enter.

"Is that really the best route?" I ask, hoping these terrorist pants of mine don't stain easily.

"Not the best route, no. But it's the only one we won't get shot on," she replies.

The captain punches some commands into the flight

navigation system, and a holographic calculator appears. From there, he issues a voice command.

"Odds of successful asteroid field navigation," he asks the machine.

The holograph does some flickering before a number comes up. Damn, that's a lot of zeroes! Wait, they're *after* the decimal.

"That clocks in at about 3,720-to-1 odds," Beecher mumbles after doing a little mental math.

"Never tell me the odds," I plead. I don't like numbers to begin with, but especially not those. Taking blasts from the space station almost sounds better, honestly. Death by giant rock just doesn't sound as American as death by glorious, righteous combat.

"Grab something sturdy, men," she orders as we go head-first into the sea of asteroids.

Beecher's body tenses. "Madam President, do you want us to take over piloting—"

"These old hands might not be as steady as yours, Lieutenant, but I'll remind you I was a pilot in my better years. If I'm going to delegate, it'll be to your commanding officer and myself. Now's not the time for trust." With that declaration, she refocuses on the incoming wave of obstacles.

"From north, turn twelve degrees west."

"North, ten degrees east."

"North, five degrees south."

Captain and Faust give azimuth-based directions back and forth as they work in tandem to pilot our clunker in far more precise increments than it was built for. The maneuvers that follow are shaky, but I can stomach them. Am I getting a little queasy from the on-and-off thruster bursts every other second? Sure. It's just a few degrees of movement, though. As long as it doesn't get worse, I think I'll be okay.

"It's about to get rocky!" Faust shouts.

Of course it is.

The president whips us up and down, grazing asteroids as we charge forward infinitely faster than before. Right as that shit starts, a wave of dizziness hits me—fuck, vertigo is about to kick my ass. While fighting the incoming nausea, I look out the cockpit windshield. We're now cramming through spaces not even fit for a shuttle, an observation our increasingly abused craft is a testament to. The thing's exterior plating is mercilessly scraping against asteroids, and at the rate we're making contact, even if these asteroids don't kill us, they're still on track to rip the damn vehicle to shreds. It's getting a hell of a lot tighter with every passing second, and the window of sight we've got in front of us keeps getting narrower as more and more rocks fill up the view 'til I'm sure we're about to get pounded right through the windshield and—

Silence.

Whoa.

We made it.

Amazingly, between Captain's and the president's skills in the driver seats, we've managed to push through without a single sheet of cracked glass, engine going offline, or essential component getting crushed, though I can't speak for the condition of the bits of the ship I can't see or hear. Thing probably looks like a metallic turd on the outside. Grimm seems unfazed, though, so I don't complain about being treated like ammo for an asteroid field pinball table. Instead, I let out a quick sigh of relief. We're officially out of the thickest stretch of the belt, now in something *a little* less likely to crack open our ship like a giant red pistachio. Even though the field's gotten less congested, the interstellar soup's nowhere near thin yet. But still, we're past the worst of it. Why is the president speeding up?

"What's with the boosting?" I spit out, barely holding back yesterday's breakfast in response to the sudden burst of speed. Space flight needs to be like cookie batter, consistent and silky smooth. AKA, the exact opposite of the shit we're doing right now.

"Lieutenant, can you see our target?" she asks me.

"Yeah," I respond, looking out the front windshield at the black outline of the station.

"Then they can see us."

Oh. Right.

"They don't monitor that asteroid field very closely, but if we're not fast, you better believe they'll get eyes on us. Our cloak is useless at close range," she clarifies.

Guess I'll just have to suck it up for a bit longer.

Or maybe I won't. My grade-A effort in patience disappears as Faust beelines for an oncoming asteroid.

"What the bloody hell are you—" Wesley roars, shouting the words on everybody's mind.

He's cut off by the massive, ship-rocking impact of an asteroid smashing us head-on. The president and captain shoot forward in their seats, Wesley and Beecher fly off the floor, and I'm finally unable to hold back the floodgates, meaning I vomit all over where Beecher's boots just were. He's lucky he went flying into the ceiling half a second ago or that orange stuff would be all over him.

After taking a moment to wipe my face with the sleeve of my armor, I take a peek around. Wesley and Beecher are on the floor, picking themselves up while the president and Captain slide back into their seats without a scratch.

"Jesus Christ," Beecher and I mutter at the same exact time.

"I told you all to grab something. There was a swarm of hornets patrolling overhead; had to give us some cover. Ramming that rock will keep their sensors in check while we go underneath."

"That stunt could've killed us!" Wesley shouts.

"Yeah," Beecher adds.

Gah, I toss in as my mouth makes more unwanted noise.

"You want to turn that *could've* into a *would've*, Wes? Take the wheel and show me how it's done," she says, getting him to back off a bit. She has a point: we *are* still alive. Just a lot worse for wear.

The important thing is that we're below the asteroid now, so there'll be no more rock-boxing for us. I look up and see exactly what the president was talking about: flying over the mess of space boulders is a fat swarm of silver hornet drones. As much as I'd like to take them head-on, she's right—our little tin can is in no position to challenge those chrome commies. Instead, we're taking the silent route, beneath all of it. No more hornets, no more asteroids, nothing but open space. For once, I'm glad there are no explosions going on around me. I admire the view and take a second to thank our lucky stars—and stripes—that we made it through the ordeal alive.

That asteroid thicket sure was one big fuckin' artery clog of rocks. Good thing space can't get indigestion.

Now that we're no longer at the mercy of asteroids, the main challenge finally appears. We've reached the station, and it's realer than any of us could've imagined. The thing hardly looked all that bad before the belt. Like, I could joke about it from that great a distance. Up close, though, it's just one big pile of "no thanks." Never thought I'd say that about something made by Russians, let alone by some two-bit terrorists I'd expect to be on a tight budget. Doesn't look like it from the size of the place, though; the New Union of the Red Star must be banking those rubles in the trillions.

"That's no station . . ." Wesley starts.

Beecher finishes his sentence for him. "That's a goddamned O'Neill Cylinder."

Clearly they know something I don't.

"What?"

"Remember a few years ago when CNES was talking about prototyping a space habitat to speed up expansion and bypass the need for planets?" Beecher asks.

"Yeah . . ."

"If they'd found a way to fuel it, what we're seeing now is what it would've looked like."

I start to see where Beecher's coming from. It does seem pretty similar to the design concept the National Centre for Space Studies, the French government's space agency, was toying with way back when. Only difference is everything's a gazillion times bigger. Take the little ventilation slits—each one's big enough to fit multiple cruisers. Actually, now that I squint, they *might be* fitting cruisers—yeah. They don't look like vents anymore, more like deflector shields. Didn't know those came in jet-black. Hell, I didn't know O'Neill Cylinders came in anything besides fiction.

"We're, um, not going in that thing . . . are we? Are we?" Wes asks nervously.

I don't blame him for the apprehension; the guy's just doing his job as the voice of reason that has no business being on our shuttle.

"Like Lieutenant Beecher said, it's a habitat. Only way you destroy one of those is from the inside," Cap tells us. "And even if our ship had missiles, it'd be like flicking specks of dust at a giant. I doubt one-hundred-thousand ships combined could take down such a target. Madam President, where's the back door?"

"See that massive ring locked around the funnel's exterior, way past the hangar bays? Should be a service duct somewhere on the six o'clock support beam. I can get us in through there."

"Then?"

"Then we take a bit of a jog to an off-map site on the other side. You can't see it from here, but trust me, all the hassle will make sense if we reach it."

Make sense, huh? The only two words I've been wanting to hear for the past day; it's about time they cropped up. I just wish we didn't have to go inside the station to get to that point. Sadly, my wishes don't mean jack shit right now. Whether I like it or not, it's time to cross borders and sneak into a designated no-Americans-allowed zone.

We begin the final push to entry. As fast as our battered and bruised craft will take us, we slide beneath the underbelly of the giant soda can, aiming for a straight shot at the service duct. Our shuttle goes pitch black as the shadow of the giant space station gobbles us up. I pass the time looking up at what we're about to be inside, struggling to comprehend how it's all so big and somehow working. The pipes alone are thicker than any cruiser I've ever seen. The fucking pipes! If bigger is better, then the shit I'm seeing is the cream of the Soviet crop. From where we started, somewhere around the cylinder's halfway point, it still looks like a good fifty-mile dash to the duct entrance near the tail. Well, maybe not *actually* fifty miles, but still a really long fuckin' way.

"We're lookin' at a Russian military wet dream brought to life," I say.

"A real Red Peril, huh?" Beecher responds dryly, unamused with himself.

"Say that again?"

"Red Peril. It was a shitty joke, I get it. Let it go."

"That's exactly what it is, yeah. Er, not the joke, the name. That's the name of the place from now on," I declare.

"Red Peril," Beecher repeats, put off by his own invention.

We close our gap with the target support beam, clearing the final hundred yards between us and our landing spot. We've made it.

"All right, Captain, I'll take over from here," President Faust says, giving him the signal to move aside while she handles everything. Then she punches in a series of codes while angling the shuttle parallel to the service duct in front of us. When her hands leave the controls, the beam's joints open up, their ends stretching in opposite directions to reveal an opening. Without hesitation, Faust slams in more codes and our shuttle tilts, sliding past the entrance's thick gating until we're snuggled inside the landing bay. It's cramped and looks like shit; no wonder it's only for repair personnel.

The president presses one last button after the service entrance's airlocks seal, lowering our shuttle's boarding ramp and leaving us clear to exit the vehicle. The captain leads, followed by an overeager Wesley, who's probably never been happier to get off a spacecraft in his life. Then the president, Beecher, and I step off, covering the rear.

I guess it's like Captain said a day ago: If there's even the chance of a threat, ain't it our responsibility to handle it?

Well, looks like it's time to get around to that handling part.

CHAPTER 8

Wesley

'**ve** made a horrible mistake.

Sweat trickles down the sides of my face as my team and I pass from the cold void of space into an even colder-looking, cramped landing bay. The airlocks seal behind us with thunderous echoes, the sheets of metal slamming shut in rapid succession. The harsh noises evoke an image in my mind—that of the locks effortlessly crushing a frail human body like a boot snuffing an ant. And though I should at least be grateful that the airlocks sound durable enough to protect me from the void of space, even that doesn't seem guaranteed. A few thick sheets of metal are all that stand between me and instant death. All it would take is one stray laser to pop the bubble and suck me out into the black nothingness that's just a stone's throw away.

The shuttle's landing gear makes contact with the bay's floor and the cabin shakes. Unlike my peers, I nearly lose my balance, probably because my sudden light-headedness is messing with me far more than any tremors rattling the tiny box I've been trapped inside for what feels like an eternity.

Not long ago, I was wrapped in silk bedsheets, eager to play hardball with a president and make a killing in the process. And now, the only killing set to happen will likely involve the end of me, aboard a gargantuan cage tucked away in the back alleys of the cosmos.

Truthfully, I expected to feel a bit gutsier by now. In reality, I feel like a poor sod who's about to get stung for fingering a hornet's nest. I'm decked out in a dead man's clothing, toting a Russian rifle that I've yet to actually fire, trapped with a dangerous president and three unquestioning Marines, all while aboard a hostile space station with the capacity to eat planets like Turkish delights.

What was I thinking?

Oh, I remember. I was going to be a superhero and get revenge on those nasty terrorists. Little me, intoxicated by the thrill of liberation from a hostage situation, thought that I could take on the world. And now destiny is going to reward my hubris.

"Forward march, men. End of the tunnel's a ways down," Faust tells her troops, beckoning us to follow. The linear path ahead doesn't give me a lot of room to argue, and besides, Faust seems to know her way around here pretty well. There's no reason for me to get myself lost when we've got a neighborhood regular as pack leader.

We trek down the lengthy tunnel in silence, serenaded by the hollow tune of boots plodding on floor grates. I'm not sure why I'm voluntarily stepping toward my own slaughter, but I don't stop. Perhaps morbid curiosity compels me forward; my subconscious mind's need to see what poison it has picked for itself. After no less than a mile's worth of marching, we arrive at the expansive repair duct's end and reach the entrance to whatever lies beyond.

"Take a deep breath, everyone," Faust says. "If you thought the place looked bad on the outside . . ."

It doesn't seem like she's pulling anything fancy to get past the entryway's security. No, she just uses a retinal scanner since, unless I'm missing something important, her eye is already on file. Why, of course it is! That raises the question: If she can get us in without a hitch, what's to stop her from trapping us just as easily? Unlike her, we don't know what awaits us on the other side of that monstrous door—

Mother of God.

I don't even realize my legs have collapsed until I land in the arms of one of the Marines. I'd be embarrassed if I wasn't so dizzy. In my dazed state, I turn toward them to see how they're faring. By the look in their eyes, they're just as far past their breaking point as I am. Everything in front of us isn't possible; it's the science of decades—no, centuries—from now.

Inside the massive cylinder is a living, breathing, bite-sized country without a sky. At its nose on our far right is the station's massive cannon, which is all but consumed by radiating, color-sapping black light. Closer to our immediate stretch of the tube is a small city with shimmering skyscrapers built around a blue tower that's nearly tall enough to form the radius of the station's interior.

The distant city is connected to the rest of the station only by a thin strip of roads that lead to the cylinder's other regions, starting with a forest biome. From there, the evergreens and emerald fields transition to industrial grays as a forge complex overtakes the landscape, the lava within contained by what I assume to be the station's artificial gravity. The smelting zone's glowing red hues eventually morph into dull whites, leading to what's immediately in front of us: the largest transportation terminal in space. Dozens of long trams shuttle in and out of the station, circling up and around the cylinder's inner circumference toward the forest and industrial areas. Strangely, no tracks extend toward the eastern city with the tall tower.

It's hard to tell from my current distance who—or what—is boarding the trams, though most beings appear to be human size. They number in the hundreds. I can't identify the bigger beings yet.

Every inch of my face is paralyzed, overcome by awe. For a split second, I'm even grateful to have come so far, if for nothing else than to have seen the sight of the station's interior with my own eyes. Of course, I dismiss that thought when I consider the fact that no matter how impressive it is, it exists solely to kill me. That dulls a lot of the charm and allows me to get back on my own two feet.

"Where *are* we?" Beecher asks rhetorically, every bit as blown away as I am.

Gourd remains silently petrified. Captain Grimm actually gulps at the sight, though he tenses his jaw in an attempt to hide the nervous reflex, probably thinking his mask will hide everything.

"We have to reach the trams and take one to the smelting platforms," Faust says, unfazed. "There, we'll reach the entrance to our target service duct. And remember, you're supposed to be escorting a political prisoner—so look like it."

No one's up for a debate, so we watch her take the first step onto the long, winding stairwell in front of us that leads to the train station's main terminal.

Faust quickly realizes we're not moving with her and shakes her head. "No. No. No. I can't be in front. Two of you get up here and at least try to look like you're in control."

Gourd and Beecher scurry up front and assume semi-dignified postures as they pretend to be two men who could actually keep the wily woman in check. Captain and I assume our positions in the rear of the formation, effectively boxing her in as we navigate upward.

"Left. Now right. Another left," she whispers to the leading duo, guiding them up the maze of stairs. Her lowered voice tells me we can't be far from human contact. I'm not looking forward to it.

Between her instructions and the natural progression of the stairwells, we eventually find our way to the tram platforms. I finally get a good view of who we're sharing the station with: technicians. Lots and lots of technicians. They're clad in safety vests and armed with tool belts, though some also sport mechanical augmentations, ostensibly for more dangerous work. Past them, a handful of men wear basic military outfits, but we're the only ones with masks and specialist-grade bodysuits. We're the only ones with armor thick enough to clank.

Or so I thought—as I look at the crowd a bit more closely, I see we're not the only ones dressed to kill. At first, I mistake the robotic units in front of us for standard civil engineering machines, the kind found all over the streets of Russia. They have the right color scheme: glossy silver and yellow to attract attention and alert people of their presence. For that reason, I write them off—until I see their arms. Where there should be a left hand is the tip of a rifle. From there, even more differences reveal themselves. Their leg design is a mechanical replication of the digitigrade footing style, which undoubtedly offers them more agility than the standard service robot. And the torso plating on these units is far thicker than the industry standard—another design evolution that'd be useful in a combat scenario.

The last major difference I catch is subtle but striking: while their crab-like heads seem fairly normal, their sole eye, located at the center of their angular faceplates, radiates black—perhaps because they're running on some form of the same mysterious energy that seems to be powering the station's cannon.

Under ordinary circumstances I'd have pissed myself by now, but nothing about the current circumstances is remotely close to ordinary. Besides, our disguises are working perfectly, and it looks like no one can tell we're not, in fact, the men under the masks they think they know. That little detail almost nullifies the current threat level, barring one immediate safety hazard standing about a foot in front of me. For every new sight in the station from hell, nothing displaces Roseanne Faust as my primary cause for concern.

As we close in on one of the trams, my very, very basic Russian skills start to come in handy. I identify enough words on the departure boards to figure out where the trains are headed, and one destination in particular interests me. I can only identify a single word of its title, *bay*, but the arrow next to it points directly behind me, which is all I need to piece together the clues. I peek over my shoulder and look up. Massive sections of the cylinder protrude inward overhead, forming suspended boxes where scores of hornet drones and other small ships are buzzing about. Those must be the hangars. I've found my method of escape.

I realize I sound mutinous, but really, why am I here? The terrorists aren't the biggest threat to my survival—Faust is. And the opportunity in front of me might be my best chance to make it out alive. The Russians can keep their station; I just want to go home. Plus, I can alert the government of my findings if I make it back. Instead of winding up a dead suit, I'll be a living hero. Perhaps the queen will knight me for my reconnaissance and brave efforts to aid national security.

"All right, boys, take the one on the first platform," Faust whispers to us.

I stay in formation with the captain, not sure if I'm actually up for what I'm contemplating.

I have only another second or two to decide—Beecher and Gourd have already stepped onto the passenger flatbed. The president gets a foot aboard as well, leaving only Captain and myself still on the platform. My feet stop moving. Captain continues forward with the other three, not looking behind to notice my hesitation.

Am I really about to abandon my crew? I won't have anyone to fall back on but myself. I'll be alone. Still, that's less dangerous than staying with Faust.

After Captain steps off the platform, the boarding ramp lifts up and forms the waist-high wall of the tram, signaling it's time for departure. Only now that they're trapped inside the train does the squad turn around, just as they begin to pull out of the station. Their last sight is a shocking one, no doubt. There I am, still on the platform. Their eyes go wide with surprise, anger, and horror, none of which they can express aloud. That limitation goes both ways. I wish I could apologize to the Marines, I really do, but I need to look out for myself, and that woman they're following is not conducive to anyone's safety. Hopefully they arrive at that same conclusion on their own while I figure out a way off the fever dream of a space colony I'm trapped in.

I turn to my right and spot an incoming tram headed for where I want to go. Time to get out of here as fast as I got in. The plan is simple: travel with a pack, avoid drawing attention, get in a ship, and handle things from there. I'm a decent pilot, so I can probably figure out how to maneuver one of the terrorists' crafts. Hell, Beecher and Gourd figured out how to; it can't be that hard.

The tram pulls into place, and its row of cars unfold their boarding ramps. I let the wave of technicians on the platform filter in ahead of me, only shuffling myself aboard when the last line of humans trickle onto the car. Behind me, robots slowly march onto our transport. As a result of nerves rather than conscious thought, I tap my foot, waiting for everyone to pack up so we can get a move on.

After an anxiety-inducing minute, the ramps fold up and we're off. As we push forward along the track, I glance to my right to see where my former teammates' tram is. After a bit of scouting I locate it, though the little gray transport has traveled far into the distance. I track it as one by one the cars fade out of view, until the tail carriage disappears and the Americans are truly gone. It's just me and a whole lot of

Russians—and not the kind that do their business in suits. Christ, I need to calm down. It's not like anyone's talking to me or putting me in a position where I need to prove anything.

"Вы там."

Shit.

I know that one. It means . . . "you there." I think. I tilt my head ever so slightly in the voice's direction and see a jumpsuit-clad technician roaming toward me. I ignore him. Maybe if I look straight ahead, he'll think I didn't hear him and drop the matter. *Yes, Wesley, that's a good plan.* Besides, what if he's not even referring to me? That's always a possibility! I'm not important here, I'm not valuable. No reason to bother dealing with me, no sir.

Now within arm's reach, the man repeats himself and taps me on the shoulder.

Damn it, brain, you've chosen the worst moment to go into hiding. I scan the massive length of track we're on to judge how close we are to our destination. The results are good: the first hangar stop isn't terribly far from our current location. If I can somehow stretch the conversation out to, oh, say, thirty seconds, maybe I can get out of my current mess before things get hairy. Half a minute, I remind myself before putting on my calmest voice and best Russian accent in order to take part in the riskiest conversation of my life.

"Какие?" I ask. It means "what," if I'm not mistaken. I guess only his response will tell. Lucky for me he can't see how hard I'm biting my lower lip; the damn thing's on the verge of bleeding.

A little tension dissipates when he responds with an indifferent tone, indicating no signs of alarm or suspicion. The only issue is, he's now using a whole bunch of words I don't recognize. I'm screwed. The game is up. My only chance is to stall and look like a complete asshole, a minimalistic goal that may still be too hard for me to achieve.

I work up a little bit of a cough in my throat, carefully letting it rumble around my vocal folds until it's phlegm-filled enough to last a while. Then, I release.

"Excuse me," I mutter in Russian, pardoning myself as I hack away until we're about to pull into the first hangar's station. I straighten up, work off the last of the cough, and regain my composure just as the tram slides into place beside the platform. The boarding ramps unfold, and I quickly pat the man on the shoulder and leave with a parting phrase.

"Wait one minute," I tell him, internally cheering as my limited Russian carries me over the finish line. By the time he realizes he's been duped, the little ramp will have folded up and he'll be whisked away, leaving me to do my business. Oh Wes, you are brilliant.

He seems confused by my statement, but I don't give him time for a rebuttal as I scurry off the tram and onto the platform, quickly disappearing into the crowd of people and robots ahead of me. As long as he doesn't follow along and crop up somewhere behind me, I think I'm in the clear. Onward and upward to the hangar I go.

Surrounded by 250-kilogram machines and a miniature army of station operators, I skim the platform's signs and hustle across another maze of stairwells, aiming for the ones that lead to the first hangar's elevators. The routine's not too different from maneuvering between tubes back home,

I suppose. Yes, it's just like my daily commute, with a few militarized robots and terrorists thrown in.

I reach my target elevator and take a quick ride up alongside some human workers who decide I'm not worth bothering. It's almost as though I know what I'm doing. *Yeah, you've got the situation under control, Wesley, you've got—*

Well, I did have the situation under control, until the elevator door decided to open. I was correct in my guess that I'd reach a ship hangar—so why did I underestimate the security that would be present? Goddamn it, I'm aboard what is likely the most secretive, high-tech terrorist hotspot in the universe, and I didn't expect the people running it to be monitoring who gets in and out?

I survey my surroundings. Dozens of crimson civilian shuttles make up the docking rows at the front of the hangar, followed by a nearly endless assortment of intimidating military fighters, all of which are closer to the rear where I am. As I should've expected, the Russians are swarming virtually every ship, which is problem number one. How on Earth-072 am I going to inconspicuously get inside one of these crafts, let alone commandeer it out of the hangar? And what about the defenses that await me outside? Oh, I didn't think *anything* through.

None of that's even relevant, considering the security checkpoint between me and the vehicles. No use fantasizing about a daring escape if I can't even get near a ship. And given the muscle guarding the hangar, maybe keeping my distance is for the better. While the militarized bots down below were definitely a warning sign that I was barking up the wrong tree, the forces up here are something else entirely.

Gateways scan each and every person before they can access any stretch of the main hangar floor. Manning these checkpoints are not the seven-foot, four-times-my-bodyweight robots I've come to expect. No, the clankers posted here are a brand-new breed of war machine, the likes of which I've never seen anything close to before. Hulking, twelve-foot-tall versions of the engineering robots guard all entrances to my escape vehicles, and in no way do these machines look built to administer warnings to trespassers.

Towering well above every other robot and human on the hangar floor, these four-meter monsters sport a glossy black color scheme to go with their triangle of black eyes. Said eyes are mounted on an ovular head shaped similarly to a Spartan helmet, which is attached to a massive torso via a busy assortment of neck joints and pistons, each of which is about as thick as one of my arms. Speaking of arms, theirs are fitted with rocket launchers and giant retracting blades that keep sliding up and down, as if to challenge any potential ne'er-do-well to make a move. It's clear these machines aren't built to take out humans. They're built to take out entire ships.

I guess I can chalk them up to one more impossible thing the terrorists are powering with their special super juice. Yep, everything makes sense. I think I'm getting the picture now. The picture is that I'm going to shit myself and die, likely not even in that order, if I don't get out of here soon.

I don't even know where "out" is anymore, though. As I've been ogling the sights, I seem to have strayed from the elevator, and the ocean of people blocking my view isn't making things easier. There's only one constant in every direction, towering over the heads of the Russians swarming all corners of my line of sight: giant death robots.

After pushing my way past a good dozen or so people, I finally see a method to the madness. Various lanes grant access to the main hangar. Since I happen to be trapped in one, I look ahead to get an idea of what's coming. As per usual, it's not good. The checkpoint robots are scanning identification tags on each individual before allowing them entry; the issue here being that I haven't got one.

My lane in particular is zipping right along. It's only a matter of minutes before things get messy. I take a quick inventory of my options: run, attract suspicion, and get killed; or don't run, fail to produce an ID tag, and get killed.

Looks like I'll be choosing death by giant robot, as I can't build up the courage to pound my way out of my crammed lane. Five people to go until Three Eyes crushes me under those boxy talons it has for feet. The worker currently being inspected raises his badge, gets scanned, and continues forward, leaving four. The process rinses and repeats, and then there are three. Then two. Then one.

That last lucky bastard marches on ahead of me, leaving nothing but a foot of space between myself and the two-ton metallic guard waiting to annihilate me. I hardly knew thee, world. Farewell. My throat is dry, my forehead is soaking, and my hands are shaking as I stealthily reach for my rifle. Here it comes . . .

. . .

And then it doesn't. I look up at the monster of a machine, and it makes a sweeping gesture at me, with a little light below its neck plate glowing green. Without question, I step forward, knowing full well that if I've misunderstood the robot, I won't have to worry about it for long.

Turns out I'm right, though.

I did it! I bloody did it! Wesley Alistair Clarke has duped terrorism! But how? How did I do it? What saved me? The armor? Does my current getup mean I have seniority? Could I actually boss around some of these guys? What am I talking about? I'm not sticking around here long enough to find out. Time to get off the oversized steel cigar I'm in and escape to greener pastures.

Finally in a position to commandeer a ship, I wander around the main floor's selection of spacecraft to determine which would look best for my grand escape. I'll take something in the middle, I think. A single-manned fighter will be perfect. It's small enough to not attract attention when leaving the station, likely kitted with military-grade fuel reserves built for long-distance travel and an engine capable of getting me home before I dehydrate . . . yes, I'm feeling good about my choice.

To think I came so far just to fight for a return trip. At least I'll leave with the pride of knowing I pulled one over on the terrorists. That's a victory in and of itself, right? Besides, when I get back home I'll report my findings, and Her Majesty's armed forces can take it from there. No need for me to stay here.

I arrive at a sufficiently isolated fighter and see that the coast is clear to make my escape. All that's left is for me to get inside that cockpit, man the sticks, and be on my merry—

"Nice ride, Wes."

—way.

"Don't let me stop you. Slide in there, get comfy."

I know who that voice belongs to, and I don't like it one bit. I turn my head slowly, praying to any and all gods who'll listen that I don't see who I'm expecting to see.

It seems prayers don't work aboard terrorist space stations. In all her pint-sized, evil glory, it's Roseanne Faust. With her crow's-feet creased, eyes narrowed, and mouth wide in a grim smile, the witch has the look of a cat who's just found its favorite mouse. My right hand inches toward my stowed rifle even more quickly than when I thought I'd have to square off against the checkpoint robot. I'd take the heartless jet-black machine over the mechanical woman with a heart of coal any day.

The single semi-silver lining to seeing her face is that I get to see the other three Americans along with it. Their eyes tell me they're none too happy with the little stunt I pulled. Understandable, as I'm none too happy with them chasing me down.

"Wes, you are a walking, talking liability. Get your fucking hand off that ship and let's get a move on," she commands after savoring a few seconds of my unease.

"No." I'm on a defiant streak today, and it's not stopping here.

"Can you imagine what that thing out there," she says, referencing the planet-eating cannon looming beyond the hangar's deflector shields, "will do to you when the Russians above us see a ship shooting out of here with no clearance for takeoff?"

I . . . no, she's trying to trick me. She's *been* trying to trick me. The terrorists won't waste an entire cannon shot on my fighter, will they? No. They'll . . . they'll probably just send out a few drones or fighters to obliterate me. Oh, bother. And dare I imagine if they actually *do* elect to test the cannon on me?

"It'll erase every atom in your body from our dimension. Now stand down." Her tone tells me she's not playing around.

Well, neither am I. I stop going for my rifle and instead reach to the highest rung of the fighter's boarding ladder. But the tip of someone's gun gently presses against my lower back. All of a sudden, the blessing of having found a secluded ship in the hangar turns into a curse.

"Do what she says, Wesley. We're in her world now."

I'd say it's the captain's charisma that nearly sways me, but I'd be lying. The hairs on the back of my neck go stiff as his rifle nudges deeper. He's let that wicked harpy grab him by the bollocks, the spineless man. I won't let him convert me to such cowardice as well.

Against my better judgment, I let go of the ladder, ball my fists, and spin around, taking a wild swing at the captain. He moves like lightning, leaning back to dodge my attack before grabbing my throat and hoisting me a few inches off the ground. As soon as his digits wrap around my neck, I realize that if he wanted to, he could snuff the life out of me right here, right now. Even though he's relegated himself to being Faust's lapdog, he's still lethal, and I am at his mercy.

"Don't make a scene," he says, releasing his grip on me.

I cough a few times as I look around at the Americans. They're not allies—they're three stooges and a vile puppet master. Realizing my only choices are to play along or die in the most miserable, undignified manner possible, I swallow my resentment for my repugnant squadmates and obey the captain's demand. A small formation of Russians passes by just in time to miss the scuffle. Once they're out of earshot, a new order is given to me: exit the hangar.

Concealed but deadly, Grimm's rifle prods me forward, and our quintet resumes the box formation from our initial entry, though now I'm in the front. It's laughable, really, that they view me as a bigger danger than Faust. When we're all dead inside a basement somewhere within the hour, I'll go out knowing I was the only one who saw it coming.

"Color me surprised, Wes. Didn't think you'd have the stomach to wander past the big guys," Faust says as we pass those massive mechanical monsters on our way out of the hangar. While I didn't necessarily choose to wander past them, I'm not going to tell her that. I'm not going to tell her anything. As a result, for a brief while, there is total silence. Our group's mute, tense state is only briefly shaken up by a fear-fueled remark from the rear.

"What else they got going on here?" Beecher mumbles a bit too loudly. I look over my shoulder and see his eyes drifting around. Though the rest of my traveling party's members remain focused on me, I'm clearly not the lean lieutenant's biggest concern. Foolish fellow that he is, he still thinks the Russians' toys are a bigger threat than his own president.

"A hell of a lot more," Faust replies, keeping her voice low. "But you don't want to meet the rest."

Our journey continues devoid of spoken word as we board a tram and head in the direction the president had intended from the very beginning. At the rear of the colony, I think I see another hangar. It's only a few miles away, but there's no way to reach it. Between it and me is a sea of generators, pumps, and pipes, all working diligently to keep the colony afloat. The machinery seethes with black energy and uncontained electricity, likely lethal to any human who gets within a couple hundred feet of it. And to even get that close, I'd need to somehow survive jumping out of the transport I'm on at its current speed.

Then a thought hits me: What if I shout? If I blow our cover, at least Faust won't get the last say in what happens to us. Yes, the idea has merit. But when I look over my shoulder at Gourd and Beecher, I just can't do it. These two men have done me no wrong. Well, no wrong besides forcing me to play into the inevitable trap Faust has yet to reveal. Hmm . . . perhaps they are guilty. Yes. They deserve what comes their way, just like the president and captain. If I don't seal their fates right now, then I'll only be sealing my own.

I open my mouth ever so slightly and feel a shout build up. I close my eyes and prepare to sound the alarm.

My throat goes dry.

I can't do it.

I try to force a sound out but can't, just like I can't block out the thought of Beecher's eyes as he fearfully looked at the monsters around us just minutes ago. I can't condemn him to being their victim—especially not after he saved me from my own execution not much more than a day ago. I owe him. Which means . . . which means it's back to death by witch for me.

We finally pull into the station at the smelting complex. Our destination explains why the temperature's spiked inside my already uncomfortably hot body armor. For something called dragon skin, I'd fancy a bit more heat resistance.

Beads of sweat form on my brow as the station's previous horizon of cold grays transforms into warm, sizzling black metals and bright pools of yellow-red lava, all bouncing and swirling mere feet below the grates that support my flammable feet.

"Off," Captain says, ordering us to leave the tram. The nearby robots don't pay us any attention, but I can't help but wonder if that single English word will be enough to alert the technicians in the neighboring tram cars. We're in a noisy environment and may be out of immediate earshot of any living beings, but the captain's unnecessary risks are making an already boiling-hot situation even more heated.

Faust looks at him, apparently sharing my sentiments. "Quiet." Then, fresh off scolding the man, she assumes leadership over our team. Her first whispered command is for us to go down a secret path that no one else is using. After all, that's the one where no one can hear us scream. It's a maze of metal stairs that wraps around and weaves between the huge support beams holding up the tram platform. The stairs stretch down to the floor of the station yet continue even further below, into the darkness of the unknown. The winding mess of steps is so concealed from view by the tram platform above that one would only see it if they knew to look for it— which, of course, Faust does.

"Why aren't we taking the main route?" I ask, speaking up once we've descended to a point where I'm sure no Russian will be able to hear us. The fact I don't have to worry about Russians is where my fear stems from. I'm not keen on going somewhere even the terrorists aren't venturing.

"It doesn't go where we need to go, Wes. And in case you

haven't noticed, it's too damn hot up there. Didn't you see how no people were going near those platforms? No more idiotic questions."

She's right; there were only engineering robots past the unloading area of the station. The human workers were either dropping off equipment or staying on the trams.

Okay, so maybe she's telling the truth about the danger. And I suppose she did give me a reason as to why we're *not* headed further along the main route. But that still doesn't explain why we *are* going in the direction we're going.

"Where are we headed?"

"Somewhere a lot cooler. Didn't I just say no more idiotic questions?" she responds, working hard to spit the words out while reserving most of her breath for the task of hustling us down another absurdly long stairwell. I find it surprising that these terrorists can afford a cannon capable of cutting through space but are picky about where elevators are installed. No wonder the place needs so many workers.

The house-sized generators we saw from the tram turn into skyscrapers down here, drenching us in shadow as we descend beyond where they meet the floor of the colony. After venturing dozens of stories beneath the tram rails and surface of the station itself, we reach a large gateway. It's reminiscent of the door that got us inside the other end of the colony, though it's far more hidden away than that one. Furthermore, the new gateway doesn't have a retinal scanner. Instead, it demands blood, of which Faust readily sacrifices a few drops from her fingertip. The small needle above the door's touchpad accepts her offering, and the gate opens.

Impossible. What am I not seeing? The Russians have her

eyes on file. Her *blood* on file. And yet, not one enemy troop has intercepted our party. No computer system has sounded the alarm that a hostile nation's president is skulking around. The only possible answer is that she's some sort of Russian agent, right? And if the three soldiers aren't protesting her actions . . . God, are they all part of a terrorist sleeper cell? Did I miss the part where she used their trigger phrase?

The idea that they're mindless drones scares me to death, but I know that fight and flight are both out of the question. My gun is useless so long as theirs are all trained on me. I'll never get a shot in. And if hand-to-hand combat occurs, well, Grimm's already demonstrated he's capable of killing me before I finish throwing a punch. Whatever happens next, I'm going to be forced along for the ride.

With the gate opened, our unit presses forward into the new area. Inside, there's a secret tram station, secluded from the rest of the colony. Several trains, unmanned and unused, are docked.

"We take the first transport. From here on out, you're clear to engage hostiles," Faust says, before turning in my direction and adding, "that doesn't mean me."

I give my response in the form of a sneer.

As we ride the frontmost tram out of the station, I look out the green-hued, transparent shell of the tube our transport's traveling through, peering between the bits that aren't covered with bundles of piping or obscured by bands of dark deflector shields. Through the gaps, I gaze at the stars I could be flying by right now, had I made my escape back in the hangar. Such a big, vast space out there to occupy, yet here I am, on a train ride to my grave.

Though every second of it is hell, it's a quick trip, lasting no more than a few minutes. It lands us at a destination that pokes out past the station's primary cylinder, reinforcing the idea that we're somewhere secret—somewhere we shouldn't be.

Once out of the shuttle, we pass through the mysterious new station's arches and start down yet another hallway. It's insanely cold and paneled to look like the interior of a giant freezer. The walls are coated in a thin layer of frost and icicles dangle from vents above us. Though the low temperatures help alleviate any earlier worries about suffering from heatstroke, I can barely hear my own thoughts over the sound of my chattering teeth. No wonder we're all alone; no technicians probably visit here unless they've fetched parkas first and something's absolutely mission critical. And as for the lack of robots, well, any robot's wires would eventually snap after prolonged exposure to such frigidity. The armor the three soldiers and I wear is well insulated, but even so, I don't know how long I can take the cold. How the president is managing it is beyond me.

"What's with the chills?" Beecher asks Faust.

"You're about to find out." She guides us to another massive gateway. With one extra-lengthy code input from the president, the door panels slide open, immediately dropping the temperature even further as a flood of bone-chilling water vapor spills out, the plumes of cold mist concealing what lies beyond. The president ushers us in.

We're in some sort of central cooling unit. Massive tanks covered in ice line the room's shelves as far as the eye can see, all of them hooked up to thick hoses that unify at the ceiling.

The coolant reserve around us must be what the pipes lining the monorail tube were channeling back to the main colony. No wonder the current area is so sectioned off and empty— empty enough for Faust to pull off four murders without any commotion, that is. She clearly knows her way around; maybe she has the place rigged.

"Let's make our way to the back. There's one final thing . . . to be done," she says between brief pauses, her face contorting in the same way it did right before she passed out on the shuttle a day ago. I consider calling attention to her mystery malady but stop myself. Whatever's wrong with her doesn't seem to be enough to stop her, meaning there's no time to wonder about her health while my safety hangs in the balance. I need to let the situation play out and wait for the best possible opening to make a move, since I'll only get one shot at saving myself.

Faust leads us past row after row of cooling tanks until we're at the back wall of the storage facility. Having moved ahead of the pack, she positions herself next to a temperature dial and, while we're still out of arm's reach, hastily clutches it.

"Just give it a second," she says, twisting the switch.

More mist pours into the room. Instinctively reacting to the danger, I do what I should've done a long time ago.

"Stop!" I raise my rifle and point it directly at Faust's chest, my hands shaking from the cold as I aim my crosshairs at the President of the United States. My motion sets off a chain reaction, the likes of which I knew was coming. I hear the clinking sound of three rifles being lifted.

"Wesley, what the fuck do you think you're doing?" Grimm barks.

"Don't you see? She's going to kill us off here. She's going to freeze us to death!" I shout back, enraged by his blindness. I hear the clanks of shifting armor plates as Gourd, directly behind me, lowers his weapon ever so slightly, susceptible to the common sense in my words. I may have failed to get him to stand down, but at least he's trying to think through the situation for himself.

"Look at her! You think she won't freeze with us? You're out of your mind!" Grimm says. But with all the tricks she's had up her sleeve throughout our journey, I don't care what her weaknesses appear to be.

"She's been five steps ahead of us the whole damn way, you idiot! Surely she's prepared to get out of here as well!" I roar, forcefully enough to momentarily startle Beecher.

The captain doesn't flinch. "You can't win, Wesley. You put another ounce of pressure on that trigger and I'll drop you."

"At least I'll go knowing I did what none of you had the stones to do!" I say, not faltering a smidgen.

"Don't do it. It's not what you think."

"Then what is it? I want answers, and I want them now!" My voice cracks. She can't be my end. I won't let her be.

Throughout our whole exchange, Faust hasn't moved a muscle or said a word. Only now, in the brief interlude between shouts, does she slowly remove her hand from the cooling dial.

"Wes, you're right." A small, wry smile forms across her wrinkly mouth.

With my rifle still aimed directly at her heart, she speaks the phrase I've been waiting for all day.

"It's time . . . for answers," she says, pausing as her mystery malady once again takes over her body. As her muscles tense up and veins begin to pop, she locks eyes with me and speaks through gritted teeth. "Think you can handle the truth?"

CHAPTER 9

Beecher

What. Is. Happening.

I keep my rifle fixed squarely on Wesley's head. A single trigger pull will take him out of the game . . . but why the hell would I do that? He's super paranoid, sure, but it's not like his fears are unfounded. No one's answering questions, sketchy shit abounds, and he's had enough of it.

Thankfully, just when it looks like Wesley is about to do something stupid, Faust speaks up and the Brit's stance falters. That's all the reassurance I need to know he isn't going to do it—not because he can't, but because he truly doesn't want to. I lower my weapon. Gourd follows suit, giving up his direct lock on the civilian's skull. We don't take our sights off Wesley completely, though, walking a fine line so as to not piss off Captain, who's still holding firm. Damn it, Grimm, just go easy on the guy. He won't do anything unless you box him into a corner.

"We have a little time, men, so let's make it count," Faust says.

"Quit stalling! I want transparency, now," Wesley snaps back, his voice wavering as he loses some of the prior conviction he had.

"And frankly, you all deserve some. Let's start with Grenada," she begins, taking us back in time. "Forget everything you think you know."

I take a deep breath as Sierra Squad and an on-edge Wesley strap in for story time.

"Years ago, the Department of Energy was quietly using Earth-068 to test a new fuel, one that utilized concentrated, liquified dark matter. They were kids playing with fire, but no one at the top stopped them. After all, the fuel was supposed to be a bigger breakthrough than electricity. 'The strongest and cleanest power in the known universe,' they'd said. With it, we'd all travel faster, farther, and kill pollution in the process." Faust seems wistful. A weak smile inches across her face. She lets out a chuckle and continues her tale.

"Mind you, all that top-secret research was underway well before I got elected. As was President Cox's desire to take the project in a new direction. In response to Soviet aggression, Cox thought it wise to focus on the fuel's military applications. Naturally, that led to his men developing dark-matter-powered weapons of all sorts . . . including bombs. They weren't testing them on the planet, just constructing them. But that was all it took. One slipup later and half of Earth-068 ceased to exist."

I can't believe what I'm hearing, and I'm sure no one else can either, but we don't stop listening. She has us hook, line, and sinker—not that Wesley seems to notice. His paranoia has given way to utter befuddlement.

"On that day, Cox had private task forces go in while planetary evacuation teams yanked everyone else out. His guys collected everything: samples, formulas, you name it. That's the gift I inherited from his administration, the classified leftovers hidden in the back of our country's fridge.

"He wasn't the brightest man, if I'm being honest. At the time, there was a mole. Cox knew it. Yet he and his men still tinkered with the Grenada findings instead of locking that stuff up and throwing away the key. He was confident the impostor would be weeded out before anything could happen. That gaping hole in national security was outside of the public's radar, of course. Off-limits knowledge to everyone but a few select politicians, and later, yours truly when I came aboard."

"So . . . they never got him?" Gourd interrupts.

"You mean 'her.' And they caught her all right, but none of her exchange records. No one knew what she'd leaked. There wasn't a smidge of concrete evidence against her, and the woman didn't crack once during interrogation. Broken bones, insect torture, rectal rehydration; those logs were something else," Faust says, a bit too casually. "The kicker? She's rotting in the Federal Prison Zone's dark sector right now, probably still getting hosed each day, refusing to talk."

Every detail divulged is shocking news, and Faust must be able to tell by our wide-eyed faces that we've already gotten more info than we bargained for. Still, she goes on, refocusing the conversation on her role in the current madness.

"But I digress. Point is, considering how fast they nabbed her, everyone went with the pipe dream that she hadn't found anything big. Cox's guys all chose to believe that, and up until a year ago, my people did too. Then we discovered something big, bad, and ugly. You're inside it.

"Of course, twelve months ago when we found the colony, it wasn't . . . as much of a threat," she says, clenching her jaw in pain. It looks like her headache is making a comeback.

"When Cox was busy playing whack-a-mole and analyzing the Grenada files, he had his best scientists reverse engineering the remaining fuel samples in order to figure out how to undo the dimensional fallout that'd eaten up half of Earth-068. In the years since, we've started to understand how to repair the damage. Our enemies, however, have focused almost exclusively on the fuel's destructive capabilities." She gestures toward the walls of the station we're trapped inside. "The station exists for many reasons, the biggest of which is to test every strand of fuel the Russians cook up. Fuel for fighters, for machines, for cannons capable of tearing apart space itself at the seams. It's all here."

The gravity of the situation finally reveals itself. Everything here is running on a different flavor of the most lethal dimensional poison known to man.

"Unlike us, they don't know how to handle the fallout. That's the only thing holding them back from blackmailing our entire country. That's why they've been testing it on planets. They've been trying to replicate our counter-reaction formula, and they can't do it. That's where I came in," she says, hurrying up her speech. She'd better get to it fast; her face is turning a deathly shade of red, and whatever's wrong with her is flaring up again, big-time.

"As I said before, my people believed Cox's people when they claimed the mole didn't get anything big. But I didn't buy that for a second, so I formed a new covert operations unit that reports directly to me. You mention their name to anyone else and you'll be laughed out of the military.

"They are Tenth Echelon, the best of the best, plucked from every branch of our armed forces. Handpicked by me. As soon as I was sworn in and briefed on everything you all just heard, I decided that, unlike Cox, I wasn't going to leave our national security to chance. I founded Tenth Echelon solely to carry out one mission that would last months, if not years. They were sent to track down anything related to the mole's intel breach. A year ago when they found the station, it became clear the Russians had stolen quite a bit of our initial research.

"My men managed to scout every inch of the place during the blueprinting phase, but the Russians were too fast. With the help of the dark matter fuel, they managed to take a decade's worth of construction and compress it into eight months. Things got too sticky for the Tenth to do reconnaissance, and sending in the military would be suicide. You've seen what that cannon can do. And it's sharing that power with thousands of defense turrets, all ready to disintegrate anything that gets too close. We're inside a fortress, the kind you can't crack from the outside."

"But you've been in here before," Wesley weakly interrupts, not entirely convinced by the yarn Faust is spinning.

After a brief fit of violent coughs, she explains. "When things got too tight for my own team to get eyes on the target, there was only one option left. I had to take the plunge. Around six months ago, I extended my hand to the New Union of the Red Star, explaining that we knew of their cannon's capabilities and had no way to combat it. As such, I would covertly share what we knew about a dark matter treatment formula in exchange for permanent asylum aboard the station when they handed their research off to the Russian Alliance and the Reds took over our country."

"Wait, so she is a traitor—" Gourd starts, but Faust cuts him off.

"It was a fucking ruse! I'm the single American citizen valuable enough to show my face to these people and not get shot on sight."

"But you told them we don't have a countermeasure. What stopped them from firing on us half a year ago?" I ask.

"Haven't you been listening?" she hisses, holding her forehead with one hand while using the other to decrease the room's temperature even further by twisting the dial almost as far as it can go.

For a second, I swear I see steam coming off her, though I can't tell if it's just a fresh influx of mist from the worsening cold.

"They don't know how to stop the fallout. These are state-funded terrorists, people. Wake up. NURS is just a front, a false flag, so Russia can play with shit beyond its jurisdiction, all right? No major government is going to risk firing on another superpower with a weapon it doesn't have the instruction manual for. You remember what caused the US to lead the space colonization race centuries ago?"

"World War Three . . ." Gourd says hesitantly, fully aware there's probably a more detailed answer. Naturally, there is.

"Bingo. And what was it fought with? Nukes. Lots of them. At a time when humanity didn't have the technology to heal its only planet. Ozone layer ripped wide open, natural resources obliterated, almost every species rendered extinct, you name it. All because of nukes. What those weapons were to our forefathers is what the dark matter fuel is to us. The Russians aren't going to make the same mistake twice. They're not whipping out their new toy until they know how to stop it from spreading to unwanted areas and can control and counteract every bit of damage it may cause. After all, we've reached the *final* frontier. One Earth? Not the end of the world. But the entire universe? Then we're literally out of space, and it's game over."

Well, shit, I never thought a history textbook recap would get my balls hiding faster than they are right now. She doesn't stop there, though; the story goes on even further. The brief glimpse I catch of Wesley's eyes as he shakes his head in disbelief tells me he lacks even an iota of the anger he'd held just minutes ago. When he demanded the truth, I don't think he knew he'd get it quite so bluntly.

"Back to the point," she yells, rushing to deliver the last of her story before her condition becomes critical. "I signed on so I could be our country's eyes and ears inside here. Obviously, the Russkies didn't trust me to be a good little camper while away from the station, so they put something . . ."

Halfway through her sentence, she buckles and falls to the floor. I look over to Captain for instruction, but he's already dropped his gun and dashed over to help the president back onto her feet. Wesley just stands there, dumbstruck. Gourd's profoundly confused as well, though it seems like he's still piecing together the puzzle rather than reacting to the finished picture.

After a few seconds, Grimm has the president standing again. One of her arms is propped over his shoulder, the only thing preventing her from slipping back to the floor. Taking a minute to let the mist of the room wash over her, she finds the strength to continue.

"It's in there . . . right now. It's been in there, for months," Faust mumbles, tapping her temples.

"What's is it?" I ask, as gently as I can.

"The chip. Monitors what I say, what I see. Entirely offline . . . impossible to disrupt with network interference. Rigged to . . . if I say anything too specific about the fu . . . the fuel."

Oh my God.

"Medical staff back home . . . couldn't extract. Too deep in, they said. Pulling it out would kill me. They implanted a second chip to counter the first. Nowhere near perfect, but . . . best they could do. Works most of the time, but can't defend against the big trigger switches in the first one . . . Yesterday in the shuttle . . . got too close to saying . . . passed out. Water . . . vapor, cold, all jam the first chip, help the second." She gulps down more mist from the surrounding air as her veins threaten to pop out of her skin. Then, as though she isn't on the brink of implosion, she keeps orating for us.

"Those damn Reds thought they could control me with it. They didn't realize . . . they gave me the one tool I needed to take down . . . their whole . . . fucking . . . operation."

Her head's gone from its original pale white complexion to something resembling the crimson of yesterday's shuttle. Now I realize what she's planning.

"Now you see . . . why I couldn't blow the lid on the place

when I first started exploring it . . . months ago. It would require a sacrifice . . . I wasn't sure our country was ready for. But over the past week . . . it came to my attention that our time was up. I'd only slipped them a little info, the least I could get by on . . . but it was enough. Out of alternatives, I made the call. Made sure . . . the current trip would be my last. Wes, you were right . . . the White House was my fault. But I never meant for you to get swept up in it. You were supposed to be out the door by then. I staged my kidnapping . . . to explain my permanent disappearance to the public. The Russians cooperated . . . thought it was my way of . . . requesting the start of my asylum and . . . leaving the country exposed. They didn't know . . . my plan."

"B-but why d-did you . . . the Nebulus . . ." Wesley sputters, mortified.

"Those planets . . . could've bought me a few more weeks. Taken away . . . their last testing resources . . . don't feel bad. I was trying . . . to postpone the inevitable," Faust whispers, losing the fight against her body's internal meltdown.

"You can't be telling the truth! You . . . you were in their systems," Wesley says, driving himself insane as he grasps at any possible straw that could help him maintain his crumbling conspiracy theory.

"Not my blood . . . not my retina . . . all synthetic. Fingerprint blood capsules and micro-contacts . . . stored on my body, impossible to confiscate . . . the perfect skeleton keys. Fashioned from the DNA . . . in the stray hairs and skin cells of my NURS escorts . . . that I gathered and brought to the labs after my trips here. I'm wearing their identities . . . using their clearance levels. No more questions, Wes." She squeezes her temples with enough force that I'm amazed her skull isn't cracking.

"Captain Grimm?"

"Yes, Madam President," he responds, his tone filled with the utmost respect as he continues to prop her up.

"My final briefing for you begins now. I started a timer . . . around fifteen hours ago. Tenth Echelon set off a distress beacon to these coordinates. Signals every auxiliary fleet we have. They'll have been . . . traveling here since last night. By the time they arrive, I will have taken out the cooling, so the Reds can't use the cannon or outer defenses. That leaves a window open . . . gives our boys a fighting chance to board the station."

So that's why she didn't want any of us here. The whole time, I thought without us she'd be screwed, but no . . . she had a plan mapped out from start to finish. One president and her secret team were going to stage the biggest, most elaborate operation in military history. Boy, did we ever fuck it up.

"You only need to hold out . . . an hour or so . . . until the rest of them get here. But . . . there's a complic—"

A surge of blood pours out of her mouth, dripping all over the floor. We're looking at the last few minutes of the 117th President of the United States.

"—complication," she continues after wiping off the dribble of blood still dangling from her lower lip.

"The blue tower . . . heart of the station. When reinforcements . . . arrive, and the Reds see they're outnumbered, they'll start the . . . data purge. All the research . . . lost."

"Surely the Russian government has backups somewhere,"

I interject, not meaning to interrupt a dying woman but wanting clarification as to why we specifically should put our necks on the line like I sense she's about to suggest.

"They have nothing recent . . . don't want to messy their fingerprints . . . risk leaks . . . until the research is complete. That tower . . . the Spire . . . has all the dozens of zettabytes' worth of data the station holds . . . all the relevant data the Russians hold," she says before taking a massive breath and continuing her pained instructions. "So much data . . . takes time to destroy. Six hours to wipe it all . . . Grimm, if you and your Marines can stop it before it finishes . . . the remaining research can defragment the rest.

"I would've settled for capture of the station . . . but with you here, I have a new primary objective . . ." she trails off.

The typically stoic and calm Captain Grimm is on the verge of tears as he shakes her frail body. The jolt summons her back for just a bit longer.

"Captain Grimm, your final mission . . . under my command. Get to the top of the Spire. Save that research. Get it in the right hands . . . American hands."

Gourd's barely maintaining his "I'm too tough for crying and other pussy shit" look, Wesley's dangerously close to having a panic attack, and Grimm . . . I'm almost certain I saw the glint of a tear in his eye, but I can't be sure.

"Now . . . let me down," she requests.

The captain gently lowers her to the floor.

"No more time to waste . . . need to get . . . those defenses down. Get your men . . . out of here," she says, blood seeping from her mouth again, boiling and steaming as it makes contact with the floor, too hot to freeze. Her head looks like a cherry on the verge of popping, and God knows the three of us do not have the iron guts to watch our president go out in such a morbid manner, not after what she's been through.

Grimm gives her one final salute before picking up his rifle and ordering us to get going. As we start to move out, it becomes apparent Wesley's going to need some assistance. He's petrified, completely frozen in place.

Without a word, Captain grabs Wesley like a football and hauls him along at the pace Gourd and I set. We press forward until we've reached the chamber's entrance, where the massive entry doors slide open and let us pass. They slam shut the second we're on the other side, leaving just enough time for us to hear the detonation and subsequent explosions echoing from the tank-stacked halls behind us. An orange glow shines through the cracks in the room's entranceway, drenching our backs in hues of destruction. While none of us see it firsthand, our shared thought goes unspoken. We know that sound wasn't just the shriek of a station being crippled from the inside or the roar of Russians realizing they've been bested. It was the sound of Roseanne Faust's final act of service to her country.

CHAPTER 10

Wesley

Various gurgles and gasps are the only noises I can muster after I rip off my face mask and puke my brains out, the umpteenth time my body has forcibly emptied itself during the unending, nightmarish journey I'm trapped in. The mess in front of me is disgusting, and once again, I feel nothing but shame and embarrassment in front of the Americans. I'm amazed I even have anything left to spew, given that it takes me a few seconds to reach the point of empty, dry heaves. The veins on my neck actually ache from the strain, as do the rest of the muscles in my body. I lose control of my legs and fall to my knees beside the puddle I've created.

"Get it together, man!" Beecher grabs my shoulders, steadying my heaving body.

I'm grateful that he's still standing by my side to help. After all, if he'd put me through what I've put him and his fellow men through, I'd never be so supportive. Or maybe they understand, or . . . or I don't know. The whole situation's a crock of shite and I just don't know anymore. I can't block it out of my mind. It just happened and the memory isn't going away any time soon. Her face keeps popping back up, and it's just so awful, and I . . . I . . .

No, keep it together, Wesley. No more retching. No more neuroticism. We're not going to let a moment of weakness transform into one of *those* episodes. Get a grip, like Beecher.

"But how did you know?" I ask the captain weakly, rasping the words out through my weary breaths.

"Morse code, Wesley. She was telling me the truth the whole way here."

Morse code? Morse fucking code?

"But y-you never, never said . . ."

"If I said anything, it'd set her off, and there wasn't a time or place to pull you aside for a one-on-one."

"I-I didn't know, Captain," I say, realizing it's too late.

"Wesley, I know. But we don't have time. With the station's cooling offline and crippled, the Russians will know there are enemies aboard, especially since they were expecting at least one American's arrival. The sabotage is obvious. They'll be sending squads here as we speak, so we need to fortify our position and prepare to weather the storm until reinforcements arrive. Lieutenants, set up on the sides of the boarding platform; we're creating a defensive bottleneck. Beecher, handle the right flank; Gourd, left."

Gourd shuffles over to the diagonal counter on his side of the platform, mirroring Beecher's angle. Looks like the plan is to cross streams and make it impossible for the enemy to slip through the sides. Not that I'd know a thing about strategy; I'm too busy glancing back at the man I've disappointed on what is undoubtedly his most important mission ever. He doesn't allow me time to feel sorry for myself.

"Can I trust you to aim your weapon at the right people and take care of yourself at the same time?" Captain asks, seeing if he can pep talk me back into fighting shape before the opposition appears. He can.

"I . . . yes, Captain Grimm," I respond, discovering a renewed sense of determination.

"Good, then we take front and center behind the tram bumper barricade."

At last, we've got things sorted out. Not a moment too soon, either. Just beyond my allies' scuffling boots and clinking ammo belts, I hear shuttles screaming across rails, their vibrations shaking my feet. I know what's coming down those tracks, and I'm ready for it.

My feet quake more and more with every passing second. At first, the tremors are small. But they keep growing. And growing. And growing. I take cover behind the shuttle bumper beside Grimm. It's not the first time I've been hunkered down behind a chest-high barrier in the past forty-eight hours. The difference is that now I have a gun and know who the real enemy is. The UK hasn't formally declared a side in the international affair, but if I make it home—no, *when* I make it home—I'm going to petition damn hard on behalf of the three Yankees who kept me alive.

The enemy rockets into the station, and Captain gives the word that it's time. I swerve up, poking my upper half over the bumper barricade just in time to be blinded by the incoming shuttle's headlights. Bloody hell, those are bright!

I sink back behind cover to avoid taking a bullet while I

regain my vision. Not the smoothest start, but at least I'm still in the fight. After seeing nothing but large white spots for a good ten seconds, I clutch my rifle and pop out again, intent on lasting long enough to fire a bullet or, if I'm lucky, two.

With my eyes finally adjusted to the headlights, I take a look at what we're up against. There's not a single human in sight, just two transports' worth of faux-engineering robots with arm-rifles and glowing black eyes. Some climb over seats to get closer to the front faster, others duck behind their peers for tactical cover, and the remainder walk down the center aisles of their shuttles with no self-preservation instincts whatsoever. The bots just trudge forward, unloading bullets in our general direction in hopes of hitting anything that bleeds.

Still not entirely sure what I'm doing, I take a chance and gently squeeze my rifle trigger. My entire body shakes from the recoil, and I hastily remove my finger from the firing mechanism for fear that I'll pop an ally's head off should I dare hold it any longer. What the hell type of firearm causes such kickback? It didn't seem to be nearly as complicated of a weapon back when the captain was training me on the shuttle. Admittedly, my gun knowledge is piss-poor, but the thing in my hands doesn't look too different from a thirtieth generation AK-NX rifle, which would use standardized armor-piercing 7.62x39 fractal rounds. I don't believe such rounds should cause me to shake so pathetically! And yet they do. The recoil is ludicrous. How are the other three handling it? I look at Captain Grimm next to me, whose massive right bicep and shoulder are holding his rifle in place, and realize I completely forgot the proper stance. I might not have the same musculature to back me up, but I'll be damned if I can't at least try to strike the right pose.

I shoot up from behind cover again, prepared to actually take out a robot. I choose my first target. It's one of the bots hiding behind cover on the right shuttle, near the back. I fire off a small burst, and to my amazement, the bullets don't go blasting off into the great beyond. Instead, they make contact with my target and its searing black eye bursts into a thousand little fragments, the head of the mechanical foot soldier ripping from its neck mount as the bullets tear it backward.

I . . . I got one! That was amazing!

The crackle of gunfire and whirring of bullets stop being the deafening unpleasantness they once were and become a call, not only to pay back some of the nightmares I've endured over the past two days, but also to avenge Roseanne Faust, a monstrous and haunting old woman who did what she had to do right up until her final breath.

I let out a battle cry and pull the trigger once again, unloading far more than a burst for my next offensive. The kicks come rapidly, one after another slamming into my shoulder and pushing me back, but they don't affect my aim. I riddle holes in the chests of the first few machines roaming down the center aisles, stunning them long enough for my three teammates to efficiently pop off their heads. Metal flies everywhere, a mixture of both our shell casings and the shattered remains of what used to be our adversaries.

As minutes pass, the robotic bodies of our foes pile up on the shuttle floors, cluttering their comrades' paths. Like oversized ants, the remaining units resort to crawling over their offline allies in a desperate attempt to finish us. Thankfully, they can't land a shot on our crew as Gourd and Beecher create an impenetrable crossfire of bullets, restricting enemy wiggle room while Grimm and I go in for the finishing blows. Even though they're soulless tin cans and not the warm bodies of villainous terrorists, the rage-fueled catharsis I feel is strong as ever.

Only a few more to go; they're dropping like flies. The four of us keep slinging lead, chipping away at the last of the automatons as they march toward their doom. That'll teach the Russians to rope me into their nonsense. They'll be taking their damn machines back in buckets when everything's over, if I have anything to say about it!

After another good minute of unloading magazines and shouting battle cries, it looks like I'll be getting my wish. We effortlessly take care of our last few attackers and reduce them to a pile of bolts without receiving so much as a scratch in return. We've got the current fight in the bag, my mates and I—

"Wesley, look out!" Beecher yells.

I pause my rifle reload and look up, twisting my head forward just in time to see it. On the floor of the right shuttle's main aisle, a thin stream of fuel trickles in the direction of my feet. The liquid isn't propelling itself forward, however. It's a trail left by the innards of a brutally dismembered robot that's been split in half from the waist down, abdomen spewing black fuel as the machine's hand claws at the ground, dragging its torso toward me. By the time anyone notices the shell of the enemy is still active, it's already made its way to my barricade and leapt up, launching itself forward with its single arm outstretched to catch me in a desperate suicide strike.

I stare in horror as its cold, glowing eye hurtles toward me; its cracked-open, crab-like head plate ready to slam me into oblivion. It's less than a meter from my face, leaving me with no time to scream.

Captain reacts at a speed I can barely process. With no time to set up a proper shot, Grimm slams his rifle to the right, waving it like a police baton less than a foot in front of my face. Miraculously, he doesn't smash my skull in; instead, he stops just short of my head to intercept the oncoming robot. With not a picosecond to spare, the barrel of the gun lands right in front of my enemy's shimmering eye. Gunfire crackles and I know I'm about to go blind. I raise my free hand to shield my eyes from what's about to happen, though the scene unfolds well before I can get my makeshift blinder in place. Grimm's rifle tip lights up as he executes the machine at point-blank range, his perfectly timed trigger pull launching a cascade of bullets directly through the head of the thing that was less than a second away from killing me. I fall on my back, stunned and all but paralyzed from shock as I watch the machine drop lifelessly to my side. Captain marches over to it and unloads a few more rounds into its head just to make sure it won't find *another* last bout of life.

Even with the sound protection offered by my military face mask, my ears ring and cause me to wince in reaction to every bullet Grimm fires. I hear the harsh screech of metal tearing apart as his bullets travel through their target to put holes and dents in the neighboring floor panel. Only when he stops shooting do the pots and pans stop falling off the shelves inside my skull.

Christ, that was horrifying. I can't even feel my body. I'm

so numb it's like I'm a spectator, like I'm not even here right now. Wait—

Wh-what is *happening* to me?

CHAPTER 11
Gourd

O ne wave of rickety Reds down and out. We're gonna make every fucker that comes our way pay. And when we're done with the bots down here, we'll go upstairs and smoke all of those, too. Then we'll put the colony's workers on trial, throw them behind bars where they belong, and take the fight to their home turf! We'll go to the Kremlin, find the Russians' top brass, and kick all of their asses! 'Cause we're fucking Americans—well, three out of four, but I'll round up and make Wesley an honorary—and we're gonna show them what we're made of: thirty percent heroism, fifty percent liberty and justice for all, bitch, fifteen percent raw skill, and five percent polyester-nylon blend . . . wait, what? Shit, I've still got my stupid face mask on. Fuck it, I don't mind. These two little eyeholes are like mini-scopes for me to take down more bots—wait, hold up. What the . . .

Something is still alive and crawling toward Grimm and Wes. Shit, I gotta say something!

Beecher beats me by half a second and shouts at Wes to look out. That thing is already airborne, I don't have a clean shot, and I'm definitely too far away to stop it by hand—but that doesn't mean I can't try. I drop my gun and dash for the scene, but luckily Captain's one step ahead. Faster than I can say "dead commie," Grimm peppers bullets right through the thing's little tin skull, dropping it instantly. That's the Captain I know.

Wes falls onto his back, panting. It looks like he made it out just in time—minus the black goop on his arm. *Oh no.*

It only takes a second for him to start screaming and for me to figure out that some of the fuel got on his arm when the robot's head popped open. Jesus H. Christ. Even if it's watered down compared to the strand the station's central cannon runs on, that's still not something I want to touch with a ten-foot pole, let alone a limb.

"Hold on, man!" I yell, grabbing a piece of dry, jagged robo-skull. Time to put some of the shit I learned in medic training to use.

I get closer to him and see exactly what I'm expecting. That black shit on his forearm isn't sitting there, no sir. It melts right through the dragon skin armor, creating a giant hole in his forearm that won't stop spreading, threatening to gobble up his bicep above and hand below. What I'm about to do ain't gonna be pretty, but it needs to happen.

"These fucks won't take two of us today!" I yell, and just as Grimm and Beecher start to protest, I swing the robot shell at Wes's elbow joint and slice his forearm right off.

"Aaaaaah!" Wes screams in gratitude, clearly appreciative of me saving his life. "What the fuck!" he yells between wails, his face sharing the expression of my squaddies.

"You guys saw that shit. It was gonna spread and eat

his whole body in seconds." I point to the spot on the floor where there's no longer a single trace that he ever had a forearm and left hand in the first place. Not a single scrap of DNA left, I'd reckon—just a small, dissolving puddle of bubbling fuel.

"But how did you know that was going to work?" Beecher asks, pointing at the red, gushing, pulsating stump where Wes used to have an appendage to jerk off with.

I kneel down, take off my face mask, and tie its soft, absorbent fabric around the wound to stem the flow of blood while I answer Beecher's question. My squadmates take off their masks as well, now that they're no longer useful.

"Think about it, man. If the metal shell can hold the fuel safely inside the bots, then who's to say it can't stop that shit from spreading across us as well?" I reply, calmly educating him while applying a tourniquet to the wound.

"He's right," Captain says through gritted teeth, scrunching his thumb and forefinger together on the bridge of his nose while squeezing his eyelids shut, massaging that shit out. I'd be stressed too if I were him, since he's the one who's gonna have to fill out civilian injury paperwork. If we make it out alive, that is.

"Jesus," Beecher murmurs, not looking too hot. Medic training never was his favorite. Good guy that he is, though, he still tries to pitch in and help Wesley keep his mind off the whole "am I going to bleed to death" question.

"Focus on me, man. Just look up here. You're alive. Big picture, right?" Beecher says to him. Nice words.

"The big picture is bullshit!" Wesley shouts back. Not nice words.

"Can you stop fidgeting, man? I can't get a secure knot with all the waving," I tell him.

"Stop fidgeting? I just got my fuckin' arm hacked off, mate!"

Like, that's true, but being turned into literal nothingness by terrorist fuel doesn't sound much more appealing. To me, at least.

"Hey man, like Cap said yesterday, no room for tourists in our line of work." When you sign on to shoot at people, you gotta expect to get shot back at in some form or another.

"Fuck, though . . ." he says, losing his will to kick up a fuss.

At first the lack of resistance is nice, but then I realize it's because he might be falling into a coma. With his kind of wound, I want him conscious, damn it.

"Man?" I smack him on the cheek as his eyes close. The hit works and he's back, for now. "Stay awake, chief. Naptime in a little bit, but right now we can't risk you going under."

We can't risk ourselves going under either, though. As I tend to Wes, tremors rumble under my boots, and it ain't me doing it, it's the ground. That better not be—

"Reinforcements!" Captain barks.

Can't save a civilian if we're KIA. Wes will just have to hang in there and hope that God saves the Queen. I think that's how that phrase works.

Beecher shoots back to his post, and I follow suit. After getting up off the ground I charge back to my spot, diving behind the counter and sweeping up my rifle just as the second set of shuttles crash into the first pair. These goddamn Reds just don't give up.

The two cars in front of us buckle as the ramming duo

push them from behind, smashing against the bumpers Captain's hiding behind. Bits of their exteriors tear off and fly toward us, as do parts of the robot graveyard we've made up front. While it's annoying that the newcomers' arrival impact partially disassembles our makeshift barricade of machine bodies, it's no big deal. Now it'll be even easier for me to see and mow down baddies.

Screeching and ramming sounds turn into clanking and clinking as enemy units, currently beyond our view, make their way across the front of their shuttles and onto the back of the two trams crushed between Beecher and me. Doesn't matter if we're down one friendly for the current wave; tactical advantage trumps quantity advantage every time. Well, except for a few. But the current fight won't be an exception to the rule. We have the choke point and three of the best shots humanity has to offer on our side. There's not a Soviet robot in existence that'll top us.

The rifle arms of the defense force's second wave reach our position. I slam my finger down and let 'er rip. The first torrent of bullets hit the mechs before they're even out in the open, pushing those clunkers back with ease. We keep the pressure on, and soon they're nothing but a clump of malfunctioning Roombas rubbing against each other, firing into and against one another, unable to get a single steady shot on us. Doesn't matter how scary they look, how many there are, or how fast they come. Nothing beats three guys with the bald eagle's blessing.

Just as I start to become desensitized to the color yellow, Beecher's muzzle stops flashing. I lock eyes with him for half a second, which is just enough time for him to give me the "reloading" sign. All right, all right, I got your back, man. Make it snappy, though. Triangles don't work with one corner cut off.

For the first few seconds, everything seems okay. I keep punching the silver Soviets back, and between Cap and me, it looks like we might be able to keep them in their places long enough for Beecher to get back in the game. That is, until Cap gives the sign that he has to reload too. Not good, man. Looks like Beecher's back up and running, but in the window between my boy coming back online and Grimm going off, two clankers slip past our bullet wall. Looks like I gotta get crafty.

Keeping my distance so I don't get any fuel splattered on me, I shimmy over a little until I'm between my post and Grimm's, a good angle for me to pop off a few rounds at the two pack leaders. Splitting them right down the head, I get back to my spot just in time for Grimm to whirl around, reloaded and ready for action. As quickly as we almost lost our defensive grip, we regain it, and while the bad guys are busy jostling each other, I get my chance to pop in a new mag. The transfer takes two blinks of an eye before I'm back in the business of kicking ass and taking names. Shit's moving quickly—not just for me, but for the fight as a whole. I might be going through bots like hotcakes, but I'm also starting to run low on mags.

My personal tally is up to about twenty of these bastards destroyed, but Jesus, they just keep coming. For every one we pick off, two more file in, and it doesn't look like the trend's going to stop any time soon. Don't get me wrong, I'll hammer these things down all day long for fun; the issue is ammo. My reserves are drying up, and it's obvious the guys we took these belts from weren't planning on holding off an army. Cap's got Wesley's belt slung over his shoulder, so he's rocking twice the munitions now. Double portions of a small serving still isn't a whole lot, though.

Pop. Pop. Pop. Another three down. We nearly have a pyramid of the busters' corpses formed, which allows us to score clean shots on new enemies' heads just because they're getting held up trying to climb over their fallen buddies. That makes things easier, and we've already got the best position in the house, but I'm not feeling too hot about taking on many more of these things. My belt's seriously light, and when I finger each pouch looking for a magazine, only one crops up near the last slot. That ain't good. And getting up close and personal with these fellas isn't on today's menu either, given that they're spitting something nasty. Wes gave us his first-hand review of that shit, and now he's only left with a second.

Then it happens. Metal stops falling down the shell pyramid, and the last bot sitting on top of it eats a big one right in the center of its eye. Beecher keeps his stance like the rest of us, waiting to see if it's a confirmed kill or if we're gonna have another creepy crawly try to give one of us a hug. After a few more seconds and no movement, it looks like we're finally clear.

"That better be the last of them," Beecher grunts.

"Fat chance. Ammo count?" Grimm says. He's probably right. The station was swarming with them; who knows how many are on their way right now. And if more *weren't* already on their way, then the ruckus we've caused will undoubtedly attract additional unwelcome visitors.

"Just one mag left," I say. My little lead farm has whittled down its harvest.

"Got three," Beecher reports.

"Here." Cap beckons us over, then hands us each two from Wesley's pouches.

Beecher gives me one of his so we're even. Nice guy.

I look over at Wes, who has only one eye open. The poor dude's clinging to consciousness like a toddler clings to his favorite blanket. The mask I put around his arm is completely soaked through and there's still fresh blood dripping onto a thickening crimson puddle on the floor. Looks like Cap's seeing the same thing I am.

"Hang in there, trooper," Cap says, patting Wes gently on the shoulder that's still linked to a full arm.

Beecher and I give him a little salute, reminding him of our promise that we have been doing, and will continue to do, whatever we can to get him home. At the moment, that doesn't mean a whole lot. Our guns aren't raised and at the ready. Having abandoned formation to restock on ammo might have been the last straw needed to take us out of the zone. We've disbanded our triangle of determination—it doesn't feel like we're in fighting mode anymore.

"You think we got a chance at holding off another set?" I want to hear Beecher deliver a wisecrack or something, anything to lighten up the mood. I don't dig the shitty gritty vibe our situation is giving off, and if there's one guy who can fix that problem in a flash, it's Beech.

All he does is shake his ammo belt a little and shrug. Well, shit. Captain reads the mood and decides to put it out there, the thought on all of our minds.

"Men."

Beecher and I look at him.

"Reinforcements are on their way, both ours and theirs. And if ours don't get here first and we're left to stand our ground with what we've got," he says, tapping his dual ammo belt getup, "we'll take every last one of them to hell with us."

I perk up a bit. That's the fighting spirit. That's why Grimm's the man in charge. He gets that battle spark of ours back in check just in time, too. Rumbles vibrate beneath my boots. Round three's coming, and it ain't gonna be pretty.

"Stations," Grimm says, getting back into captain mode for what's probably the last time.

Headlights appear somewhere down the tube, their white beams poking past the tin graveyard we have blocking the entrance.

"And men," Grimm adds, keeping his eyes front and center, "it's been an honor serving with you."

"Aye, aye, Captain," I mumble. Shit's getting emotional and I can't fight with the sad butterflies whirring around, damn it. C'mon, Lieutenant, straighten up. The next round's the big one. Either beat the third strike or you're out.

The lights get brighter, the screeching grows louder, and my heart beats faster. I've seen some stiff odds before, but right now is a whole 'nother level.

The shaking beneath my feet reaches its peak, and I know it's that time. The front row of shuttles crash forward against the bumper yet again, the second row now adding to the slam as the pile of metal bodies shifts around on top. Then comes the sound of robots marching forward, their harsh stomps telling me we're only a few seconds away from seeing wave three creep over that ridge. I give Beecher one last look, and he shoots me a thumbs-up. I give him one back, take a deep breath, and shift my attention toward the bottleneck. It's now or never.

The pile of robot corpses begins to shake, and pieces fall from the top of the mound. At first, it's just one or two bits, then a few more, until finally a wave of scraps comes down in an avalanche and the first steely hand grips the top of the garbage pile. The machine pulls its body over the edge of the graveyard barricade, rearing its ugly head just in time for Beecher's first shot to pop it. One down, God knows how many to go.

From there, it's a madhouse like the last two waves, the issue being that now we can't keep a stream of gunfire going; we're stuck having to choose our shots instead. More bots are able to stumble over the metal mound while we focus on knocking out eye sockets and shredding heads, rendering that damn body barricade of ours all but useless. One by one the machines fall, and two by two more march forward to fill their comrades' places, moving with the kind of suicidal determination only a commie could program.

It's not long before I've taken down a good few dozen of them with Beech and Cap and I'm on my last mag, popping that sucker in with the gusto of a guy who knows he's fucked.

It's been a long road, and I've learned a lot along the way. Between Grimm, the best captain I've ever met, and Beecher, the best friend I've ever had, I'd say I've lived in good company. Hell, I'd say I've lived a good life. One with meaning, at least. I did right by my country and it did right by me. And here in a goddamn rolling pin from hell, I did what I had to do and I'll go the way I have to go, fighting a threat far bigger than the robots closing in on us right now. I'm sorry to my ma and lil' sis that I can't make one last call, but I know them, and I know they'll be fine. Even though I'll be gone, God will take good care of them. Hopefully he does the same for me when I come stampeding through his doorstep in the next few seconds.

I fold up my bipod, press the butt of my rifle up against my shoulder, and squint hard down the sights for my last few shots. Crack. Crack. Seven bullets left. Crack. Crack. Crack. Down to four now. Crack. Crack—

A deafening roar blasts through the station, one that completely erases the sound of gunfire. Right in front of me, roughly two dozen commie bots get vaporized as a wall smashes through the tram tube, speeding across my line of sight with no sign of stopping even after decimating the opposition. Sparks fly everywhere, and we hide behind what little cover we have as the goliath object eats the station alive, inching dangerously close to us as it burrows through the tube.

Beecher's mouth moves, and though I can't read it or hear him, it's pretty clear he recognizes whatever the hell the thing is, which is great 'cause I sure as hell d—

Wait a minute.

Hold on.

It's them. They made it! They fucking made it!

CHAPTER 12

Beecher

Those glorious sons of bitches sure know how to crash a party, all right. A few seconds after the cruiser makes its perfectly timed entrance, it slows and screeches to a halt. It completely fills in the shattered upper edge of the tube it's just carved open, leaving only a sliver of a gap for the black glow of the station's deflector shields to shine through as their energy fields protect us from the vacuum of space. Hopefully they don't go offline now that the cavalry's arrived to tear up the place. Our guys accounted for the shields before crashing the party with a maneuver that would've otherwise killed us, right?

The portion of the cruiser parked right in front of us sports a hatched airlock, which swings open to reveal a smug Aussie who knows R Company just saved the day. I swear I see a halo hovering over his head.

"Hey, fellas, I reckon we're not interrupting anything, are we?" Sergeant Milo Toufexis calls out, hopping down onto the mosh pit of dead bots. He nearly falls over as he lands on the shaky metal scraps. "Oof, did you guys make the mess here?"

"Y'know, cruisers aren't built for that docking shit you guys just pulled." I let out an overwhelmed, overjoyed laugh. "Stop eating crayons on the job."

"How'd you find us?" Gourd shouts, sliding over his platform's chest-high cover and scrambling toward Milo to give him the hug of a lifetime.

"Hey, you're welcome!" the sergeant says, straining to withstand the tight embrace. "Bet you're glad we asked for those exothermic sigs way back when during recruitment, yeah?"

Jesus, I totally forgot we had those. Still, they only work at close range, meaning the reason our guys are in the Nebulus sector to begin with isn't because of us . . . it's because Faust's plan was real.

"Besides, one of us was gonna have to breach here. Every attack cruiser from the Wisconsin unit to South Carolina's fleet is breaking in right now. All major entry ports and critical channels are getting slammed by our guys as we speak."

I can't believe our president was telling the truth.

"Insane, man," Gourd says, just as shocked as me. After a second of cooldown, the wave of amazement washes past us and we realize not everything's hunky-dory yet.

"Wesley," Gourd and I say in unison, turning our heads to see if the poor guy's still hanging in there.

Captain's way ahead of us. Already hauling Wes along, Cap charges forward with the injured Brit tucked safely under his shoulder. "We can talk inside," he says. "Med bay first."

After a dash to the bay, we lay Wes down on a bed and the medical officers get to work on stabilizing his condition.

"He'll make it," one tells us, giving our party the all-clear to leave, if we so choose.

I decline the offer. He hasn't come so far just to lose an arm and be abandoned by his squad without a proper good-bye. I look at Gourd and see he feels the same way.

"Right, well, now that we've got that taken care of, I think an explanation on your side is in order. Let's get you lot to command so you can spin a yarn or two," Toufexis says, signaling we should step outside the room.

Shit. After all the stuff we lied about to get here, how the hell are we going to avoid an on-the-spot court-martial—

"I'll take it from here," Captain Grimm says, giving us both a nod and Wesley a salute before guiding the sergeant out the door. Looks like he's planning on covering for all our asses, leaving Gourd and me to chill with the injured civilian.

I look at the tubes connected to Wesley's stump, watching streams of liquid flow through them as vital fluids are pushed into and sucked out of his wound. The medics will no doubt get him suited up with a prosthetic arm soon enough, but for now we have no choice but to look at the remains of his severed limb.

"You awake, man?" I say, after an uncharacteristically shy Gourd makes it clear he doesn't want to start the conversation. His apprehension makes sense; Wes might be a bit salty toward him, considering the big guy is the one who hacked off his forearm in the first place. Still, we're all responsible for letting it get to that point.

Though Wesley's eyes remain closed, his mouth moves a little. After a bit of struggling, he forms a word, overpowering the pain meds' efforts to render him dormant.

"Yeah," he responds weakly. His eyelids begin to part, and

before I know it, he's staring right at me. He's not the scared, twenty-something business guy we rescued on that shuttle yesterday. No, that Wesley is gone.

In his eyes, I see a man who's witnessed horrors, someone who's been exposed to too much too fast. I know that feeling. Hell, I'll probably have nightmares myself when everything's over. But therein lies the upside.

"At least it's over, yeah?" I say, trying to ease him into a goodbye. No simple way to do that, considering the guy is one limb worse for wear and will probably have serious PTSD for months, if not years, to come.

"Ha, sure," he says, regaining a bit of strength in his voice. "Not for you two though, I assume."

"You got us there," I say after a deep exhale, looking at Gourd's weary eyes and knowing they're nothing more than a reflection of my own.

My partner finally speaks up. "Wes, I'm so sorry, man. I had to. It was only gonna spread, and I didn't want to wait and see . . ." The words cascade out of his mouth in a troubled ramble.

Wesley hushes him. "You were right. The fuel was spreading, and it would have eaten me alive if it wasn't for you. I'm grateful you did what you did. And as for that stuff . . . God, it shouldn't exist."

His statement brings to mind the president's dying order, a thought I try to block out of my head. "Think you're gonna hold up okay?"

"Unlike you blokes, the stuff I do probably only requires one hand anyhow," he jokes. The guy lost half an arm and he's joking. Wow. He really has changed. Power to him, though. "Anywho, having a 360-degree rotating wrist should be interesting."

Looking on the positive side of things, eh? The new Wesley seems like he'll be a cool guy. Or maybe it's just the pain meds making him a little more docile and chummier than usual.

Captain knocks on the glass door and gives us the one-minute notice to wrap it up. I guess it's time for farewells, then.

"Well, Wes, it's been a pleasure serving with you. Maybe we'll cross paths at some point in the future. If we do, the beer's on me," I say.

"Yeah, Wes. You're a good guy. Best of luck when you get back to work—if you go back to—like, if you choose—" Gourd stammers, completely fumbling his farewell.

Wes shrugs it off like a champ. "Ha-ha, thanks. I know what you mean, and yeah, my career might have to go on hiatus for a bit. I'll figure something out. Regardless, best of luck up ahead." He extends his remaining hand for a goodbye handshake.

Gourd meets it with the lightest grip I've ever seen him use, then does a little head bow and quickly exits the room so he doesn't run the risk of looking any more awkward.

Now that it's down to just Wes and me, I feel a bit of a social obligation to avoid dragging my exit out any longer than it needs to be.

"See ya down the line?" I ask him, extending my hand for a shake.

He meets it and responds confidently. "For sure. It's been an honor to fight alongside you." He's eyeballing the door. Maybe he wants me gone too?

"The honor is all mine." I take his cue and turn to leave.

"Beecher," he blurts out, his voice filled with uncertainty.

"Yeah?"

"I overheard your chat with Gourd back in the shuttle the other day. I know you . . . well . . . you think for yourself," he says, stalling every few words as he finds the right way to articulate whatever it is he's trying to get across.

"I'd like to think I do."

Then the conversation takes a turn.

"That fuel . . . the research. You know none of it should ever leave the station," Wesley warns, his tone grim.

I really hoped he forgot that bit from Faust; God knows I've been trying to.

"Make the right call," are his last words to me as I swing the door open to leave.

Not wanting to say anything, I give a subtle wave of acknowledgment before exiting the room to regroup with Gourd and Grimm at the end of the hallway. As I pass by the last glass-paneled wall of Wesley's room, I feel his eyes following me.

"All set, Lieutenant?" Grimm asks.

"Um, yeah, good to go," I respond, not entirely convinced that's the truth.

"All right, then here's the deal. I've secured the last two ACA suits aboard the cruiser for you two, so get suited up and meet me in the hangar. I'll brief everyone there. Clock's ticking, men."

With that, he announces he's leaving to suit up in his personalized armor's duplicate unit, since the original is now floating in space somewhere. That leaves Gourd and me clear to head toward the back entrance of the hangar's standard-issue ACA deployment area.

For the first few seconds, we're totally silent. It's been a rocky couple of hours. Hell, days even. We've seen so much shit that our minds haven't had time to digest it all, let alone discuss it in small talk. So we walk in silence, until I find the nerve to ask Gourd a question.

"Why'd you go for it, man?"

"Go for what?"

"His arm. I've never seen you just do something like that— so decisively, I mean. You didn't wait for orders or anything, you just did it."

He takes a few seconds to craft his response.

"It's like you said yesterday. It's about doing what you gotta do, not doing what you're told to do."

I gulp down a breath's worth of air, taking a moment to refocus my attention on the conflict immediately ahead of us. We reach the deployment area and prepare to re-don the ACAs, the bulletproof super suits we've been sorely missing for the better part of the past day. They're taxpayer money well spent, even if there's only enough to fund a few of them per year. It still hurts to think about the ungodly sum of money my squad dumped into space back on that shuttle when we ditched our last suits; what a waste of armor.

We step inside the Advanced Combat Armor fitting modules, relieved that we've been privileged with the last two suits the cruiser has on board. Through the modules' glass panels, I see Gourd is as pumped as I am when the metallic arms start to unfold from the ceiling hatches, each carrying bits and pieces of our exoskeletons. Limb by limb they're fitted and fastened over our dragon skin, snugging us into the aluminum-titanium interior frames. Then larger sets of robotic arms bring down the armor's plating to further bulk us up, and once that's all fitted, a thick spray of catalyst is applied, activating the suits' projectile-spitting nanogel layer. From there, the last bit of our exposed flesh is covered as our helmets' faceplates slide down, preparing us for the penultimate suit-up procedure. *Here's where the fun really begins.*

My suit's HUD boots to life and I hear the familiar buzz of my comms line activating, which lets me know Gourd and I are officially connected via radio and almost ready to rumble.

The fitting module has one more attachment to install. Two small compartments open behind my feet, revealing microthruster-concealing shin greaves. They latch onto my armor's calf plating and are bolted down until I can feel the small thruster engines whizzing and whirring against my titanium heels.

With our fancy rocket boots saddled up, the only thing left is weapons assignment. The overhead menus in our fitting booths display the gear we've been authorized to use for the upcoming mission, and it's a hell of a step up from the tracker pistols and two-foot laser sabers from yesterday. We're each getting two forearm-mounted buzz saws for cutting shit up close and a heavy pulse rifle for anything that can't be sliced. Something tells me Cap got a word in when it came to picking out these bad boys.

"Least we can't run out of ammo now," Gourd says with relief.

It's true, the pulse rifle generates its own ammo in the

form of laser shots, so we're not going to run into *that* situation again. As long as there are visible wavelengths in the electromagnetic radiation around us, the rifle will absorb and congeal the resulting photon energy into segmented beam bursts and pump out all the firepower we'll ever need. In short, screw physical bullets. One less thing to worry about on an otherwise lengthy list of concerns.

One by one, our modules' thin metallic claws come down again, clutching the weaponry. I stick my arms out and wait for the first clamps to latch on. Their strong grips wrap around my wrists as the braces for the buzz saws are fitted, alongside the activation switches placed on my palms. Then the blades themselves lower and carefully lock into my forearm mounts. At the end of the process, half of each jagged death wheel is visible and the rest is sheathed. But even when partially concealed, these deadly discs still add an extra twelve inches of bulk to either side of my figure. As a result, I feel bigger, more dangerous, and for the first time in a long time . . . good. Good to not be reliant on some guerilla-style terrorist garb but instead be back inside the United States' bleeding-edge military equipment.

Below our modules' overhead menus, the firearm deployment cases unlock, and there they are—the cherries to top off our weaponized cake. I swipe my heavy pulse rifle off its tray and look to see if Gourd's ready.

"Good to go?"

"Never better." His voice echoes through his helmet's voice modulation filter.

We get a move on to the hangar. Time for a Grimm speech.

"Feels good to be back, you know?" I say, drawing

attention to the sick blades on my arms. These things are going to dominate.

"Damn right. We better not have to bail on them like last time."

The heavy stomp of my feet on the metal floor boarding reminds me just how attached I am to these suits. The armor doesn't make the man, but it sure makes it easier to be one, especially after the day I've had. The more barriers between me and the outside world, the better, even if it's something as simple as a few inches of armor covering me and my exhausted face.

"Wait, man, what good are these blades?" Gourd says, interrupting my train of thought.

"They're gonna cut up bots like a chef salad. What's the issue?"

"Yeah, but, I mean, won't that splat the fuel all over us?"

That's a good point . . . but no, these suits probably have that stuff in mind. Right? The ACA's development came after most of the Earth-068 research was done, from what I'm to understand. Based on what Faust revealed, why wouldn't our military secretly slip some next-gen acidic immunity into the nanogel on these things?

"Faust said the lab rats back home figured out the counter-solvent a while ago, so maybe the gel is packing some form of it. Why wouldn't it be?"

"Maybe," he says, not entirely convinced.

He shouldn't be, honestly, since I'm just talking out of my ass. Still, we have rifles to make sure enemies don't get that up close and personal in the first place.

"Pack the ranged heat and we won't have to worry about disintegrating, yeah?" I bounce my gun in my hand.

"Good plan," he responds, ending the conversation as we enter the hangar.

R Company's quartet of sergeants are suited up in ACAs alongside our captain, the five of them standing on the briefing stage, looking eager to bark some orders at the dozens of Marines below. Gourd and I slip into the back row, trying to play it cool as we awkwardly clomp behind rows of standard-armor troops. Subtlety never was our specialty.

As we stand at attention, waiting for Captain to give us the word, my long-range ACA audio receiver crackles to life, and before I realize what it's doing, the thing auto-tunes itself to the frequency Grimm is transmitting on. Did he forget to set his broadcast to private? I don't say anything, but it sounds like I'm about to get a sneak preview of the game plan.

"Sitrep, Colonel," he asks Colonel Bertram Artemis, the man in charge of Virginia's 2nd Battalion. I saw him on the news once; seemed like a dick. Hell of a mustache, though.

"Not pretty up here, Cap," he responds with his trademark southern accent. "That tower town ain't a sand castle; anti-air defenses are way too strong for a frontal assault. Our transports can't fly near without getting shot down."

"Then we go to the Spire on foot. Status of the Russian trams?"

"The enemy's shut them down across the colony—wait, wait, the techies are telling me there's a chance they can get the woodland habitat's rails back up and running in under an hour."

"Affirmative. Keep me posted."

The comms chatter goes dark as Artemis disconnects without a goodbye, leaving Captain to address the men and women in front of him.

"At ease, Marines," he says.

Thank God; I didn't realize how locked up my knees were until now.

"You're here today because you've been assigned the most important mission of your lives," he starts.

Way to ease us into it, Cap.

"Today is a day of great sorrow but also great triumph. Our president is gone, but we have an opportunity to fulfill her dying wish and make America the strongest superpower on the map once again. Our mission is simple: reach the Spire, retrieve the data, and cap the station, terminating every Red aboard with extreme prejudice. And make no mistake, they are Reds. Each and every one of them. NURS is just one head of a Russian hydra, one that we'll burn at the stake when the time comes. For now, we deal with the biggest threat to liberty and freedom in our nation's history.

"You came here because of the president's sacrifice, and you will stay here to avenge her. The colony we're inside houses the most dangerous piece of military hardware known to man, and we cannot let the Russians maintain their grasp on it. They've set off a timer to destroy every last kilobyte of data on board, each of which contains vital intel. We're in a race against the clock, Marines.

"Here's the plan. We filter out of here via the security hatch that's lined up with the other side of the tube we're lodged in. Then we move up to the forge zone and fly transports into the woodland habitat. From there, it's back on foot toward the Spire."

Sounds simple enough.

"Make no mistake, we will face firm resistance, the likes of which you've never seen before. Next-generation mechs, fighters, and enemy AI populate the station, varieties of which we are not prepared to engage. However, we have no choice. Some foes may be faster or stronger than us," he says, really hammering it into the minds of these poor troops without ACA suits that they're completely fucked.

Not that the few of us equipped with the aforementioned suits are much better off, but at least we have a bit of extra defense. Thankfully, Grimm course-corrects the speech with his next sentence, refocusing on optimism instead of the fact that we're all cannon fodder.

"But there's not a chance in hell any are better than us. When we join forces with our stateside brethren up top, we'll be among the best minds in the free world. And it's time to put each and every one of them to use."

Wow, he really turned that around.

"You all have the plan. Now, time is of the essence. Romeo Company, move out!" he commands.

As everyone swarms to their respective commanding officers, Grimm reverses the status quo and takes the initiative to seek us out. Through the blur of gray and beige uniforms whizzing past, I see the unmistakable navy blue and gold plating of our captain approaching.

"Anything you two want to ask before we mobilize?" His voice is calm and considerate. He even tries to make a crack at me. "What, no bullshit one-liner, Lieutenant?"

Lucky for him, I'm all out of questions and quips.

"No sir," I respond firmly. Let's just get to the shooting part.

"All right, then form up on me. We'll lead the spear tip and set the pace for R Company. Remember, we can't move too fast. The black boots are gonna have to jog it out." He nods toward the rows of regular Marines.

One drawback of the ACA suits' expensive nature is that those who do get to wear them feel like complete assholes at moments like the current one.

All of R Company filters through the cruiser until we arrive at the blast door on the other end of the tram tube that's perfectly positioned to spit us into the main body of the space station. Jostling and bouncing each other forward, one by one we exit our home away from home and dive back into the colony.

The glow of the green tube is a lot more vibrant when I enter into it for the second time today. Glancing to my right, I see why. The massive black pipes that were previously obstructing our view of the starlight are completely shredded thanks to the cruiser's perfect entry. And even if they were in one piece, the lack of an active cooling system would still mean no cannon. The station feels a smidgen less menacing now that I know instant vaporization isn't on the menu.

"Man, not to be weird or anything, but I need you still while I get these things on, just to help balance. It's been a while . . ." Gourd trails off, bracing his hand against my shoulder as he prepares to activate the microthrusters in his boots. Jesus, if it weren't for my armor's exoskeleton, just the weight of him pressing down on me would be enough to dislocate my damn shoulder. Even now, it's not the most comfortable thing in the world and—fuck!

"Gourd!" I shout, recoiling from the sudden push downward as his hand digs into me the moment his boots light up. Now that he's a couple inches off the ground, I work on fixing the feeling that my left deltoid's a couple inches out of place.

"Sorry, bro, it's tricky."

I rotate my arm until I hear a nice little crack and know everything's back where it should be. I guess I can't be mad at him; the guy's never been too good with these things, especially when it comes to the boots. Time to show him how it's done.

I press two fingers down on the armor plate of my left thigh, instantly launching myself a good foot into the air before I level out at a steady hover. The pressure sensors kick in and drop me back to the ground, though they're now primed to engage my thrusters whenever I need them.

"That's how it's done, buddy."

"Show off," he mutters as we walk toward Grimm, who has situated himself at the very head of the pack.

"Everything in order?" Captain asks.

"Sir, yes, sir," we respond.

"All right." He turns from us to face the whole of R Company. "Squads, are we ready to move?"

"Roger," the four sergeants respond in unison.

As quickly as that final confirmation is spoken, we're off. Drenched in glorious emerald light and separated from the cold emptiness of space by nothing more than a shattered shuttle tube, we march forward. Grimm slides into his slow, rhythmic rocket-skate pattern, leading our charge without a foot on the floor. After the first couple yards I find my groove as well, and slowly but surely Gourd manages to get his own flow going, rendering all of Sierra Squad airborne. The sergeants behind us kick on their thrusters, and soon enough the head of our spear is entirely off the ground, consisting of seven ACA-clad warfighters jetting toward the station's belly with dozens of jogging Marines in tow. My rifle weaves left and right as I skate forward, armed to the teeth and equipped with the finest armor in the galaxy. Deep in enemy territory, surrounded by unknowns, I know one thing for certain: no matter what happens next, I have the tools to make a stand.

CHAPTER 13

Beecher

"Jesus, I thought these were bad with four people," Gourd says, hustling alongside me and the rest of R Company up the network of steps leading to the forge platform.

"No one ever said our job was easy!" I reply.

"No one ever said it'd be so hard, either," Gourd complains, clearly upset that we don't have enough space to kick on the rocket boots and skip leg day.

Even with our metal exoskeletons bouncing us up the steps, our quads still get one hell of a workout. And that's not including the extra effort needed thanks to the serious overcrowding and bumping going on among the troops. Whatever happened to column right and march, people?

To distract myself from the clomping boots and Captain's bulky blue-and-gold-armored ass, I glance at the scene above us. Well over our heads, hundreds of feet in the air, a fellow company's fighters dash around, locked in a colony-spanning dogfight with a swarm of hornet drones. Trams offline, anti-aircraft defenses live, hornets out in full force . . .

something tells me I was right to warn Gourd that our mission won't be a cakewalk.

"Move!" Captain yells as one of our fighters takes a full load from a hornet, its thrusters ripping off as it nosedives into a stack of generators about a mile away from us.

The torn-up ally ship, the guy inside it, and the machinery he just made contact with all burst into flames, sending a small shockwave through our stairwell as the crash's splash damage spreads. At the rate lasers keep firing overhead, that definitely won't be the last ship we see go down. Much like the captain, I have no plans to wind up as collateral damage, nor does the rest of our group. In response to the new danger, we up the pace and before I know it, Grimm's stepping onto the forge zone's entry platform, his armor reflecting the bright red hues of the nearby lava.

"Move! Move! Move!" he barks, waving each one of us aboard until we're all off the stairs.

Six transport jets are waiting, hovering idly on the opposite side of the platform.

"Sergeant Marx, Yankee Squad stays here and guards the entry. Anything comes from those catwalks," he says, pointing to the sizzling platforms only a machine could traverse, "you shoot it. Those trams come back online and anything comes your way without prior notice, you shoot it. Anything comes from above or below, you shoot it. Got it?"

"Sir, yes, sir," Sergeant Marx shouts back, fighting for her helmet-augmented voice to be heard over the hissing lava and droning transport engines. She posts her Marines at various spots along the tram platform's perimeter while the remaining fifty-something of us keep our eyes and ears glued to Grimm for further instructions.

"Sergeant Barton, your squad's taking the transport on the far left."

"Roger that."

"Sergeant Toufexis, the one next to that."

"Roger, Captain."

"McGregor, take the third in sequence. We're bunking with you," he tells Delta Squad's leader. It makes sense, since Delta has a few less Marines than the other squads and we only have three men total in ours.

"Aye, aye, Captain," the boisterous Scotsman replies.

"Marx!" The captain redirects his attention to the sergeant tasked with defending the platform. "Just got word the other three shuttles are reserved for Kilo Company, so keep your eyes open for part of Utah Battalion. They should be trickling in soon."

Trying to shout over the sudden burst of laser fire that erupts overhead would be useless, so Marx gives Grimm the okay with a hand signal. It gets the job done, and Captain moves on with the mission.

"All right, let's go!"

At his command, Gourd and I scurry toward our transport, climbing aboard the doorless minijet as fast as humanly possible. After finding spots to stand in the troop hold, we grab the overhead railing on our side of the craft and prepare for liftoff.

Our transports' thrusters stir to life, and before I know it, Sergeant Marx and her Marines become distant ants as the rest of R Company races across the edge of the forge zone, keeping as close to ground level as possible so we don't get swept up in the chaotic mess of fighters and hornets soaring overhead.

Since Gourd and I piled in on the left side of the transport, we don't get to see the battle for the Red Peril that's raging on behind us. With the uncomfortably warm breeze of mass fires whipping against our faceplates, all we get is a front-row seat to the never-ending rows of scorched towers and sizzling walkway mazes of the lava complex. Steaming pillars of yellow goop erupt beneath the zone's scaffolding, bubbling violently as if to say "do not come near." I ain't got plans to, thank you very much.

"Looks like me ex-wife's apartment," McGregor says from behind us, not sounding very amused with his own joke.

Now that he's had an aerial view of what's going down here, I think he realizes that trying to survive the colony's dangers isn't much of a laughing matter. Join the club, buddy. It seems just about everyone is getting a wakeup call about what kind of threat we're facing.

"Your ex-wife's place looks like a dragon's den, Sarge?" I want to keep the banter going so my mind can't focus on the robot version of hell we're nowhere near far enough away from. We're just outside of the standard bots' firing range, but they're no less intimidating by any means. What they lack in power, those little fuckers make up for in numbers, as I saw not too long ago. Thank God they're just roaming down there, patrolling. Doesn't look like they're headed for Marx and her squad . . . yet.

"Nah, lad. Dragon dens look like me ex-wife's place."

Ha.

"Bahaha. Nice one, Sarge," Gourd chimes in.

Glad he got a kick out of it, at least. The laugh ends quickly as we're nearly whisked off our feet by a blast that rocks the transport.

"Fuck!" I yell, accompanied by a lot of other curses from a lot of other Marines. Considering these damn ships of ours are open-faced, I guess we're lucky no one got shot or knocked off. Still, rocking the boat isn't good. And what the hell fired at us, anyway?

Scanning the environment with my helmet, it doesn't take me long to spot something out of the ordinary. Atop one of the towers in the forge zone, a red homing dot glows in our direction, its light emanating from a rocket launcher attached to the arm of one of those massive mechs I saw guarding ships in the hangar bay. Shit. We can't take punishment like that; our transport isn't capable of withstanding heavy blows. Evidently, Captain's on the same page as I am, since he's already busy yelling at our pilot, demanding alterations to our flight course.

The two of them work out a new strategy too late and our ship doesn't swerve in time, meaning we eat the black bot's second rocket whole. It slams into the reinforced floor panel we're standing on, catapulting the transport an extra few yards into the air and throwing everyone off their feet. We're all white-knuckling the rails, and I'm worried if I squeeze any tighter my ACA's gauntlet might crush the bar altogether.

Just as I manage to get myself secured, I see a much bigger problem: McGregor has no grip on anything and his body isn't staying put. Even with the weight of his modified armor, the guy is defenseless against the launching power of the rocket that sends him over the edge of the troop bay. In a great save by Gourd, he manages to connect a single hand with the sergeant's augmented ACA fists. But just when I think they're in the clear, my hopes are quashed. The connection isn't strong enough, and Gourd's fingers lose their hold on the sergeant. He goes flying out of the shuttle with his back to the flames, falling toward the lava-encrusted inferno below. He slips out of view entirely after just a few seconds, much to my shock and horror. Gourd and the handful of troops who saw the scene unfold alongside me all let out a series of panicked, angry expletives.

"Shit!" I yell, instantly queuing Grimm up on my comms. "We lost McGregor!"

"You what?"

"That last shot rocked him out of the ship!"

"Un-fucking-believable—wait, I'm still reading his signature." Cap's rage gives way to confusion. "McGregor, come in! Can you hear me?" he shouts on the same comm line I'm on.

No response comes through, but like Cap said, his exothermic sig is still active.

"Maybe . . . maybe his helmet's damaged or something," I theorize. "Maybe we should go back for him?" Or at the very least, find some remains of him. If he melted to death, that sig wouldn't be online. And inside an ACA suit, I doubt the drop or platform temperature would kill him.

The launcher-wielding robot is multiple towers behind us now and we're not under fire at the moment, so Cap tells our pilot to ease the throttle. I look out and see the other two transports continue forward, relatively unharmed. At least they're doing fine.

"Colonel, I'm requesting immediate air support over forge zone, ASAP. Looks like Oregon missed a couple launchers," Grimm reports, calling for backup.

Artemis's voice trickles in over comms. He doesn't sound happy to hear from us.

"The hell are y'all doing? Ain't no reason to be in there in the first place!"

"One of our sergeants got knocked in—Gordon McGregor. I want to make a sweep."

"Ain't no one surviving those temps! He's dead, Cap'n! Move on!" Artemis says with a hard edge in his voice.

"He had an ACA, and his sig is still showing on my scanner."

A few seconds of radio silence pass before the colonel musters up a response.

"Well, shiiieeet," Artemis whines, playing up the unique twang in his voice that only a Virginian could produce. "I'll send three fighters your way, but that's all I got to spare. No more fuckups."

"I'll take it," Cap responds, ending the conversation. He then redirects his attention back to our craft. "Pilot, one-eighty us. Gourd and Beecher, other side."

Gourd and I push our way over there. The herd has thinned ever so slightly since those two rockets shook our ship, leaving the other side of the troop bay down by a few Marines. Not good.

Our craft circles slowly, inching forward while we wait for the three promised fighters to make a sweep of the area where the rocket bot was stationed. Lucky for us, Artemis keeps his word, and as we approach the danger zone, Virginia

Battalion's support force roars onto the scene, their trio of heavily armed ships ready to clear our path.

Their jet streams disappear behind the towers in front of us, and after a few seconds, explosive sounds of cluster missile fire fill the air. I pick up some hostile audio as well. That bot isn't going down without a fight. There's also a new noise that takes me a second to identify: a metallic slash. Considering how low the fighters were flying, I can only assume the slicing sound came from the besieged rocket mech taking a melee swipe at our ships with its wrist blade. Still, I don't hear the distinctive screech of fighter engine combustion among the series of ensuing pops as our allies rain hell down on the enemy, so I assume the conflict resolves itself in a one-sided manner.

Artemis confirms my hope with his next message. "You're clear for now, Captain. I'll keep them circling for a minute, but don't waste my boys' airtime."

"Roger," Grimm responds, ignoring Artemis's attitude. He turns back to the pilot. "We have a tight window to get men on the ground. Hit it."

We pick up the pace and speed along the forge zone's fiery border walls, a blur of gunmetal towers whipping past as we backtrack. When we pull up to our destination, everyone on our side immediately starts looking for signs of the fallen sergeant. At first glance, I see nothing but a haze of swirling lava, metal girders, and scaffolding; nothing unusual. Gourd's faster, however, and spots a clue right away.

"His helmet! On that middle platform!" he says, pointing to a small blue speck in the distance.

Now I see it, and it looks like Cap does too. If anything, it's the exact opposite of encouraging, but it's enough for Grimm to order the transport into the zone.

"Get in as close as you can! We need to make the drop-off on that platform!" he says, pointing to a tiny sheet of metal that resembles a cookie tray floating in a pool of liquid death.

The pilot shoots us inside the fiery complex's borders, attracting some light fire from the standard-issue rifle bots, but nothing our ship can't handle. To the sound of crackling rifles and open flames, we close in on the platform, keeping a safe distance so none of the standard-armor troops' shoes melt off.

"Lieutenants, get McGregor and beeline for the front entrance. I'll tell Marx to expect you," Grimm shouts. "Now go!"

With a single glance at each other, Gourd and I lock eyes then stare down at the drop zone. Only one way to the bottom.

CHAPTER 14
Gourd

I t's getting hot in here, and I guaran-fucking-tee it ain't just me.

I shoot out of the troop transport alongside Beecher. Even though it's not a huge drop, that doesn't ease the scare factor; every moment in midair feels like an hour as I hurtle toward our target: a little metal dinghy surrounded by a sea of molten piss. I keep my shit together, though. Gotta be stoic. Gotta be badass. I shred through the air until touchdown, at which point my boots give out a tiny rocket burst to ease my landing. As much as these things freak me out, I gotta admit, they're nice to have around when I'm in the business of no-cord bungee jumping.

Beecher slams down next to me, the half-second burst of his boots' thrusters followed by a loud sigh signaling that he's good to go.

"Think they could've packed some suntan lotion in these things?" he asks, tapping on his armor.

"Hey, we ain't got it that bad. Imagine how Greg's doing without a helmet."

"Right," he responds, reminded that we're not here for a day at the beach. He walks across our landing platform and scoops up the Delta Squad leader's helmet. "Shit, man, look at these dents."

The thing is covered in scuff marks and small impact craters from bullets, some of which are still lodged in there. None have actually pierced the armor, but they shouldn't be stuck in it to begin with.

"What's the deal?" I ask, grabbing the helmet and flicking off a flattened bullet, hoping Beecher's got an explanation handy.

He does, of course. It's just not a good one. "My bet? The nanogel can't function properly in these temps."

So if we eat any bullets down here, we're gonna have to swallow them. *Great.*

"So glad the pits of Russkie hell get to be the setting for our first extreme environment mission." I hand the helmet back to Beecher.

He grabs it and reaches inside, pulling out a little chip that's split right down the middle. There's our explanation for why McGregor didn't say hi over comms. He's blind and deaf down here.

After a little more gawking at the helmet's dents, it's clear the thing isn't going back on anyone's head anytime soon. At least, no one with a head that's not a squashed pumpkin.

"So . . . what do we do with it?" I'm not sure if we're supposed to keep it around for the sarge when we find him, or if we should just—

Beecher tosses it into the lava pool next to us. That works.

He gestures that we should get off our current platform.

Pointing at a gap in the neighboring catwalk's railing next to us, he takes the lead. Giving himself some room for a running start, Beecher sprints and rockets a few feet forward, over the lava and onto the metal. Looks simple enough . . . except for that hop. Oh, I don't trust these moon boots enough for that.

"Come on, man!" he shouts from the other side.

Eh . . .

"We gotta get moving!"

He's right. We've got a sergeant to locate and a ticking clock to beat if we want to save the station's data; no time for dillydallying. I take a deep breath.

All right, man, you can do it. Just gotta back up a few feet and make the jump.

My heavy stomps backward push my little raft platform deeper into the lava, and while the stuff isn't exactly chasing my heels, it's still uncomfortable. I'm in the dead center of a pool I don't want to dip my feet into.

You can make the jump, Lieutenant. You just gotta dash like a motherfucker and pounce like a lion. You can do it. You can do it. You can—

"See? Wasn't that bad," Beecher says.

Oh. I'm on the catwalk now. I'm not burning in lava. Looking back, it was only a two-foot jump. No biggie.

"What's the plan?" I look around. The complex is huge, and we have no easy way to track our guy without his transmitter. To make matters worse, the temps here seem to be fucking with our exothermic heat sig tech, rendering its data increasingly unreliable. Our target's just one tiny blue needle in a big, burning haystack.

"We shout."

"We're not playing hide and seek, brother. You think he's just gonna say 'hi' back?"

"Got any better ideas?"

Well, he's got me there. Guess we're doing things his way.

"McGregorrrrr," we shout in unison, like parents who lost their kid at a playground as we aimlessly roam around an endless series of walkways. And we can't even do that without screwing something up; after a few seconds of killing our throats, I hear stomping. Goddamn it, Beecher.

"Look what we did, man. Now the bots know we're here."

"They were going to find out eventually."

Whatever, dude. Playing Marco Polo was a stupid idea.

The incoming bad-news sounds don't originate from just one spot—they come from all over. Nearby platforms shake and quake, a telltale sign that we've just become the main attraction for every damn machine within earshot. Time to see if these wrist-saws are as sharp as they look.

Beecher unloads a few shots from his rifle before any baddies appear on my side. The robot he's nailed screeches as its cut-up corpse cannonballs into the lava below. Its glowing black eye melts beneath the surface of the orange goop, its wail continuing until the machine's speaker is fully submerged and dissolved. I know it's just a bot, but . . . ugh. No time to dwell on that nasty bit of business, though; something tells me we're gonna be roasting a lot more robotic Russkies in the coming minutes. It's not a war crime if it's against machines, right?

After Beech takes down the first wave of unwanted guests, the yellow-and-silver grunts start cropping up on my side, coming at me from the fork at the end of the platform.

Back-to-back with Beecher, I dish out red hots from my rifle. The clankers fall like dominoes into the hot sauce below, shrilling their hollow scream all the way down. Ignoring the absolutely *fucked* fact that they're apparently programmed to make noises like that, I can't I blame them for their techno-rasps of terror; I'd be screaming too if I had to fight me. Still, like back in the shuttle tube, for every one that goes down, another pair of the fucking wind-up toys appear. And unlike back in the shuttle tube, we don't have a whole lot of maneuvering room or even a decent position. In fact, all we have is a single-file hit line—one we're trapped in the middle of. Uh-oh.

"Beecher, we gotta figure something out, fast!"

"I know!" he shouts back between another burst of pulse rifle fire.

"Why don't we just charge 'em—"

"The fuel, remember!"

Shit! He's right. I don't want to be grease on a hot frying pan. So how the hell do we keep the icky sticky shit away from us while still pushing toward a better spot if we're entirely surrounded?

"We'll bum-rush my side," Beecher says, reading my mind. "I'll bounce over their conga line and distract them. You follow right behind and, while they're aiming up, knock 'em into the soup!"

Ballerina shit, man, ballerina shit. Still, it's better than eating commie lead, so I'll take it. Time to get out of the kill box.

"Tell me when you got a window on your side," Beecher shouts, waiting for me to buy enough time to safely turn my back.

After a few more seconds of nonstop fire, I have a little pile of dead bots built up at the center of the fork. The makeshift barricade should do the trick nicely.

"Clear!" I slide my rifle into my suit's back-mounted magnetic sheath. It's time we blow the current shitty pop stand.

I swivel around and Beecher takes off, speed skating toward the enemy while unleashing a torrent of hip-fire shots. I get a run going and quickly shift into rocket-skate mode behind him, weaving left and right as I increase my pace to match his.

I sync speeds with him at the perfect time, and Beecher launches into the air. Just as he predicted, he instantly attracts all enemy fire. One by one, the bulky gears and pistons of our enemies' robotic limbs squeeze tight, arcing their rifles up toward my partner. They're exposed now, which leaves me wide open to take out the trash.

While Beecher is airborne, I get to work. I grab the crabby skull plate of the bot in front of me and jerk it to the left, forcing the upper half of its body over the guardrail. Top-heavy fella that it is, it tips right over. I swap hands and do the same to the next bot, shoving it to the opposite side. Heh, the action is starting to remind me of my professional hockey days. Seems NURS should've spent a little more time working on their robots' tactical AI, or better yet, their contingency plan for what to do when I showed up to kick their ass.

Sizzle, screech, crack. Sizzle, screech, crack. It's the steady beat of my own little robot annihilation reggae song. Sizzle as a bot meets the lava, screech as the next one in line falls in after its friend, and crack as the one after that hits the railing and begins the one-way dive as well. Oh, and I can't forget the loud slam every time Beecher lands back on the platform, though that's only once every three bars.

We close in on the end of the catwalk with a few tons of melted robot drowning in our wake. I crack some more mech skulls over the edge, and at long last, Beecher can stop playing bunny rabbit and take a second to relax his legs.

"Phew," he says.

Yeah, I bet looking like that much of an asshole is exhausting. Nah, I'm just messing. Not like he knows the difference.

"Got every damn one of them," I say proudly. Put as many baddies in their place as I do and you start to feel a little giddy about it sometimes. Comes with the territory.

"We ain't out of the woods yet." Beecher points back at what used to be my end of the catwalk. All the bots I left behind are pretty unhappy about not scoring the prom invite, it seems.

My turn to be the smart one. I go over to the railings of the bot-filled walkway and kick up my saws, their blades giving a high-pitched whir before slicing through the suspended platform's poles like a knife through warm butter. Mmmm, butter. That'd go great with some toast right now. Yeah, some toast with butter, and some scrambled eggs on the side . . . I miss real food. I don't like being here. Vitamin pastes fuckin' blow.

"What're you waiting for?" Beecher shouts, interrupting my daydream.

Guess I'll have to settle for scrambled Reds instead. Now that both railings are split from the catwalk and its structural integrity is weakened, I give the floorboard one good rocket-powered stomp, hoping the thing will break apart right there and then. It doesn't. So I stomp again. Second time's the charm. Every bolt holding it in place snaps off in rapid-fire sequence. That's more like it.

The machines' end of the catwalk, now totally detached from our portion of scaffolding, buckles under its own weight. It bends downward into the lava, submerging the bots' feet in a fresh bath of hot goop. Before the bots know what hit them, they're knee-deep in the drink. They try to turn around, desperately clawing at each other to retreat to the safety of the other side, but their efforts are in vain—the lava pools over their heads and melts them all out of existence.

"Nice call, man," Beecher says.

"You know it."

"All right, so shouting is out of the question if we don't want to become diner food, aka hot and greasy. How are we gonna—"

"Lee-ew-tennant Beeeecher," McGregor's loud and proud Scottish accent echoes from somewhere up ahead.

"Sergeant!" we yell back. Turns out the shouting worked? Marco?

"Lee-ew-tennant Goooourd," he continues, encouraging us to find him. The nearby sound of bots clanking means we don't have much time.

"Sergeant!" we keep yelling, sounding our way down the platforms in front of us until his voice is louder than the crackling of the lava and stomping of the machines. Almost there . . .

We make our way around a massive tower that all the noise bounces off of until we finally spot the man of the hour on the other side. His hulking ACA brawler fists are the first thing to come into view as he waves at us from across the way.

"Ay, lads! Talk about a hot zone, eh?" he says, still full of energy. Dude's got bruises and a few budding heat blisters on his face as well as a piss-ton of damage to his suit, but he's acting like he just got out of a bachelor party or some shit. Props.

"Sergeant, you all right?" Beecher asks, witnessing the same miracle I am. If such an incident had befallen anyone but McGregor, they'd have been totaled. He's one hell of a tough cookie.

"I'm feeling a bit dizzy from the warmth, so let's get out of here, yeah? Where we headed?"

"Closest exit is back with Yankee Squad at the entrance."

"Don't be telling me we're out of the fight, lad." There's sadness in his voice. For a guy as battered as McGregor, I'd expect him to be happy finding out we're almost in the clear. Turns out he wants more!

"Hold that thought," Beecher says.

Crackling in my helmet's earpiece tells me we're about to make a call.

"Captain," Beecher starts.

"Have you found him?"

"Yeah, here's here."

"Condition?"

"Still kicking."

"Then get moving."

"We going forward after we reach Yankee Squad? Or are we reinforcing them?"

"Utah Battalion is saving a shuttle for you at the LZ; not a chance in hell you three are done yet."

"Roger," Beecher says, switching off the line before giving McGregor the good news. "We're still in the match, Sarge."

"Then let's go! Me head can't take much more of the heat. Blistering, blazing barnacles, is it ever hot in here."

"You'd think he's playing into the stereotype for chuckles," Beecher whispers.

How rude! Maybe he's just proud of his heritage. Hmph. Besides, regardless of the guy's funny talk, McGregor ain't lying about his current condition. He's drenched in sweat so thick I can hardly tell where his eyes end and the waterfalls begin, and even with all that perspiration pumping out, his increasingly noticeable heat rash keeps worsening. And I thought *we* had it bad.

Beecher and I pull up Sergeant Marx's barely traceable exo sig on our HUDs. Beech takes front and center of our triangle and assumes the role of travel guide, marching us across walkways, bridges, stairwells, and yada yada yada. Put simply, we do a whole lot of walking, and the ache in my legs becomes increasingly noticeable as a result. Damn it, quads, why can't you be as strong as my biceps?

"Last set of slopes until we're just a few walkways from the entrance," Beecher tells McGregor. Since we still have a ways to go, I might as well strike up a little chit-chat.

"So, Sarge, how'd you find us? Did the shouts work?"

"Maybe the first one, sure. Thought I heard one of your voices. What really did it was the fighting; swore I heard an army going at it down here. Was hoping it'd be ours."

"Yeah, that'd be us," I say with a chuckle.

We start down the stairwell of the final slope, walking toward a—wait a minute. That's not just some weird pipeline down there. That's a mold for something. Something big.

"You seeing that?" I ask, magnifying my helmet's vision to get a closer look.

"Is that a cruiser nose mold?" Beecher asks.

I have no clue if that's what it is, and I sure as hell don't want to find out. We're in the heart of the shitstorm here.

"If it's a cast, where's the filling?" Sarge asks.

Then it occurs to me: we haven't taken a peek behind us yet. Shit, am I about to turn around and see something I don't want to—

Yep. Right behind us on the inside edge of our stairwell is a big, big hatch with a massive valve on top. The thing is stupidly huge. Like "large enough to fit the nose of a cruiser" huge.

"Let's not stick around to see that open up, yeah?" Beecher suggests as we speed up our shimmy down the insanely long flight of steps ahead of us.

"Right," McGregor and I respond, bouncing down stairs as fast as possible, trying not to look back at the massive hatch that only gets taller the farther we travel alongside it. And I still hear bots trailing us, as if we don't have enough problems.

"Just gotta move a little faster . . ." Beecher says, further upping the tempo of our descent.

Working to keep my mind off that massive piece of piping behind us, I scan the environment ahead for enemies. I can't tell if I spot something up high or if it's just a blur of smoke and my peripheral vision playing tricks on me, so I choose to disregard it in my haste to step off the never-ending stairwell and onto the massive mold platform.

"Almost there, just run for that walkway on the right—"

Beecher gets cut off by the arrival of a new challenger, one that doesn't look like it's going to let us stroll out of the current arena without a scuffle. *Shit, so that's the thing I thought I saw.* Resting atop our escape lane's biggest industrial smokestack is a three-eyed ship-wrangling bot, its launcher aimed and blade drawn. The blade's layered sheets extend themselves over what appears to be a plasma cutter, hiding it inside a sharp metal shell. But that shell ain't just a fancy carrying case for a multi-tool—it's doubling as a sword built for skewering ships and absolutely decimating unlucky fuckers like me.

The enemy bot looks like the same model the fighters were supposed to take out—the one we *needed* fighters to take out. There's an ear-splitting screech as its clawed feet dig into the stack it's perched on, scrunching up metal until it's so disfigured I couldn't even call it scrap. I hope I don't look like that by the time the upcoming fight is over.

No one has time to shout a strategy before big, black, and ugly starts lobbing rockets at us. I manage to dive out of the incoming projectiles' blast radius with a harsh boot-boosted side-step that blasts me way too far forward, well away from Beecher and McGregor. They both slide back in the opposite direction. Shit, now is not the time to split up. And where'd my rifle go? Sometime in the last few seconds, it must've been rocked out of its magnetic sheath. Double shit.

While I'm busy recovering, the mech launches more volleys at my allies. Beecher's and McGregor's reckless dodges land them inside the pit of the mold. Their incautious maneuvers pay off and the rockets miss them by a few feet, eating the mold's rim instead, but they're fish in a barrel now. I don't know if they're disoriented from the blast or ready to dodge the next wave. I gotta help them out of there—

But twelve-foot-and-angry ain't having any of it. Now that we're separated and disoriented, it spots an easy opening to get up close and personal with that giant blade it's wielding. Fuck.

With a colossal leap, the machine bounces off its perch and comes right at me. The metal monster clomps and stomps in my direction right as it makes contact with the platform, propelling forward way too fast for my liking. Given the size of its blade, my odds of survival are nil. No way in hell am I handling that thing solo.

Doesn't mean I can't try.

I rocket myself away from the lava-spitting fringe of the molding platform just in time to miss the robot's first charge, its failed rush causing it to lose its footing and nearly fall into the sauce. So close! Damn it. Recovering in less than a second, it twists around, and the thousand piston-pumping joints in its body all refocus. Now I'm one clear stretch across from the mech. No diversions, no distractions. Just me, it, and a flat patch of platform.

I push off from the ground, rushing to get back onto my feet. It swings its foot in my direction and begins its push. I get back on my toes. It takes another step. I give myself a quick kick-off and spring forward. By the time I'm finally up and moving again, the enemy is charging at full speed. I raise my arms and hope these saws are as strong as I need them to be. Meeting in the center of the arena, the mechanical monster swings its blade toward me and we collide.

My entire body buckles as that son of a bitch puts every bit of force it can muster into its sword, but somehow I'm not dead yet. I'm not dead yet! The edge of the bot's blade is caught in my saws' ruts as I block the strike. The saw wheels twitch and jerk, both trying to spin upward while the enemy's sword keeps pushing downward, making for the perfect deadlock. Even though the enemy towers over me, pressing forward as hard as it can, I manage to match its force, raging against the pressure with the added support of my boots' rockets. The scene must look pretty fucking cool from the outside: one guy shooting blue-orange flames out of his socks while using saws to arm wrestle a bot twice his size.

But while it probably looks cool, I'm not feeling the part. I gotta say, the bucket of bolts I'm dancing with really knows how to keep the heat on me. The machine can't see it, but underneath my helmet my teeth are grinding harder than Charlize Cormanne and I did at my high school prom. Every muscle in my body strains to the max, and even the ACA exoskeleton isn't digging the current degree of stress-testing. My HUD warns that the suit's skeletal integrity is faltering due to exceeded pressure limits—a fancy way of saying joints and pistons will start snapping apart in a matter of seconds if I don't do something.

More sparks flash between us as the saws keep jutting upward, scraping against the bot's blade. Jesus Christ, I can feel my boots digging into the platform. Literally digging in. Wait, that's not me . . . that's the ground getting softer. Shit, my boots' jets are melting the platform. Oh no.

My sinking stand collapses into a kneel as big-bot starts to gain the advantage, locking me into a pose that almost makes it look like I want to propose to the metal asshole. My right knee plate meets the rapidly softening metal ground as the machine pushes down harder and harder until I can't hold it any longe—

"Heeehah!" A shout erupts from behind the mech as it's about to plant me into the ground.

As a result of being shoved forward and knocked off-balance, the bot presses down on me even harder. I slacken just enough to avoid getting every bone in my body crushed. My enemy's disorientation is undoubtedly thanks to McGregor's big-ass ACA fists. Instantly, the machine's attention is off me. It loses interest in my dainty saws and decides the guy with the motorized, cinder-block-sized knuckles is the one to worry about.

Collapsing to the ground, I catch myself and get in a push-up position, which helps me avoid sinking into the melting floor. Not giving McGregor a chance to do-si-do with the enemy, I rocket forward parallel to the ground and waist-tackle the bot, knocking that fucker and myself right into the mold pit below. It crashes hard on its back, and I land in a perfect position to rain hell.

"Beecher, cut the lance arm!" McGregor yells.

I don't spare a second to see what those two are up to. Right now, it's clobbering time, and the bad bot's head is first on the to-do list. Squeezing my plated fists as tightly as possible, I let 'er rip and start hammering the thing's faceplate until it goes from being a three-eyed droid head to a splattered mechanical black cherry. By punch number six, I manage to break off a bit of metal covering something that looks like a motherboard. Like I give a fuck what it is. To me, it's just one more thing to shred.

The machine's neck pistons twitch in an attempt to shake

me off. Not gonna happen. I launch one fist right into its mechanical Adam's apple and get a good grip on the tubing inside, ripping with all my strength until I've got its robo-vocal cords severed and flopping in my hands. Black fuel starts spraying, but luckily I'm just out of spritzing range. That's right, big guy! You bleed, and that's all I need to know to kick your ass—

While I'm busy gloating, the robot spots an opening. It kicks behind me, and the force of the buck sends one of my fellow Marines flying. My split second of shock enables the bot to knock me off as well, flinging me onto the molding floor basin. *How the fuck is it not dead?*

Beecher sprawls out on top of the mold's rim and he's slow to get back to his feet. At least he's out of the line of fire. But McGregor and me? We're still trapped inside the mold with the company of one very violent robot. Not to mention it looks like the battered machine now has a plan in mind: it's actively cornering us against the massive filling hatch. I don't like what that suggests.

At least the bot's missing its sword arm thanks to Beecher and the sarge, meaning all that's left is its big rocket launcher—wait, that's still really fucking bad. Robo-baddie lines up a shot just slowly enough for me to react. Time to dip! McGregor skates up the right side of the half-pipe while I move up the left. We need to make it to the edges before the one-armed bandit gets a shot on us. The rocket discharges, and I see the smoke, but I don't know if we're out of range—

Then the rocket misses the ground entirely. It shoots right past us, in fact.

"You're welcome!" Beecher yells, dual-wielding pulse rifles as he unloads on the robot, disorienting its aim.

So that's where my gun ended up.

I cling to the edge of the mold, pulling myself up just in time to spin around and see where the rocket winds up. It makes contact with a bolted portion of the big hatch behind us, popping one of its security fasteners right off. Now there's a huge hole where the bolt just was—one that doesn't stay empty for more than a second before lava starts guzzling out. Even if only one hole is exposed, it's still bigger than the three of us combined, and it's pumping out a thick stream of bad news. A few yards beneath my feet, the hot lava flows past, and our mechanical adversary sizzles, eating it head-on. What a pain in the ass that thing was.

"Lucky as hell, man," I tell Beecher, sliding back on top of the molding platform, safe and sound at last. I try to ignore the fresh wave of brutal heat radiating from the nearby orange piss.

"At least it's over."

Then I hear metal tearing, followed by a deafening snapping noise. My guy just had to say something, didn't he . . .

On the filling hatch's lid, a second bolt pops off. Then another. And another. And a whole lot more than any of us ever asked for.

"I'm gonna have to argue that one," McGregor says as the pool of lava goes from a small stream at the bottom of the mold to a rippling river, the rapids rising at a ridiculous rate.

I'll tell Beecher to say that one five times fast if we make it out of here alive.

"That's our cue to leave, I think," McGregor shouts at the two of us.

And as if we need any more of an incentive to get the hell

out of Dodge, it seems all the bots I heard earlier have finally found our location and are vaulting down the steps behind us. Rising molten tides *and* killer robots that want to make us eat lava soup for dinner. Yeah, that's definitely our cue to leave.

We shoot for the exit catwalk, shortcutting our way across girders as the stream of hot sauce rushes toward us, the wave moving so quickly that it's probably already swallowed up all those bots. Their mechanical hisses and moans—the sounds we should be hearing—are drowned out by the oncoming tidal wave aggressively eating up every square inch of safe space we leave behind.

"Just a little bit farther!" Beecher yells as all of us rocket forward faster than humanly possible, relying entirely on the thrusts of our suits' boots to save our hides.

The LZ better be just a hop and a skip away; the lava behind us is coming up way too fast for comfort. Thankfully, the air color around me starts changing from orange-yellow to yellow-clear, indicating we're within shouting distance of the foundry's entrance. Marx better be readying the welcome mat for our torched asses.

"I see the station!" Beecher shouts, his filtered voice rasping around the popping lava.

Just a few more yards . . .

Through the haze of smoke and soot, Marx flails her arms like an air traffic controller. We get it, lady, we're coming as fast as we can. Trust me, I want to be where you are just as bad as you want me there!

I glance behind. The lava wave has died down and spread across the various pools near the zone's entrance, but that doesn't stop me from hurling myself onto the transit platform like it's a Hawaiian beach. At least the current floor won't melt underneath me—I hope.

"You okay, Lieutenant?" Marx asks.

"Never better, Sarge," I say, lying facedown on the ground, kissing the unmelting floor with my helmet.

"Ay, no time for breathing, lads. We got a ride to catch!" McGregor shouts.

I pull my head off the ground and see he's right. Kilo Company is shouting at us to get a move on from their position in front of our ticket back to R Company. Beecher gives me a hand to help me back on my feet. It looks like my five seconds of naptime are over.

"All aboooooooard," McGregor yells as we ditch Yankee Squad, hustling to the transport.

Beecher lets out an exhausted sigh and finishes sliding inside the troop bay as we begin takeoff. "And this time, let's all stay aboard."

A-fucking-men to that.

CHAPTER 15
Gourd

"**S**itrep, Lieutenants," Grimm asks via comms during our second pass over the foundry complex. He's getting testier with every interaction.

I can't blame him. After that bullshit detour and the precious time spent getting R Company ready in the cruiser, we're left with just over four hours or so 'til the commies flush our treasure down the drain. No more stupid fucking rocket bots better pull any funny business; there isn't time for it. Plus, my suit's nanogel *just* cooled down from my last volcanic adventure. I don't want to expose it to that kind of heat again. My HUD's still giving me error readings on internal suit temperatures—I think some sensors are busted.

"We've cleared the area and are en route to your location, Captain," Beecher responds.

Speaking of their location, R Company's exo sigs are moving around stupidly fast on my HUD. What gives?

"Virginia got the woodland trams running. We're detecting

large amounts of enemy activity at close range, so we're moving forward. Can't wait for you three at the station."

"So how're we supposed to form up?" I ask.

"Drop in." With that, Captain ends the call.

Great, more drops! I ain't a fucking Shake Weight, boss.

To everyone's relief, our transport zips along without a bump. Still, I can't take my eyes off those tower tops. All it takes is one more pop-up motherfucker and we'll be tossed right back into that oversized toaster. Oh, hey, there's what's left of the catwalk I dunked earlier. I can see its remains all the way from here, my own little contribution to the forge. I'll call it "Red on Red." My masterpiece.

I shift my eyes away from the sizzle spa and peek over at Beecher. He has his sights glued on something else. It ain't the towers, the fires, or the platforms. He's looking farther. I glance in the same general direction and can't see shit, besides big steamy pipes and the bottom rim of the colony in the distance. Not really an attraction, so I don't get it—oh, maybe he's trying to meditate, like I do. At last, he takes a page from the master's book. Attaboy. Just gotta think of nice things, like warm milk before bed or walking in a big field. Or drinking warm milk in a big field.

"Warm milk or fields?" I ask. It's an important question; it tells me a lot about a guy. I'm betting on fields.

But he doesn't look over at me. Shit, he must be in real deep.

"Milk or fields, man?" I give him a nudge on the shoulder. That snaps him out of it.

"Whu, huh?" he responds.

"I saw you meditating. What's your calm place, man?"

"Oh," he blurts out.

Jeez, that's a jumpy response. That's not how calm thoughts work.

"Um, field."

Knew it.

He pauses for a second before speaking up again. "Hey, have you ever thought . . ."

"Of course I have. What kinda fuckin' question is that?" Like, really, dude. You can't go around calling people stupid like that.

"Never mind," he responds. He doesn't sound pissed, though. Sounds like he just wants to go back to mind-wandering with that thousand-yard stare of his. Maybe he had something else to say . . . oh well. Probably not that big a deal if he didn't open with it.

If he's gonna go back to his thoughts, then I guess I will too, since McGregor's busy chatting it up with the Kilos, and God knows I don't want to talk to those guys. The pilot's probably not in the mood for small talk either. Yep, it's just me and my own two eyes left to keep the party going. Guess I'll spectate the lightshow happening overhead since the guys around me have lookout duty covered.

Above us, the biggest, most chaotic dogfight I've ever witnessed is taking place. Trying to keep track of individual fighters should be a good way to pass the time, since hundreds of allies are whipping around upstairs creating headaches for the legions of enemy hornet drones. Thankfully, my HUD minimizes visual riffraff by highlighting visible friendlies so all I have to do is enjoy watching the most interesting ones. Hoo-boy, our guys are really handing their shiny chrome asses to 'em. Mother Russia's getting a good belt-whipping from Father Freedom today, sir, yes, sir.

I lock my eyes onto one of our side's speedier fighters, a glacier-blue ship that's roasting hornets left and right. That'll make for good entertainment. It arcs around the entire field, ditching formation to swing to the rear and take out the hornets tailing it. In a very Beecher-esque move, the star pilot slips right underneath a swarm of silver commies and, one laser at a time, pops their heads off. Left! Right! Left! The turrets screech, alternating shots to pick off two rows of incoming hornets simultaneously. Good shit. No match for that kind of maneuvering, the drones' chrome shells explode one by one until the last of the swarm gets sent down in flames. From a ground troop's perspective, it probably feels like the sky is falling, since those ten-ton behemoths are dropping like flies. Good thing we aren't down there.

"Approaching drop zone," the pilot cuts in, pulling my attention away from the aerial spectacle.

Shit. More action already?

By now, the greens of the habitat below us have completely phased out the reds of the previous zone. It's just trees and open fields as far as the eye can see.

"Time to work for a living," Beecher mutters.

"Man, did you see that guy up there—" I start, but he's having none of it.

"There are thousands of guys up there. Stay focused on you, me, and the rest of the guys down here." He pops his head out past the side of the transport's troop bay and gets a face full of wind as he looks ahead.

"Drop zone in fifteen seconds, prep up," the pilot nags.

Beecher slides his helmet's faceplate down in preparation for the dive.

Where the fuck are we even dropping? I'm not hopping out of here just so I can get dry-docked by an evergreen—

"Drop zone in ten."

We fly over another thicket of trees and enter into a large field. The new environment isn't so bad, except for the giant dust cloud forming in the distance. Hold on a second . . . giant dust cloud. What is that doing here? And what are all those little things kicking it up?

"Pulling up now."

Tracks appear below us as we pick up speed, our transport charging forward until the tail end of a tram slides into view. We gain ground on it car by car, flying a couple dozen feet overhead until we're directly on top of a flatbed filled with troops. Is that Grimm? And the rest of R Company? Took long enough, but we're back with the pack.

"Stay sharp, lads!" McGregor shouts, wishing his Kilo pals well before bailing on them to join Beecher and me at the edge of the platform.

With all three of us ready to go, the pilot gives us the OK to ditch these Utah Battalion nerds. "Northeast drop zone is clear. Angle your descent accordingly."

I'm gonna have to jump and pray I make it down fast enough to land on the flatbed; otherwise the car behind it is gonna come up and shred me. Two things moving so fast should not have people bouncing between them. And to make matters worse, my HUD won't even help me calculate a drop path. Ugh, that's probably because some systems are still fried from the forge. Or maybe my suit's tactics processor just isn't capable of formulating path projections between rapidly shifting variables like a soon-to-be freefalling idiot, a live aircraft, and a moving train.

After a single grunt, Beecher launches into the air and leads the drop. Without pause McGregor follows suit, flinging himself out of the transport. Guess it's just me, then. Here goes nothing!

My surroundings blur as I leap out of the craft. I slant a bit to the right since I see the edge of the flatbed coming up fast behind me, though it's hard to tell how close I am to impact when everything's shaking. If I don't stick the landing in the next half second, I'm fucking toast. My suit's thrusters let out short, sporadic bursts, pivoting me like a human gyroscope, but I don't know if that'll be enough to stop me from landing with a splat. ACA impact stabilizers, don't fail me now.

R Company has cleared a space for me and my two compatriots to land without hitting anything important, but the question is: Will I hit anything at all? The whole world's moving so fast around me I can hardly—

My feet smash onto the flatbed, accompanied by one hell of a thud. That sound . . . I did it! Er, piece of cake. No problem. Having done its job, the transport we just abandoned circles around overhead and ditches us, leaving me with the all-star team on an easy ride to Spire City.

"Nice to have you back, Sergeant," Captain says to the helmetless Scotsman.

"Nice to be back, Captain." McGregor gives a parting wave then bails on the three of us to go regroup with his squad at the other end of the car.

"So, what's the situation, Cap?" I ask.

"That enemy activity I was telling you two about is catching up with us." He points to the little black dots creating dirt clouds in the distance.

"You telling me those are—"

"Yes. Our sensors indicate those things will close the gap and topple our tram within the next five minutes. We're setting up defenses on the left flank to make sure that doesn't happen."

We have a wave of stampeding droids headed our way that plan to knock us off the rails. So much for an easy ride.

"Join Alpha Squad on the car in front of us. They need some extra manpower."

"On it," Beecher and I say, moving toward the next flatbed to help out Sergeant Barton and his team.

After a little pushing and shoving, we make it past the Marines blocking our path and slip onto the rickety little four-foot bolt-bridge connecting the cars. Once across, we find Alpha Squad going full throttle, bustling ammo crates and mobile turrets around like nobody's business. Barton might not be my favorite sergeant, but when it comes to queen bees, no one runs the hive quite like him.

"Delecord, space that mount out some more, we need room to swivel those things without taking each other's heads off," he shouts at an Alpha, who reflexively nods and gets to work adjusting her turret's placement.

"Hey, Sarge," I say.

"Ah, Lieutenants Gourd and Beecher! Didn't know if I'd ever be seeing you two again," he replies, continuing to give directions and relay instructions to his Marines while talking to us.

"Well, we're here and ready to help. Where do you need us?" Beecher asks, briskly and businesslike. Sounds like his meditation didn't work out.

"Centerfold, boys. Man the two lead turrets."

"Roger," Beecher says.

Maybe it's the fighting that's bogging him down. I mean, I love a good punch-'em-up as much as the next guy, but the shit we're dealing with is relentless, and I can totally imagine close to two days' worth of nonstop chaos weighing down on someone. Plus there's the noise of fighters overhead, which could probably cause a headache. Oh, and speaking of those fighters, there's the risk of death by flaming jet since they keep crashing down like meteors. Not to mention the giant wave of robots chasing us. Wow, that *is* a lot of exhausting shit. No wonder Beecher's so grumpy.

Whatever. I can think about how tired we are after we take the Red Peril, which ain't happening until we mow down every single robot inside the colony—starting with the wave directly in front of us. Grabbing hold of my assigned turret, I extend its stand to meet my height, pulling it a few feet over the flatbed's waist-high side paneling. After a little fidgeting, the turret's in position. I grab a bandolier and shove that puppy in the receiver, waiting to hear the nice little click that confirms it's locked. There, all set and good to go.

The dust storm's getting bigger and the commie bots are getting closer, though they're still far enough away that I can't quite make out what they look like. As long as we do our jobs right, we won't ever have to find out.

"You good to go?" I ask Beecher, who's just slammed in his own bandolier.

"You bet," he says flatly, not sounding super convincing.

I hope whatever's bothering him doesn't make him a bad shot in the next few minutes.

I reach behind my back and pat my heavy rifle, making sure it has stayed in its sheath since Beecher gave it back to me on the transport. Good, it's still there. Now all that's left to do is wait.

"Hey, you remember those super old stories of the cowboys who'd try to rob trains and the sheriffs who'd have to shoot them off their horses?" I ask Beecher.

"Yeah?"

"Guess we're the new sheriffs in town. Heh." I think I'm funny, at least.

"Ha, I guess so."

There we go, man. Gotta keep morale up somehow. Especially when robo-dirt storm 2395 is headed right for our speeding tram.

"Positions, Marines!" Barton yells behind us.

Seems like we're kicking off the main event a little earlier than expected. I zoom in my visor's optics and take a closer look at the Bolshevik baddies headed our way. I can't get a close enough scan to see the finer details, but I get the gist: they're fuckin' cats. We're being chased by a wave of metal tigers pouncing toward us at full speed, which unfortunately seems to be just a tiny bit faster than *our* full speed.

"You seein' that?" Beecher asks.

"Looks like we got some kitties to put down." I ain't going down like a pussy, or by one either.

"Ready!" Barton yells.

I tense my knuckles on the turret grips.

"Aim!"

Got my sights set on the first wave's right wing already.

"Fire!"

Way ahead of ya.

All other noise is instantly drowned out by a wall of non-stop gunfire. Turrets rip and shells fly, the metal piling up around my boots while bullets tear holes in those clanking cats. They might be almost a mile away, but that doesn't mean we can't put a few to sleep before they're knocking on our front door.

The first row tumbles over as R Company opens fire. Not that it matters; as usual, the robots behind the dead wave don't pause even for a second. They claw over their destroyed comrades and continue to rush us. There's no bottleneck, no squeeze-spot to pick them off from. There's just an unfiltered horde of thousands of these things coming at us out in the open.

It doesn't matter, it just means more exercise for my gun. The chunk-chunk-chunk of my turret keeps on rumbling as I unload bullets nonstop, keeping one hand on the trigger at all times. The metal barrels glow brighter and brighter shades of orange with every bullet I spit out, but I don't dare worry about overheating my gun. I'll risk a blinding cloud of exhaust smoke or even a full-on weapon jam before I give the enemy so much as a second to freely gain ground.

Speaking of blinding clouds, pretty sure the field would look like a droid pet cemetery right now if it weren't for the fact that the damn robo-cats keep kicking up dust behind them, hiding their destroyed litter from view. It's a shame, since I could really go for a motivational boost in the form of a takedown tally right about now. Something—no, anything—to remind me that if I keep popping their caps it'll eventually be over. Seriously, at the rate the machines keep coming I'm starting to think they might be spawning from a wormhole or some shit. I've wiped out at least a couple dozen by myself, and the rest of R Company combined is probably inching toward a thousand confirmed kills by now, but the gap between them and us is shrinking, and the holes in their formation keep filling in as more robots charge forward from the rear.

They're close enough now that I can see them in greater detail. The incoming bots have catlike skulls, fangs, and the general appearance of supercharged black panthers, which honestly sounds right in line with all the other insane shit we've encountered thus far. All they need now are some stupidly pointy blade tails to really sell the image—wait, yep, they've got those too. Fucking blade tails. No way do I want those things within petting range.

What is up with the station's wild fuckin' defenses? I must be witnessing what Faust was talking about when she mentioned the testing going on here and that the cannon was only one piece of the puzzle. Maybe the bots are prototypes for Russia's next-gen ground forces. Looks like us Americans arrived just in time to be live bait for an impromptu weapons demonstration.

More chunk-chunk-chunk noises sound off as my turret's muzzle flashes a solid stream of bright orange-yellow. The sheer number of casings on the flatbed's floor starts to make me nervous; there's more than enough of them to be a legitimate mobility hazard. If I slip on those things like a pack of loose marbles, I swear—

"Check the rear!" Barton shouts through our comms, his voice barely audible over the sound of gunfire.

Good thing he said that, otherwise I would've almost begun to think we were holding out decently enough. Turns out, while we were slamming the fuck out of the main herd, a couple, oh, I dunno, hundred of them decided to push toward the back. Now we have a sloping wave of fucking panther robots closing in on the tail cars. How are we supposed to handle them when we have the rest of the wave right in front of us to worry about?

Keeping one hand on the turret trigger, I use the other to grab my rifle. Only way to hit two sides at once is with two guns, after all. Thank God for the ACA's pneumatic pump joints; otherwise the recoil of dual-wielding these guns would tear off my arms and get everyone around me killed. Free-handing both weapons, I angle myself so my ninety-degree fire range won't take off any friendly heads, then I let loose with everything I've got. My turret handles the tail of the panther wave since that requires the most range, leaving my right hand free to clutch the heavy rifle and shoot the piss out of the bots directly in front of me. And I do mean right in front of me—the gap from a minute ago has shrunk yet again; now they're just a hundred or so yards from clamping their claws onto the side of the car I'm on.

"Might wanna double up," I say into my helmet's mic, hoping Beecher will hear me and take my lead. Even though he's right next to me, there's no way I can shout over the robo-cats' stomping, our tram screeching across rails, and a couple dozen turrets firing. Hell, thanks to our train's raw speed, the wind we're getting slammed with is probably enough to mute all but the loudest roars. Though the sound barrier my helmet provides keeps some of the commotion outside, my ears are still getting pounded with way too much noise.

"Roger that," he responds.

Right away, another outbound stream of red laser fire appears, and I know we're packing as much heat as possible, for whatever that's worth. And actually, that's probably worth around . . . oh, I dunno . . . seven or eight dead mech kitties a second. Good rates on an overall shitty deal.

Out of the corner of my eye I see Grimm and the rest of the guys to my left focusing all their fire on the rear-flanking Russkies, but I'm not sure how much good that'll do. The bots are almost within jumping range of the last car, and—

"We're boarded!"

Well, that confirms it. If they can't knock us over, they're gonna try to chew us out from the inside.

The tram gets a lot shakier, and something tells me it ain't happening 'cause of a bump in the tracks. Even the turrets can't drown out the scraping sound coming from behind us. If these things can close a miles-wide gap in a handful of minutes, I can't wait to see how fast they cross ten train cars.

"Sierra Squad, form up on me. Bring some firepower," Grimm says over comms, barely audible over the surrounding chaos.

Sounds like a plan, Cap. After latching my rifle onto my back sheath, I rip my turret off its detachable mount and make my way toward the next car where Grimm and two of the sergeants are stationed. Since everyone's busy holding the line on our left flank, it's easy for Beecher and me to get where we're supposed to go. Besides, we're the ones swinging around detached turrets. It's not like anyone wants to be on the blocking end of these things.

After a quick trudge across the connector bridge, we're back on the car from our initial drop. Grimm is setting up an ACA-exclusive defense line at the back. While the normies hold the sidelines, it looks like the suits will be responsible for hands-on animal control.

"Beecher on the left, Gourd on the right. McGregor will handle the bridge"—makes sense, since he's got the fists— "and Toufexis and I will fill in the gaps. Clear?"

"Roger," Beecher and I confirm before splitting up to get in position. Not sure if the plan's good enough to succeed, but if Cap says it, it's probably the best option we have. I plop down my turret and get ready to rumble, scoring a few seconds to adjust my optics before one of the crates in front of us goes blasting off the train. Piece by piece, the bulky cargo separating us from the enemy is sent flying. Prep time's over.

Our car rumbles heavily. The scraping noise is raging now, which means those mechanical mewlers are about to break through the last of the crates. Our firing line braces itself as the final stretch of our barricade is blown to shreds, exposing the threat in full: a wall of pointy-fanged panther bots.

They pounce into the air, and our muzzles light up in perfect sync. McGregor kicks the sailor talk up a notch as he doles out haymakers. On the edges of the car Beecher and I guard, the fight never gets up close and personal. We turn up the heat the second we see any machine launch its death paws into the air and knock it out of the sky with a good old-fashioned dose of lead soup well before it can get near us. My team's system works pretty well—for the whole ten seconds we get to keep it going. Then I look up.

The first thing I spot is the outline of a fighter. A second of squinting reveals it's the glacier-blue fighter I was rooting for earlier, the one dogfighting like a champ high in the skies above us. Then I notice its flaming nose, shredded thrusters, and flight trajectory. It ain't flying high anymore—it's falling fast and headed right for us. If my HUD is accurately assessing the speeds of our tram and the falling fighter, then that ship's projected crash point is going to be directly beside the stretch of track our car will be rolling over in . . .

Three seconds.

Fuck.

Before anyone has time to dive out of the way, the fighter smashes into the ground right next to our car, the roar of its two exploding thrusters swallowing all sound in the area. A wall of fire shoots up from the wreck's impact, and the resulting explosion knocks us halfway off the tracks for a split second, tilting our car hard-west as the right set of wheels become airborne. I see a perfect opening to nail a pair of jumping panther bots trapped in the space between cars. I fire a quick burst that hits them both with maximum stopping power, knocking their metal bodies out of the air and down onto the rails where the tram is going to land. With the immediate stretch of track covered in robot shells, the rear car we're facing only makes it halfway back down, crunching the bots stuck between it and the rails. The resulting angular friction twists the couplings between the cars enough to snap them, as well as the bridge McGregor is standing on, disconnecting the flatbed full of kitties from our car entirely. Sparks fly as we crash back down onto the tracks, now the last link in the train. Thank fuck. I like our new, human-occupied caboose a hell of a lot more than the previous one overrun with frisky death cats.

No more than a second goes by before we're dozens of yards away from the mess of derailed cars and crunched bots, buying us some much-needed distance between ourselves and the remaining pack of panthers that aren't sure how to proceed. *Jesus Christ, that was insane.*

"Nice moves, man!" Beecher says over comms. Damn right.

"Never settle for less," I respond. Play it cool, Lieutenant. You just saved the whole fucking day with a single trigger pull. No biggie.

"Spectaaaacular!" McGregor roars in approval, falling flat on his ass from the recoil of our car bouncing back onto the tracks.

Bringing fists to a gunfight works, I guess, but only if you're okay with letting the other guy do all the cool shit. Like me. Nah, I'm just fuckin' around. I like the compliments, sure, but that isn't what I'm most happy about. As the few remaining fragments of metal panther guts fall off the rear of our car, disappearing into the distance as we pick up speed and outpace the cats for good, all I can think about is taking a moment to breathe. I crack my knuckles and relax a bit, looking over at my tired allies, then back at the miles of green grass around us. I've been needing a calm field for a while, and I finally have it. Easy ride express? It's about time.

CHAPTER 16

Beecher

"**Y**ou, uh, don't think these are actually empty, do you?" I ask Grimm, joining what's left of R Company as we step onto the trio of long roads leading to the Spire and its surrounding town. We might've had an easy tail end of our woodland tram ride thanks to Gourd, but I'll be damned if that's the last of the surprises the Russians have in store for us, especially so close to the brain of the Red Peril's whole operation. Still, hopefully nothing's as death-defying as that tram. I'm gonna be paranoid about rail travel for months now.

"No, I don't. But R Company is ahead of the pack, and there's no time for pissing in the wind. We move forward," Captain responds, his voice gruff and cold.

So much for safety first. He's right, though; time is in short supply. It's been hours since Faust . . . since the new mission was established.

I glance at the blue tower in the distance. According to my HUD, we have a little under three and a half hours left. If anyone makes it up there in time . . . well, it's going to be tight, to say the least. Too tight. Still, there's no use thinking about the endgame. The shitshow isn't over yet, and I have no plans to leave my fellow Marines dangling between now and then.

"All right, everyone, file formation. McGregor, Delta Squad takes the left road."

"Aye, Cap."

"Barton, Alphas on right."

"Roger that."

"Toufexis, Bravos are here with us in the center."

"Roger."

If I had a fear of heights, these roads would make me shit the bed. Not only are they incredibly high and dangling over a sea of insta-death generators, but they're barely supported—hell, I don't see *any* supports. Beyond their connections at each end, these things hang freely. For that reason alone, walking across them is tough going. I can't believe they're the only way into the city. The Russians *really* didn't want the wrong people getting in.

Once everyone has their position sorted out, we begin our march into the heart of the storm. And storm's the right word for it, hands down. There's no skyline over the Spire, just a giant, gaping spiral of dark matter. Even the stretch of road we're on is losing the warmth of the Red Peril's artificial lighting with each step taken.

"Spooky, yeah?" Gourd whispers, pointing at the handful of abandoned transport trucks littering the main road. Their doors are still open, a sign that whoever was inside must've been in a real hurry to get the hell away from here. The question is, where did they go?

"Yeah, definitely . . ."

The bluish-black glow of the dark matter cannon's interior reflects coolly off the road's white tiling. The farther down the road we move, the farther our shadows stretch in front of us, as if drawn to the darkness ahead. Pretty sure that shouldn't be happening, but with the colony's wacky science, I'm not making any bets on what's normal and what's not.

Other than the weird visuals, the walk is pretty low-key and uneventful, barring a few bombs we detect in some of the abandoned trucks along the way. The traps are obvious and our ACA sensors detect the trace amounts of Semtex residue scattered about well in advance, giving us ample time to neutralize the explosives before they can detonate and take out any of us or destroy our path forward.

Beyond those brief moments of activity, there's nothing but eerie silence as we make our way across the lengthy roads, those of us with ACAs hovering slightly ahead of the rest of the group. I now see why the trucks are there in the first place. Making the trip on foot clearly isn't ideal.

We're about halfway across when the first legitimate cause for concern crops up. For a fraction of a second, something blips on my radar.

"Hey, did you—"

The second I open my mouth, the blip disappears. Strange.

"Yeah, I saw it too," Gourd responds, confused.

"Keep moving. If something's out to get us, we'll find out soon enough," Grimm says, ordering R Company forward.

After a couple more yards, the blip comes back and goes away again, just as fast as the first time. Strange.

"Barton, slow down," Grimm tells the sergeant, ordering

Alpha Squad to take a firm position at the rear. "McGregor, double time."

It's a smart move; we need eyes and ears watching in front and back. If there's anything coming for us in the first place, that is. Maybe it's just the dark matter messing with our sensors. I hope it's that and not something more serious, like the dark matter affecting our cognitive processes. After all, who knows what the stuff can do. I follow suit with the rest of my peers, sliding my rifle out of its sheath. Can't afford to take any chances.

We trudge forward as the blips continue on and off, appearing and disappearing at regular intervals. I keep my ears open but can't hear anything out of the ordinary. All I detect are the sounds of R Company's clomping boots. I'd hear if something was coming, right? Right?

"I'm getting goosebumps, man," Gourd says. "I got a bad feeling."

That's my cue to raise my rifle and enter a firing stance. I don't need an official order to tell me what my gut's feeling. Gourd senses it, I sense it, our sensors sense it. It's not just our paranoid imaginations playing tricks on us. It can't be.

"Stay calm and keep moving," Grimm orders. He can say that as much as he likes, but being calm isn't really a choice, given where we are right now.

Just keep putting one foot in front of the other, James. You've been on plenty of narrow stretches before today and gotten out fine. No reason the current one will be any different. Besides, it's not like there are any enemies around. Can't be scared of bad guys that aren't even real. Well, I mean, I know they're real, but they aren't visible. Wait, what if *that's* it? What if they're invisible? Damn it, now I'm just freaking myself out. Cloaking devices don't work on anything smaller than a shuttle, and they definitely don't work at such close range. Unless, of course, the station I'm in is testing a new kind of cloaker. Not like I haven't seen impossible shit here already.

I hear my own breathing, and it's not sounding too good. My body tenses. Shit, if I'm freaking out inside an ACA, I wonder how the Marines in regular body armor are doing right now—

Then I hear it: the loud, unrestrained scream of a woman getting shredded from the inside out, her pain producing a screeching of the vocal folds so awful that R Company stops dead in its tracks.

The two glowing black eyes of a robot panther are the only thing I manage to glimpse before its fangs sink into an Alpha Squad member's chest, her body armor no match for her foe's industrial-strength mechanical jaws. None of her squad-mates even have time to turn around and help before the bot flings her gushing corpse into the abyss. With two steely paws firmly latched to the right road's guardrail, the machine pulls itself over the edge and onto the platform, now a threat to all of Barton's squad. By the time it's gotten that far, every gun in Alpha is filling it with holes, but that's just one down, not nearly enough to assuage anyone's fears that the worst is over. Now we know the machines are capable of climbing beneath us. Silently. Off the radar. We're all fucked.

Suddenly, I'm slammed to the ground. My head rocks around inside my helmet as I crash onto the road tiles. I can't lift my legs. Both my arms are pinned. From my trapped position, the only thing visible is the gaping maw of a bionic cat. It's a second away from chomping my skull off, which means I have even less time to stop it.

I might not be able to move my arms, but I can still move my hands, turn on my saws, and shake shit up. But what if I cut the beast open and it spews fuel all over me? Can the nanogel take it?

Y'know what, whatever. I'll be dead in a second anyway if I don't try something.

I squeeze my right fist, and a saw kicks to life just in time to slice directly into the robo-cat's metal rib cage as it lunges. There's a split-second pause as my blade stalls against the bot's armor. I'm not sure if it's going to be able to dig in—but that invaluable pause is all I need. Before either the bot or I have time to react, the blade starts chewing at full speed and slices into the beast's wiry guts, sparks and black goop pouring over my helmet. I sit up and struggle to push the enemy back.

That's my answer, then. If I have time to sit up and recognize that the fuel's all over me, then clearly it hasn't burned through my armor and melted my head off. I'm still alive. The robot's not going to be for much longer, though.

Pushing forward with maximum effort, I unstick the thing from my blade and send its twitching, cut-open body sliding across the ground, smearing the tiles with fuel. Before I have a chance to get up and finish the job, Grimm slams a foot down on its head and terminates the bot once and for all. The assist buys me a second to pick myself up off the ground and get my bearings. Both Barton's and McGregor's squads are engaging the enemy on all sides as an endless swarm of droids crawls out from underneath the roads, attacking Alpha and Delta from every possible angle. The center strip that Bravo and our squad are trapped on is looking pretty crowded as well. Toufexis and his Marines chip away at the units on the railings' edges, but every few seconds a cat makes it onto the road and sticks a claw in someone. It seems like each time I blink, another soldier without ACA protection gets disemboweled. R Company's strategy has to change—fast.

Gourd's busy kicking them off the edge with his ACA's thrusters, afraid to get down and dirty. "Wait, so are we safe," he blurts over comms, pausing to boot another hostile into the void below, "from the fuel?"

Gourd's frantic tone tells me he needs a guarantee, so I march over to his side of the road where a clawed paw is climbing up. Before the machine can raise another one, I grab its forearm and yank it up, quickly wrapping my right hand around its robotic throat. I shove my other arm's saw blade deep into its skull, my helmet less than a foot away from the bionic cat's cranium. The fuel spews all over me at point-blank range, covering my visor in pure black. But I don't need to see it to know what happens next as the sliced-open head stops struggling. I crush the machine's neck until the rest of its body falls off entirely, spiraling toward the generator pit below.

"Yeah, we're good." I toss the bot's skull over my shoulder, wipe all the shit off my visor, and scoop my rifle off the ground. The fight isn't going to be hard at all now—well, at least not for me. Most of the troops don't have ACAs, though. If the goop gets on them, they're toast.

I scan my surroundings to see where the cats are coming

from. I might be wrong, but it looks like the wave we left behind in the fields is playing catch-up. "Captain, we gotta move the privates ahead of us."

He concurs. "Sergeants, tell your troops to push forward and maintain distance from the enemy!"

The sergeants acknowledge, and squad by squad the privates run ahead on all three roads. Now it's just Toufexis, McGregor, Barton, and Sierra Squad left to deal with the droids hand-to-claw. Once the standard-armor troops get in position ahead of us, they unleash everything they've got in our direction, knowing our armor can easily take the few stray bullets that will inevitably hit us on such a narrow battlefield. Our ACAs spit out any incoming friendly fire while the rest of the bullets zip past and start shredding enemy units. At their range, however, the privates aren't going to be able to catch every cat. That leaves the remainder for us.

Gourd juggles an especially feisty one a couple yards away. Time to help him out.

"Give 'er a toss, will ya?"

"On it!" Gourd flings the clanking kitty high into the air.

I run toward the airborne hostile with my rockets engaged, keeping them live just long enough to reach peak thrust capacity. I kill both for a split second in order to hit the ground and jump, reactivating the juiced-up kicks mid-ascent. Blasting a good ten feet into the air, I arc my right arm back, ball my fist, and wait for the right moment to release.

Time slows as I reach the apex of my jump. Once the mechanical cat's razor-sharp teeth are within spitting distance, I send my armored knuckles forward. My punch rips right through the guts of the machine, rocketing it into the road tiling beneath me with such force that it leaves behind a small impact crater.

"Got 'em!" Gourd roars.

That's what I'm talking about.

My momentum doesn't stop on the way down, either. The second I'm into my jump's downward slope, I slide out my rifle, kick the rocket boots back on and segue into a skating motion, not touching the ground once before I'm gliding toward a bold bot who's about to rush me.

The bot's hind legs crunch into the ground and it leaps, claws outstretched and teeth bared. Two can play at that game. I launch into the air like a human drill bit and, buzz saws on, spiral-nosedive that bastard. My rifle shots shred the beast's exterior armor before I smash right into its chest, my head sliding through its innards while my blades tear its torso open from the inside. The cat's reduced to little more than four dismembered piston limbs by the time I slice through the other side, exiting without a scratch.

My untouchable streak ends when another cat slams into my side, knocking me off balance and prompting me to wind up a punch. But as I'm about to deliver the swing, I pause. The bot hasn't gotten back up.

"Sorry 'bout that!" McGregor shouts.

I look over and see where it came from: Sarge is launching machines all over the place with those fists of his, taking them out by the dozens with nothing but blunt force. Since that's the only method of attack that will keep the bots from tearing apart and squirting fuel all over his exposed head, I can't fault the guy for being a little cautiously reckless.

The six of us hammer away at the army of full-metal

felines, exterminating the opposition with ruthless efficiency until we've whittled their numbers down to single digits. Almost defeated, the once intimidating wave of machines is reduced to nothing more than a few suicidal stragglers. Grimm decks one over the edge, Barton headshots another, and Gourd decides we should finish the last remaining opponent with style. Taking the last one in his arms, he tosses it over the all-but-bottomless pit between McGregor's road and ours.

"She's all yours, boss," Gourd shouts.

Challenge accepted. Building up a little speed, I go for the showboat kill of the day. I see Grimm shaking his head as I rocket-vault over the perilous gap between roads and slam dunk that motherfucker right down the middle, landing gracefully on Delta Squad's side.

"That's enough. Get back over here," Grimm orders.

He's right. Even though we narrowly saved the majority of soldiers, that doesn't mean we can rest easy. Too many good men and women died for our "victory" to be anywhere near clean, and we're still on the roads. I don't think we've seen any actual defenses kick in yet. Those bots were just leftovers—the consequence of a sloppy job back on the tram. I doubt the real show has started.

One jump later and I'm back on the center road with Gourd, Grimm, and Bravo Squad. Now that animal control duties have been taken care of, the six of us catch up with the other troops and continue marching forward.

"One hell of a show back there," Gourd says.

"Got that right." I can't even begin to explain how good that felt. The whole time we've been pissing ourselves over the Russians' bots, but now we know we can handle them without burning to death in seconds. Good stuff.

"Nah, really man. You went apeshit on those things," he says. It's almost like he doesn't expect me to be as much of a badass as him out in the field.

"What can I say, it's been a long day. Gotta vent somewhere."

"At least we're done fighting robot cats. That shit'll make for a good story back—"

I don't get to hear the end of his sentence. In an instant, all nearby sound is drowned out by the roar of a stray incoming fighter. Instinctively reacting to the threat, Gourd and I dive away from our current position as far and fast as our rocket boots will take us. As we land, a burst of black-and-orange flames erupts behind us, splashing dark matter fuel next to our heels. It takes me a moment to realize what just happened.

"*Kamikazes! Move!*" Grimm shouts through our comms.

It looks like we've triggered the Russians' plan B. Gourd and I don't waste a second in dashing toward our objective, though we're not quite fast enough to escape the blast radius of kamikaze fighter number two. The second explosion knocks both of us to the ground—which is now covered in a thick coat of fuel.

Unlike whatever's juicing the bots, the fighters' strand of fuel isn't leaving the ground untouched. I don't realize it at first since my nanogel remains impervious to the stuff, but as I try to get back on my feet, I feel the soles of my boots sinking. The surface tiling is melting from the heat of the explosion. The ACA can handle that. What it can't handle, and what comes a second later, is the entire area burning clean through to the bottom, leaving absolutely no road where my left foot just was. I sink into the puddle of rapidly dissolving goop that's eating up the road beneath me, unable to think straight. My fear-clouded mind tells me one thing, and one thing only: I'm about to fall to my death.

Thank God for Gourd. Without a moment's hesitation, he grabs my arm and flings me forward, the speed of the hurl enabling me to land back on my feet and continue skating away from the disintegrating ground behind us. After a few seconds of sprinting, he reaches my position and we're together in the mad dash to catch up with the others.

"Why the fuck can't we just shoot them out of the air?" Gourd half pants, half shouts, his question almost immediately answered by an American fighter that swoops in overhead and takes out an incoming dive-bomber. Right after tearing through the suicidal Russian, the ally fighter gets torn to pieces by an anti-aircraft turret within the Spire's walls. It's a firm reminder that we're on our own down here.

"Shit!" Gourd yells, wasting precious breath during our forward scramble. That selfless American might've bought us a few extra seconds, but his sacrifice won't stop the rest of the Russian fighters coming our way.

The road is a blur as we shoot across it at top speed. The two of us have almost caught up with Grimm, and the rest of the troops are already closing in on the city's entrance gate. I'll be damned if the Russians cut us off so close to the finish line.

The ground shakes violently, signaling another fighter has crashed. I peek behind to see the damage, and it's not good: the road Alpha Squad's on is melting way faster than ours, likely thanks to its smaller surface area. Not that the science behind it matters right now; what matters is that Barton and his Marines are dangerously close to getting the rug pulled out from under them. Maybe if I hop over there and link up with their sergeant, we can carry—

My plan turns to dust as the fourth kamikaze fighter lands a direct hit, wiping Barton and his entire squad right off the map, erasing them from existence.

"We lost Alpha!" I shout over comms.

"Those fuckers!" Gourd roars.

"Focus!" Grimm orders. We still have to save our own asses before we can avenge anyone.

With the right road lost, it's down to McGregor on the left and our two squads in the center to stay in the game if we stand a chance of tackling whatever awaits us beyond the city's gateways. Just a little bit further and we'll be out of bombing range.

Suicidal fighter number five blasts down from the sky, beelining for Gourd and me in a bid to see if Sierra Squad can be eliminated as easily as the Alphas. With reflexes I didn't know either of us had, we fan out just in time to avoid the aircraft tearing through our bodies. A moment later, the fighter births a maelstrom of fire and fuel-drenched metals directly between us, crashing with an impact that sends us flying forward and plasters our backsides with chunks of road.

I slam into the ground, pick myself up, and keep moving. My squadmate does the same, and soon we're once again in a position to play catch-up with Grimm and the rest, all of whom have made it off the road and are safe inside the city's first building, which rests just beyond the blown-open entrance gateway that our allies have breached. At least Bravo and Delta are safe from the madness. All that's left is for Sierra to finish the race.

Easier said than done. Gourd and I can't dodge what comes next: the last kamikaze fighter rockets down right in front of us. We're about to be on a platform that's dissolving from both sides.

I kick a boot in front of me to stop my forward advance. Gourd follows suit, so neither of us are blasted too far back when the fighter slams into the strip of road directly ahead of us. Recovery time is minimal, but the damage is anything but. We have about forty yards of road behind us and ten in front that aren't completely disintegrated. At the rate both ends are dissolving, that's not a lot of wiggle room to make the impossible jump to the platform R Company's on.

"We're fucked!" Gourd shouts, the frenzied panic in his voice reading like that of a caged animal.

I feel it too; the situation looks bad. We have a shrinking launchpad and a growing gap from our target. Time to shatter a few long-jump world records or die trying.

"Back it up, I'll give the signal to kill the boost and bounce!" I shout. The two of us scuttle backward to get some build-up room. It only takes a few yards to hit max skate speed, so I think we can reach it before our runway fizzles out of existence.

"Go!" I yell. We charge forward as fast as our exoskeletons will allow. With every motion we make, our rocket thrusts expedite the dissolution of the road beneath us. But there's no better option; irresponsibly spiking the likelihood of our own demise is the only chance we have of escaping it.

"Wait for it . . . wait for it . . ." I say, knowing we're going to be cutting things stupidly close when the portion of bridge in front of us burns away entirely and our remaining stretch of platform starts to freefall into the abyss.

"Wait for it . . ." It's the third stall I give before we have less than three feet to make our jump or fall into the sea of electrical components miles below.

"*Now!*" I shout, just as we hit max speed. Gourd and I kill our boots in perfect sync before jumping and reactivating our thrusters as the last tile of platform dissolves into the ether. With that, the road ceases to exist. As for us, well, the situation's not looking much better. With arms outstretched in a desperate reach for the incoming platform edge, we flail toward it, but we're not covering enough distance. Our target isn't coming up quickly enough, and our speed isn't staying maxed-out long enough. Gourd screams my name, and the platform passes out of sight. That's when I know—beyond a doubt—that we're well and truly fucked.

CHAPTER 17

Beecher

"**E**ven ACAs weren't built to lift you, Gourd!" McGregor says, using his massive mechanical fists to lift the combined weight of my best friend and me up from below the platform's edge. A second earlier, a rapidly falling Gourd grabbed onto my ankles for dear life, a move that would've sunk us both had McGregor not caught my hand when he did.

"No fucking kidding. I think he pulled my legs out of their sockets," I grumble, crawling onto the platform but lacking the strength to stand up afterward. My feet were not meant to suspend freefalling ogres, damn it. Seriously, my ACA even gave me a "faltering skeletal integrity" HUD warning due to the stress of supporting Gourd's weight.

"Sorry, but I had to, man. Bigger guys sink faster. It's gravity and shit."

Look out, fellas, we got a scientist on our team.

"Well, smarter guys go on diets and end up being lighter guys who clear the platform," I counter, still lying facedown on the ground. I feel a sharp kick against my boot and know he heard me.

"Colonel, why the hell weren't those Russian fighters taken care of before they reached us?" Captain hisses over comms.

Sprawled out next to him, my ears just barely pick up his seething words. He's turned off his mic's speaker and set his broadcast to private, so it's unlikely anyone but me can hear his helmet-muffled rage. And it's definitely rage, no doubt about that. I've never heard him use coarse language with a superior officer before.

"Simmer down, Cap. We stopped the drones heading for you, but some manned fighters slipped through the cracks," Artemis responds, his audio coming through just loudly enough for me to overhear. "Forces are spread thin. M'boys got a lot to juggle right now, and we can't be babysitting you every inch o' the way; not when we're busy cleaning up the messes Romeo Company's so good at leaving behind."

"Care to come down here and say that to the faces of the *remaining* men and women who almost died thanks to your inability to prioritize?"

"No can do. Not with those AA turrets around," Artemis replies glibly.

That cheeky motherfucker. And what the hell was that previous comment referring to, anyway? If he and his team were any good at "cleaning up messes," we wouldn't have had to deal with that rocket bot in the foundry.

"I don't know what your game is, Bertram, but I'm onto you, and when we get out of here, I'm going to personally ensure you never see another combat mission in your life," Cap spits back, his voice low and menacing.

I can't believe what I'm hearing. I knew these two had a bit of a nasty rivalry, but I didn't realize it was so bad. Has the colonel been *trying* to get us killed?

"Harsh words for a Devil Dog trapped deep inside hostile territory without air support. G'luck to you and your Marines, Cap." With that, Artemis disconnects before Grimm can say another word, meaning I'm the only one who can hear his slew of curses. Then, for some of the longest seconds to ever pass, he says nothing. The silence is deafening. Once the fuming period is over, Grimm turns his mic's speaker on to address what's left of R Company.

"Everyone," he says, "we're officially on our own from here on out."

That's the cold, hard truth. Even if the rest of the US forces secure the station, there's no way they'll be able to mount a full-scale anti-AA strike soon enough to back us up while we're still on the clock. As far as our current mission goes, whatever happens here lives and dies with R Company.

That splash of verbal ice water reminds me it's probably a good time to get myself off the ground. Depleting what little energy my muscles have left, I lift myself back up onto my feet, both of which ache like a bitch. My suit's internal vitality scanner detects my weakened state and offers me a tactical anabolic stimulant injection. I ignore the offer on my HUD without a second thought. I'm never, ever voluntarily taking one of those stimulants. They give me headaches so bad that any health benefits are completely negated. Pretty sure they fuck up most other Marines the same way, actually. And besides, drugs aren't the solution; the solution is getting my buddy to eat a salad for once. One of these days, I'm putting

Gourd on a scale to prove that his weight is comparable to that of a baby elephant's.

"What's the plan, Captain?" Toufexis asks. That's the question, all right.

"We use our scanners and stay frosty. Aim for the tower."

That's Grimm-speak for we're winging it—hard. Winging it has been the name of the game for a while now, though, so I can't say I'm shocked.

"If there are no other questions, let's get moving. Forward, Marines." Grimm stomps ahead to lead us.

Guess it's time to say farewell to the nice, roofed fortress that kept us safe from kamikaze carpet bombings. Taking a look around, something dawns on me: the current building doesn't look like it belongs inside a terrorist colony. It looks like a stolen slice of architecture airlifted from Moscow's ritzy financial district.

As we exit through the checkpoint building's massive golden doors and filter into the city itself, I'm greeted by even more visual decadence which stretches as far as the eye can see. None of it fits in with the war bunker narrative we've been fed thus far. What we're seeing in front of us is a civilian sector. It's an entire artificial world, perfectly pristine and quarantined not only from the outside universe, but also from the rest of the station it resides in. It's expensive, urban, and everything else wealthy first-world citizens could possibly want from a human habitat among the stars.

Rather, it's everything a person could want if there were any here to want it. Currently, there doesn't appear to be a soul here besides us. Still far from the desolate blue tower lying in wait beyond the city skyline, we walk along the streets of the empty civilian hub. Sliding my rifle out of its magnetic sheath once again, I tighten up formation with Gourd and Grimm, uneasy as we lead our expedition through the main thoroughfares of Spire City, Red Peril.

The high-rise buildings gradually give way to smaller, more town-like offices and apartment complexes as we move from the first metropolitan portion of the city to the residential region that precedes the thicket of towers surrounding the Spire. The colony's architects really had a place planned for everyone, didn't they?

Throughout our travels, everything remains abnormally spotless and shiny, as though we're moving through a giant, newly constructed dollhouse. There's a movie theater with an unlit marquee, a bar with no name on its sign, and a chapel. I find that last one funny; who's there to worship? There is no God here. As I stare into the black nothingness radiating from the front of the colony's interior, its darkness spreading across the rows of rooftops in the immediate foreground, I start to piece together why such a place might exist.

The colony and its pulsating heart of darkness have all the resources and infrastructure of a small nation. As such, I can't imagine the immense city we're exploring is meant to be just a temporary home away from home—it seems like it's meant to be a complete substitute. After all, who needs to take care of planets when you can just manufacture a sleeker, smaller living space using the most dangerous power source known to man? The station is self-sustaining, running an entire ecosystem on fuel that could burn the whole place down in an instant. But that little detail doesn't matter, at least not to the people who built the colony. What matters is that any elites who don't want to live on the frontlines of a universe ravaged by dark matter can just live here while the Russian government destroys every planet in existence.

Having seen the things I've seen today, there's no denying that the fuel and the research behind it could do a lot of good across the galaxy. And it's no secret—at least, not anymore—that the substance can empower whoever controls it to change the way the universe runs. I just don't know who should be imbued with such influence.

If we don't nab it for ourselves, the fate of the US and every other nation is at risk. And who's to say Faust was right? Maybe the Reds do have the data backed up somewhere. Plus, even if they don't, there's a decent chance the Russians will win an all-out war with normal weaponry entirely through superior political and military power, as much as I hate to admit it. Leaving the fate of the universe up to a handicapped military facing off against people who would build something like the colony I'm in . . . it's not a savory prospect. Maybe . . . maybe the United States is the right country to own such technology and assume the burden of defending the universe from Russia. Besides, once something's discovered, it's only a matter of time before someone, or something, replicates it. What's the worst a head start could do?

I look around and receive my answer.

I . . . I can't think these thoughts right now. I need to focus on getting to the Spire first. The clock is ticking.

"Not digging the vibes here," Gourd says, sharing the unease of the rest of R Company. The place is quite a sight, even if we can tell it's not a good one.

"It's like a giant simulation of what life's supposed to be," I muse.

"Yeah," he replies, his tone guarded. His walk is stilted, the uncomfortable aura of our surroundings clearly getting to him underneath that armor.

I think we're all a little on edge, frankly. It's like being in a ghost town that hasn't had time to populate, depopulate, and become a ghost town yet. It's like Chernobyl born broken.

Metal blast grids are rolled down over all the windows and doors of the buildings, probably a result of whatever security measures went into play when we crashed the station. Not that it matters, it's just weird not being able to see inside anywhere. Our discomfort grows stronger as we pass the last block of high-rises and enter an area full of residential homes, all of which are boarded up, devoid of life and soul. And as if that isn't creepy enough, it seems dark matter is manipulating the dimensional properties of each house's lawn decor.

Levitating fountains shoot streams of water downward, only for said streams to magically guide themselves back up, cycling freely through the air. Flowers decorating the yards change colors and petal shapes on the fly. Even the sidewalk is affected, floating up and down to ease our steps as we walk across its slabs.

The peculiarities don't reek of military intent, that's for sure. They look like the products of some well-funded scientists and landscapers who had too much time on their hands. Truthfully, if it weren't for the lifelessness of the area, its bizarre appearance might be appealing.

Maybe we've shown up at a good time, though, before the new neighbors have had a chance to move in. After all, property values are probably pretty low right now, and something tells me these homes are going to become prime real estate if we can't wrest control of the station from the Russians.

At the end of the first stretch of houses, we come upon a divide that reaches all the way to the bottom of the station, cutting us off from the next chunk of city just beyond our reach. Between us and our target is a large, circular garden loaded with cherry blossom trees and rimmed with flowers of every shape and size. Pretty as it is, that's not what draws R Company's focus. Instead, we stare at the large disc the garden is situated on, hovering freely above the miles of open space below. It's not attached to anything, meaning dark matter's likely involved. It's no doubt dangerous. It's also our only way forward.

Suspended dozens of feet in the air on either side of the gravity-defying botanical platform are two floating pods, each made of three chambers. They look like human cryo-sleep cells, but . . . bigger. The pods have yellow-and-black banding on them, along with some Russian text I can't quite make out from my current angle, even with my optics zoomed. Whatever those things are, their warning tape gives a bad first impression. If it's marked like a trap and placed like a trap . . .

"I don't feel so good," Gourd whispers to no one in particular, acting as a voice for all the troops too spooked to speak.

Everyone has cold feet about proceeding. No one trusts the magic disc to let intruding Americans safely pass over it. Judging by Grimm's tone when he finally speaks up, it sounds like he feels the same way. Too bad his words don't reflect his apprehension.

"We have to cross it."

He's right. It perfectly bisects our path to the Spire, and there's no other bridge across the gap—not that I can see, anyway. On one hand, we don't have time to search for another path, and the distance between us and the other side of the disc is definitely too big to jump across, even for ACAs. On the other, no one's willing to put a foot on that platform.

"That's an order. We move forward." Grimm's voice slips at the end, losing some of its fearlessness.

It really has been a day . . . er, days . . . for firsts.

"Sierras and Bravos, onto the platform. Deltas, stay put and watch our six."

McGregor fails to fully stifle a sigh of relief. "Sure thing, Captain."

Thanks for the vote of confidence, Sarge.

Guess we're the guinea pigs. I don't need to see it to know that Toufexis is sweating bullets under his helmet as he and Gourd file up behind me. I follow Grimm onto the disc, since he bravely volunteers to be the first to step over the foot-wide bottomless gap between us and the platform. It doesn't even shake in response to his presence, nor does it react to any of the twenty-plus other Marines that step aboard behind him.

It looks like everyone is trying to keep their eyes focused on what's in front of them and not think about what they're walking on. As for me, I can't help but look around. My helmet auto-translates newly detected Russian characters as my gaze sweeps past the floating pods again, now from an angle where the text can be accurately processed. The translation on my HUD isn't encouraging: Residential Peacekeepers. I don't like the sound of that.

What I don't like the sound of even more is McGregor's massive fists smashing shit behind us. Our entire squad twists around to see the sergeant vault out of a broken window frame and lunge toward a badly beaten station technician, whose tiny body slams into the front lawn of the house he's just been tossed out of. The lone Red lies in a pool of his own blood, covered in shards of glass. Like a true Russian, he refuses to surrender, weakly getting his back a few inches off the ground before raising his shattered hands in an attempt to swat off the attacking American. It's a futile defense against McGregor's knockout punch.

"Captain! They're hiding in the houses! They've been watching us!" the sergeant shouts over the sound of his Marines scattering to kick in the doors of the houses preceding our disc. It's too late, though: a single window's metal slats split open for a fraction of a second, revealing a pair of eyes watching us. The trap's been sprung.

Before those of us on the platform can evacuate, the floating pods pour out steam, blinding us to what comes next. There's no doubt we all feel it, though. Or rather, don't, as our bodies are overtaken by a state of instant weightlessness. The garden disc falls out from under us, hurtling toward the station's fuse-covered flooring.

As I plummet, spiraling through the air alongside my fellow Marines and that goddamn platform I knew we shouldn't have trusted, I catch a glimpse of a few lucky bastards who were able to grab the edge of the city block we were just on, which is now far, far away. Besides those fortune-favored souls and Delta Squad, R Company is screwed. Even if the four of us in ACAs survive the drop, standard armor isn't going to stop all of Bravo Squad from becoming bloody mush down below.

Unless.

"Gourd!" I shout through my mic, flying damn near blind thanks to a stream of cherry blossom petals ripping off of the falling platform's trees and smashing me head-on. "Save Bravo!"

Even if I can't save everyone, one fewer life lost is all that matters. I kick on my boots and rocket toward the nearest Marine, a mixture of flailing and sporadic boosting getting me within arm's reach of him. Completely paralyzed by fear, the guy's in no position to help himself, so I save him the trouble. Roping my arm around him, I pull him in close for a life-saving bear hug as we continue our dive, backlit by the trail of flaming petals my boots have ignited.

Out of the corner of my eye, I spot another skydiver without a parachute. Time to play Canadian doubles. My ACA's tactics processor, struggling to run even a fraction of the calculations necessary for proper path projection and navigation assistance amidst the aerial madness, generates a flight assistance offer for me on my HUD. I accept. Even if the suit's software and hardware are being pushed beyond their limits here, I'm not about to turn down what limited computer assistance I can get. Hopefully when combined, some smart eyeballing and my ACA's automatically emitted rocket spurts will allow for the kind of heroics I can only dream of—the kind I need right now.

With the most careful flail I can muster, I head toward warfighter number two, narrowly avoiding burning off the feet of the guy currently squeezed against my arms as our four legs kick wildly through the wind. No telling how far we've fallen or how much farther we have left to go, but we can't continue at our current speed for much longer without hitting something.

Inching closer to the next Marine, I apply one more rocket kick that slides me directly underneath him, allowing me to grab him with my other arm. Ride's full. I pray to God I don't spot another person on the way down, since it'll probably kill all four of us when I try to save them too. But hey, that's how it goes. No man left behind.

Lucky for me, the next thing I see isn't another human, it's the garden platform, which is no longer boosting downward in its faster-than-gravity drop. It's chosen an odd distance to halt, given we're still nowhere near the bottom of the station. Unless it's stopping there just to catch and splat us early so our bodies don't messy up the station's flooring. Hopefully I can get my two passengers and myself upright in time.

Curling into a somersault, I shift the bulk of my weight to my feet, rotating our three-man jamboree forward until I'm able to chop downward with my legs and get us in a heads-up dropping position. Now that that's dealt with, I look down to see the green grass and silver steel of the platform, which is coming up fast. Time for my final party trick. Loosening every muscle in my body less than five yards from impact, I kick the boots on and use the thrust to cancel out as much momentum as possible in the millisecond I have left before landing. I then toss both of my hug-bound Marines onto the platform with as much upward force as possible, hoping that'll mitigate the pain of their impacts. Their body armor doesn't provide them with nearly as many durable layers of protection as ACAs, but I wager they're still buffered enough to avoid having their brains turned into mashed potatoes.

Now it's my turn. I slam onto the disc with enough force to completely muffle my rockets for a full second before they bounce me back up. As I come back down and kill my thrusters, the men I rescued are struggling to pick themselves up. At least no one's dead.

The platform doesn't budge when the next person thuds aboard. Gourd has a total of three men clinging to him when he lands, tossing them all to the side in the same fashion I did. Not five seconds later, Grimm and Toufexis arrive with a few guests of their own, for a sweeping total of nine Marines saved by our four suits. But that still leaves three or four missing, if I'm conservative with my estimate of how many managed to grab hold of the ledge and save themselves before the fall . . .

It doesn't take long to locate the missing few. As I figured, a handful of the Marines must've lost their grip on the edge of the city block above, since flailing Americans are still coming down from on high. One rockets past the platform, his scream so brief it doesn't even register until I see his speck-sized outline disappear into the field of generators below. As I arc my head up from the brutal sight, I spot M.I.A. free-faller number two. I won't let him suffer the same fate. Dashing as close to the edge of the platform as I can get, I don't hesitate for a second. With one good rocket hop upward, I catch the guy, do a little spin, and hurl him to the ground as gently as possible to avoid snapping his neck. He'll be wounded from whiplash, but that's an unavoidable byproduct of getting to keep his life. My boots die instantly, and I fall back onto the disc alongside him.

A third Marine is headed for the center of our platform, too far for me to reach. Gourd's got him, though. With a good running start and a valiant leap toward the middle, he catches the flailing screamer in midair, tucks him under his shoulder, and braces for impact. They both crash onto my side of the disc. Once they're sprawled out on the ground, the man falls off my squadmate and flops over, exposing some serious wounds. While most of him looks okay, his left arm is totaled. His ulna is split down the center, and both ends are jutting right the fuck out through his skin. Glancing over at the last guy I saved, it's clear he's not doing too well either. At first I thought he was fine, but now that the commotion is over I see he's not just pressing a sore chest, he's covering a rib that's poking out from beneath his armor. My immediate reaction is to blame myself, but given how much force he was coming down with, it's nothing short of a Christmas miracle his spine didn't snap in half when I grabbed him.

As it stands, two of our Marines are seriously injured and the other thirteen of us aren't doing much better after our impromptu skydiving session. In fact, none of the non-ACA-equipped troops have even picked themselves up off the ground yet, let alone gotten back into fighting positions.

None of that would be a major problem if it weren't for the fact that the trap we're caught in seems to have another stage. Above me, I see the distant hovering pods' lids pop off, releasing six distinctly humanoid figures. Three head toward Delta Squad's position while the other trio aim themselves downward, directly toward us. They're not falling, however. They're flying.

As they get closer, the new enemies' appearance comes into focus: they're bots with mannequin-like faces and silver bodies designed to imitate human musculature, each with three angular rocket thrusters bolted onto their backs. Jetpack androids. And what the fuck are those long pole things in their hands—oh, lances. Of course they have lances. Dostoevsky's *Crime and Punishment* must've had a pretty descriptive chapter on how to handle people in the wrong neighborhood. "Residential Peacekeepers," my ass.

Stopping far above us, they hover in place and look down. In robotic voices pretty similar to the generic male ones used in most AI assistants these days, they start speaking to us. Only problem is, their words are fast and in Russian.

My suit's audio translator should be auto-converting the words for me like how my HUD converted the Russian text earlier, but it's not—I'm just hearing loads of sinisterly accented gobbledygook. Fuck. Whatever heat damage my suit sustained back in the forge zone must've resulted in some melted sound-processing components.

"Gourd, you catching any of that?" I ask, frantically tinkering with my suit's controls to try to restore audio translation functionalities.

"Nah, my audio isn't converting right," he replies.

Some of the injured Marines around us try to deduce what the machines are saying, vocally translating bits and pieces via what little Russian they know. Their jabbering results in a series of siren noises emitting from the robots' mouths.

"They're telling us to be quiet and accept our trespassing charges," Toufexis says through what sounds like gritted teeth, angrily gesturing at Bravo Squad to shut the fuck up before anyone irritates the bots further. Unfortunately, Toufexis's actions themselves seem to do exactly that. Fuck, does the enemy think Toufexis is trying to resist? Are we being put under arrest by these three fuckin' robo-cops for entering a residential neighborhood without permits?

The lance bots' thrusters' black jet streams surge as the trio comes blasting down, ostensibly to finish what the garden platform started. Now that "peacekeeping" talks have completely imploded, I guess it's time to whip out the ol' pulse rifle and give them the classic one-two—

Shit—where's my rifle?

Oh, fantastic. It's not in its sheath, meaning it's somewhere at the bottom of the colony.

Doesn't look like any of the other troops have their guns either, including Gourd, Grimm, and Toufexis. Not good. My saw blades whir inside their wrist mounts, now acting as my last line of defense. Let's see how these things hold up against jetpack androids with lances taller than my body.

Grimm activates his elite ACA's custom wrist attachments. They slide open to reveal rifle barrels. So *that's* what he's been hiding up his sleeves. Two PDWs slip out of his gauntlets and land directly in his hands, affording him some ranged heat with which to take on the incoming bogies. Toufexis, on the other hand, is trapped in the same boat as us. Saws for life, I guess—oh, all right, Captain. Give him your spare gun. I see how it is. Nothing for me. That's fine.

"Form up in the center," Grimm commands.

They can't pick us off one by one if we're a cluster with two guns, I guess. My squadmate and I do as we're told, and within seconds the four of us are back-to-back, Gourd standing opposite me while Toufexis and Grimm man our flanks, their rifles aimed at the sky.

"Stay down, Bravos," Toufexis orders his Marines, most of whom have already shuffled their sore bodies off to the sidelines. Those who can't move themselves or be repositioned by allies remain sitting ducks. I get in a fighting stance, my blades spinning in sync with Gourd's. Four guys with two guns fighting jetpack androids with lances. What could go wrong?

Three pointy poles rain down on us, primed to turn our heads into kebabs. Toufexis and Grimm open fire less than a second before we all get skewered, not giving our foes any time to reassess their attack strategy. The bullets break up the incoming triangle of death, and the three bots part ways, abandoning their head-on approach. Now circling our four-sided formation like vultures eyeballing a pack of dying rabbits, they ominously glide along the circumference of the platform before figuring out exactly how to break our defense and lure us out. Simultaneously, the three of them swoop low and go in to lance the injured troops huddling on the outskirts of the disc.

With a measly two guns between the four of us, Toufexis and Grimm only have enough firepower to dissuade their pair of incoming peacekeepers, leaving me to stare down the one that's preparing to stab the guys I saved earlier. I will not let them survive the fall of a lifetime just to get speared.

I charge from my position at full speed, rocket-boosting directly toward the android as it prepares to thrust its lance. Just when its arm is about to jab forward, I jump, soaring over the troops about to get their intestines blended. Right arm outstretched, I grab the bot by the throat, squeezing its metallic jugular tight as I knock it away from the platform. On the bright side, I've temporarily saved my allies. Unfortunately, I've also just hurled myself off the platform and am now at the mercy of the jetpack bot I'm—um—hanging onto for dear life.

With one hand braced around its neck and the other clinging to its shoulder, grasping for any sort of hold possible, it almost looks like I'm trying to ballroom dance with the thing. The android seems to think the same thing, meeting my gaze for a moment. I look into its unblinking, glazed-over, synthetic eyes. It stares blankly at my visor. I think I feel a connection. But before I can take things to second base, the machine blasts us both sky high.

Guess the bot's not the kind to wine and dine before it— fuuuuuoooooh we're going way too fast now. I dig my fingers into the bot as deeply as possible, unwilling to move a single muscle for fear of losing my grip. It rockets halfway between the platform and the city above before pausing. It's one hell of a drop from here, and the machine knows it.

Trapped in altitudinal limbo, I don't give the bot a chance to make its next move. I press my left arm against its shoulder and set my saw to work, praying it'll make a dent. I only get a few millimeters deep before the machine stops me. It sheaths its lance and frees up its second hand.

The bot digs into my exoskeleton's armpit and cripples my suit's deltoid brace, its needlelike fingers crunching the intricate network of pistons so vital to my upper torso's mobility. Then it manipulates its hold on my suit's inner workings, forcing my sawing arm off of it. With my last line of defense officially taken out of the equation, the droid has me pinned like a schoolyard bully, and I *guarantee* it wants more than just lunch money. My HUD's going crazy, telling me the obvious by warning me that parts of my suit's core functionalities are going offline. I'm checkmated, and the bot knows it. My left hand can't reach anything, and if my right loses its hold on the droid's wiry neck veins, it's game over.

Keeping its right hand in a vice grip around my suit's deltoid brace, it slowly moves the other one toward the back of my helmet, sensually caressing it before jerking my head backward and ripping the armor right off. Any further back and it would've snapped my goddamn neck in half, but it seems to know that. The peacekeeping machine simply seems to want to identify and catalog a suspect. It scans my bare face with its eyes, forcing me to stare at it as I hang thousands of feet above a very painful death, devoid of HUD or cranial protection.

Now that the peacekeeper's gotten its mug shot, it's time to wrap things up. The bot tosses my helmet into the abyss and refocuses its attention squarely on me. It pulls my right hand off its neck, forcing me off as I violently struggle to grab hold again. My upper body is useless, and I'm running out of options. I whip out my last-ditch plan. Slamming my feet together, I dual rocket-blast the machine's shins, the sudden action catching it off guard. The flames singe its synthetic feet, and I know the attack has succeeded when the bot's hand loses its grip on my deltoid brace, letting my arm free. Time to see how bad the droid wants to personally deliver the finishing blow. If it truly is a peacekeeper, it won't want to let an active threat escape; it'll try to subdue me no matter the cost.

I fall away from it—without a helmet or backup plan. My drop isn't even remotely aligned with the platform, meaning if the android doesn't find me worth the hassle, then I've just secured myself a one-way ticket to smearing my guts all over the colony's power lines below.

I tumble through the air, the wind all but blinding me now that I don't have any eye or head protection. I hope the lack of a helmet doesn't make the landing extra painful—well, *if* I'm going to land, that is. A trio of thrusters kick to life, signaling the peacekeeper has decided to play ball. It blasts toward me in a terminal-velocity-based game of tag. That's right, come to papa. After how that first dance went, I'm sure as hell ready for a second tango.

Seems the machine wants to go about it a different way. Instead of trying for the hands-on approach, it points its lance at me and preps for an aerial impaling. Critical oversight on my part. Oops. I thought we were gonna fight mano-a-roboto, fist to fist. It's no fun if I can't throw a punch!

In all seriousness, I'm probably going to be speared to death in the next five seconds.

Tilting in the direction of my enemy, I thank God for the everlasting utility of my rocket boots and aim them directly at the droid's weapon. Let's see how much I can spice things up with my microthrusters. My left ankle swings into position just as the tip of the peacekeeper's lance slides within a yard, and I kick my boot to life and engulf the weapon in flames. While the action irresponsibly accelerates my fall and gives me less time to execute my plan, the risk is rewarded when the android doubles down and dives closer, refusing to let me get away. As the bot shoves its lance further forward, I feel the tip just barely poke the interior of my thrusters. That sensation disappears almost instantly, meaning my gamble has paid off and the flames are melting robo-cop's sharp stick like butter. A second later, the machine tosses its useless weapon and reaches for my ankle. Wrong move, buddy.

The peacekeeper has given me a platform of propulsion to work off of. The second it grabs my foot, I activate that boot's rocket and, with the sole combustion of one heel, manage enough force to shoot my entire body up so that the droid is the only one facing downward. It figures out what I'm planning to do far too late, and before it can let go of me, I twist my waist, place a boot directly over its android skull, and flame on. Its elastic outer shell lights up, and the goop that once comprised its silver skin sizzles off.

The bot and I continue our perilous plummet toward the generators below. The liquidized residue flying off its body slows my next move; without a helmet I can't afford to get any of that shit on my face. After a second of blind finagling, I fry its central AI chip. The body, still gripping me tightly, loses consciousness and ceases its struggle against my attack. Score!

The remainder of the head's liquefied material flies past, forcing me to duck below the peacekeeper's neck. Now that my left arm's exoskeleton is useless, I have to partially rely on raw muscle for the next part. Crouching above the droid's clavicles, seated on top of the thrusters shooting instant-death streams directly behind me, I dig my hands into its shoulders and take a shot at slave-piloting it. Luckily, as with the rest of its body, piercing the outer layer isn't that hard thanks to its material favoring flexibility over durability.

Its malleable silver musculature caves right in as I get a grip on its inner skeleton.

I guess a steering wheel would be too much to ask for, but the corpse sure handles like shit without one. The bot made it look so easy when it still had a head attached. Shoving one hand deep into its shoulder blade, I get it to swerve left, nearly flinging myself off with the force of the turn. At least I know I can make angles now. Pushing harder against its frame, I contort its deltoids to swing another ninety degrees and almost toss myself off the machine a second time. All of these maneuvers would be a hell of a lot easier with a helmet and a HUD, but my wind-whipped, watering eyes will have to make do.

Thankfully, I'm now in the general direction of the disc platform. What happens when I get there? Do I just crash my ride before it bucks me off? Or . . . do I try to give the fellas on the platform a lift? It's not like we have many other tickets back to the surface. The one I'm riding on right now might be our best shot.

Yee-haw, here comes cowboy Beecher on his trusty flying android steed. The mechanical corpse and I rocket away from the miles-deep void below us. Its limbs twitch in response to my tightening grip. I maintain my hold, press the android forward, and we blaze across hundreds of feet in seconds, right toward the sunken garden disc.

I hope I can slow the thing down enough to get a word in with Gourd, since I'm coming up on him and the gang in three . . . two . . . one. I yank hard at the bot's back, do-ing my best to get into some sort of idle hover position, but it's a wasted effort. Even though its jetpack reverses angles, it results in me flying over the platform, leaving Gourd and the rest of Sierra and Bravo as nothing but specks below. No chance in hell they'll hear me from up here. Guess when I fried the CPU in the thing's head I forfeited my only chance of altering its acceleration.

I'm not going to be able to take my ride off its top speed, so it looks like the only option is up. I yank forward a little harder and aim the machine's limp body north, forcing its thrusters to angle beneath me. The deceased droid and I speed straight toward the center of the colony. The wind current doesn't go easy on my exposed face or weakened left arm, but against all odds, I hang on for dear life and turn my lemon of a situation into lemonade.

Halfway through piercing the sky, I start to think I'll actually make it to the residential block—until I get distracted by a lurching sound from below. Even over the roar of the wind and thrusters, I hear it loud and clear: the sound of a gravity-bending platform rising. I look down to confirm my hopes, and it's true. The platform, it's . . . it's moving back up! The other Marines aren't trapped!

That's great news for them but it quickly turns into bad news for me. While I was gawking, I accidentally relaxed my control over the slaved android a smidge—just enough for it to tilt forward. Not by much, of course. Just by 180 degrees.

Aaaaaand downward I go. I was so fucking close to successfully handling the machine! Shit. Now I'm faced with two options: enjoy the last ten seconds of my life, or do something. And after the day I've had, there's not a chance in hell I'm going with the former. Yanking up with every last bit of strength I have, I force the android in the direction of the rising platform, resulting in a risky downward diagonal slant. If I'm even above the disc by the time I get within range of it, it's going to be one hell of a bumpy landing. Christ, I do not need more bouncing around; I'm disoriented and queasy enough as it is. I'm going to vomit my brains out if I don't stop moving soon.

Focus, focus . . . one dive and you're clear. That's all it is, one simple dive. At racing speeds. On the back of a twitchy dead robot. Narrowing my eyes to protect against the wind as much as possible, I slam my steed forward in a final dash for the platform.

My target quickly comes into view, going from distant speck to chrome cookie to giant fucking garden disc that I'm about to crash and burn on. Shit, physics is not on my side here. Doesn't matter, though—I have to make the situation work.

Seconds before impact, I release my hold on the android, press my feet against its shoulders, and jump off, hurtling toward the platform. The android slopes downward and disappears below my line of sight. Everything around me turns into a blur, my body flailing in its blast toward the giant metal disc intent on flattening me like a pancake. Knowing rocket boots would just expedite my death sentence, I rely solely on momentum, hoping my landing will be soft enough to survive. Wishful thinking. Looks like I'm about to eat it—

My body lurches violently to the left as the weight of a fucking gorilla smashes into me, knocking me out of the air and onto the platform. I crash against the disc, a crushing weight blocking my vision and squeezing my lungs. Only once the world stops moving do I see who my rescuer is.

"Gotcha," Gourd says weakly. He uncurls and releases me, flopping flat on his back in exhaustion. He's spent.

I give him a big thumbs-up before stretching out on the platform, releasing every muscle in my body at once. Everything hurts. Tank's empty. Let's all just get back up to ground level and call it a day.

On our backs, locked in a much-needed moment of respite, Gourd and I stare at the underbelly of the Red Peril's central city without exchanging a single word. Do I care how Toufexis and Grimm took down the other two bots or how Gourd managed to tackle me out of the air at that speed? Not really. And does he care that I learned how to fly a corpse's jetpack with the body still attached? Probably not. Let's just enjoy the scenery, ogle the underbelly of the city in the sky, and be happy we're not fighting shit right now.

As I gaze at the city's bottom, something catches my eye—a dark, angular patch amidst an otherwise curved, airtight industrial framework. Might it be a secret entrance to a path forward? A maintenance tunnel, perhaps? Hmm. Could be useful. However, I'm tired and not concerned about it in the slightest. Heck, I'm not even sure of what I see, and whatever it is, it's too late to find out now. Our platform rises past it, finally landing us back on the same level as Delta Squad. A bevy of Bravos lie flat on the ground alongside Gourd and me, while Toufexis and Grimm . . . wait, where are they? I tilt my head and see they're seated back-to-back, resting on each other for support. Jesus, the fight's even sapped them. Cap never breaks proper stance.

Of course, finding energy reserves I can't believe he has,

Grimm manages to stand in order to address McGregor with some captain-like dignity.

"It's good to have you back, sir," McGregor says, his massive fists clutching a sparking remote that looks like it was ripped out of something. "And you're welcome for the lift."

"What's that?" Grimm asks wearily, not sharing his level of energy.

"The security system's master switch! It can make that thing go up, down—" He creeps a finger toward it like he's about to demo the platform's functions again.

"Don't," Grimm roars, catching the joking McGregor off guard.

"All right, all right. Wasn't going to."

"Where'd you get it from, anyway?" Toufexis asks.

"From a guy inside . . . there." McGregor points to a decimated house across the way.

"Where is he? We need him for further questioning," Grimm demands.

"He, um, isn't available for interviews right now," McGregor answers.

It only takes one quick glance toward Delta Squad's former battleground to see why that might be. Several houses' metal lockdown frames are smashed open, absolutely everything is riddled with bullet holes, dead Russian technicians litter the lawns . . . and there are even three smoking, smoldering jetpack androids lying around. Seems like our guys had quite the ball up here.

"Typical," Grimm mutters.

"Least we know how to operate the big planter! And

besides, I got some intel out of him. Nuuuh worries," he says, pouring on the accent.

"Share."

"Well, it's not happy news. If the fellow's word is anything to go by, there's more of the pods up ahead. Plenty more. Not to mention the hundreds of Russians hiding out here who'll be rigging traps."

"Goddamn it, we don't have time for that," the captain responds. "We're almost down to two hours."

"There's no way we'll make it through more of these defenses with a window that tight . . ."

Though McGregor's remark was almost definitely rhetorical, Grimm seems to take it personally. "I'm *aware*, Sergeant. That commentary isn't necessary." He grouses some more after that, yet fails to pose any solutions. He sounds stumped.

Toufexis? Gourd? Anything, guys? No? Well, shit. We have a squad's worth of injured troops, some looking like they're minutes from the grave, a piece of my suit is totaled and another is missing altogether, and there are only two guns floating around between the entirety of Bravo and Sierra. We couldn't take on a pack of enemy humans in our current state, let alone more peacekeepers. Maybe it's time we acknowledge we're a bit outmatched.

"Captain, permission to speak?" Gourd asks Grimm.

"Permission granted."

"I think I saw something a few stories down. Looked like a door, maybe."

Shit, he saw it too.

"If McGregor lowers us down a little—"

Grimm's eyes flare up with the ferocity of a rabid animal

at the mere suggestion of moving the platform, so Gourd cuts himself off immediately. After a beat, however, my friend finds the courage to continue.

"—we could see if it's an alternate route."

Sure enough, within the next few minutes, McGregor has lowered us down and we have a dedicated team working on opening the maintenance hatch, which just so happens to be within arm's reach of our disc's rim. Lucky us. Between Toufexis's saws and McGregor's fists, the door caves pretty quickly, granting us an entrance to the city's tunnel network.

"Here's the plan," says an exhausted Grimm. "Bravo, you stay here. Guard the critically injured and drop the platform the second we're out of sight so nothing from the other side can reach you. We'll signal a rescue team to these coordinates once we've taken the Spire."

So we're taking all the remaining guys with guns for ourselves. Smart. I sure hope no rocket bots or flying androids with lances find their way down here and spot a left-behind, unarmed squad full of injured troops—cough, cough.

"Delta, you're coming with us. Lieutenant Gourd, are you seeing the broadcast signal that I'm seeing?"

Gourd nods. McGregor and I, with no helmets or HUDs, are left to wonder what it is that the captain and lieutenant are talking about.

"Good, then we're both intercepting some fragment of the Spire's data output," Grimm continues. "Even if we can't decode it, we can see its origin point. Since that's all we're picking up, let's assume any transmission capable of reaching us in the maintenance tunnels shares the same source. When we lose sight of the Spire underground, we'll follow the highest frequency signal we can find, and hope it leads us where we need to go."

That simple, huh?

Shortly thereafter, the captain's theory turns out to be right. For a brief stretch, the cramped and only intermittently lit maintenance tunnels transition into open-faced catwalks dangling beneath the city. Here, there are enough gaps in the levels above us to see the tip of the big bad Spire itself. We're too close to miss the thing now.

I almost crack and ask Gourd something I know will end awfully for both of us, but as I open my mouth to speak, cowardice seizes control of my voice. Silently and subordinately, I keep walking alongside Sierra Squad, unable to do anything else. We're nearing the end of the tunnels. The finish line is nigh. Yet even now, whose team will—or should—win is entirely up in the air.

We keep moving forward until the thick, reinforced hallways return, guiding us to a passage somewhere on the third sublevel. Just when I think it's safe to assume the weird shit is over, I'm once again proven wrong. As the generic piping along the walls starts to gradually fade away and curl out of view, the remaining gaps reveal something big and crimson. It looks massive. Heck, it's practically as large as the mold from the forge zone. Actually . . . y'know what, I'm not going to dwell on it. Considering the heat it's giving off, it's probably a ventilation shaft, or generator, or something. No big deal.

As we're going up the next flight of stairs to the second sublevel, the mysterious crimson tube-thing starts to move. Its activity shakes the maintenance tunnel and nearly sends all of Sierra and Delta airborne, though luckily we maintain our footing long enough to be ready for the next surprise. Behind us, the tube's oncoming sections are mounted with large, bladed fins—fins that slice through the gaps in the walls and head for us like giant horizontal guillotines. Shit. If those things are part of some giant cooling fan built to dissipate the temps around here, they're failing miserably; I'm feeling more heat than ever.

"Run!" Grimm shouts, as though we haven't already figured out that part.

By the time the words have left his mouth, all of Sierra and Delta are scuttling up the stairs at full speed, the troops in the back making it off the steps with just a few seconds to spare before the first massive fin slides by and cuts through our previous walkway like tinfoil. Christ, why are parts of the tunnel damaging other parts? Is it the station's last-ditch way of trying to keep unwanted groups away from the heart of the Reds' operation? Are we experiencing a fever-like defense that cripples the entire body in order to kill the virus, also known as . . . us?

The platform we're on begins to slope downward now that it's not secured to the infrastructure below, threatening to detach from the city's underbelly altogether as strands of twisted, warping metal stretch beneath our feet. We dash across the sinking hallway and see that it also runs parallel to the mobilized tube. Said tube's bladed length races R Company to the penultimate stairwell, and miraculously, we all make it through unharmed and hit the first sublevel, where the fins finally stop following us and damaging our path. Now that we're on a walkway that isn't tearing off and falling out from under us, it's just a straightforward sprint to the finish line.

Our ticket to ground level is up ahead, and we're within a few yards of it when a massive rumble knocks us on our asses. Grimm, Gourd, and I stumble backward and collapse onto McGregor and his squad. Once we get back on our feet, we take a peek at what tossed us off our feet. The ceiling above us is splitting open, violently shaking everything beneath it as its sides part. What the hell is going on?

The gargantuan red tube to our left slopes upward and slides through the new opening. The ultra-thick ceiling panels continue to move away from each other at the top of our floor, opening wide enough to provide us with a perfect view of the Spire, the sought-after landmark now almost immediately in front of us.

"Keep moving!" Grimm orders.

We rush the final stairwell, dashing hard and fast up the steps that'll get us to ground level. By the time we ascend to the halfway point, the big tube we've been running alongside picks up enough speed to slide past us, getting skinnier and skinnier until its crimson tip whips by and slips out of sight.

A few seconds later, my boots leave the last step of the tunnel stairwell and slam onto the border of the Spire's courtyard. Back above ground, covered in the black light of the station's front interior, I realize we've actually made it. We're here, one oversized front lawn away from—

What the *fuck* is that . . .

The tube from the maintenance tunnel disappears behind the tower, a trail of shredded patio tiles and torn-up grass in its wake. And then I hear it, the robotic screech of something that shouldn't exist accompanied by the shattering of the Spire's outermost glass panes. The thing that was racing us out of the tunnels wasn't some sentient ventilation pipe. No, it was a hostile—one that is actively twisting itself around the Spire.

Once coiled, the monster reveals its face to us in full, the two-fanged machine's dead, pitch-black eyes glowing violently. It lets out a hiss of nightmare fuel, allowing us a glance inside its gaping maw of dark matter.

It looks like we've discovered the Reds' final line of defense: a skyscraper-sized crimson basilisk. First the anthropomorphic crab bots, then the panther droids, and now the thing in front of us. *Why, Russia, why?* Are these beasts the contingency plan in case you accidentally wipe out all remaining animal species in the universe with your fuel?

Doesn't matter. Whatever sick fuck of a zoologist thought up these mechanical monsters is going to have hell to pay if I make it out of here. Until then: robot bestiary writers, it looks like a new entry is in order.

CHAPTER 18
Beecher

NURS really wanted to save the best for last. Seriously, a fucking snake? Sure, it's a flexible, dynamic solution to any building's defense problems, but on the other hand, it's a skyscraper-sized fucking snake. Why not build a tall fence or have some turrets pop out of the ground or something to defend your shitty tower? The Reds just *had* to be creative. Ugh.

If one thing's certain, it's that the bitchin' bot in front of us is not going to play nice with our schedule. We have less than two hours until Uncle Sam's greatest asset ceases to exist, and the giant piece of deadly strawberry licorice we're faced with appears intent on bleeding that timer dry.

Wrapped around the entire bottom third of the Spire, the basilisk's body creates an impenetrable blockade that cuts off the tower's ground entrance. Wriggling its coiled form snugly against our target, only its scaly head peeks out past the building it has entrapped, hissing at us with the ferocity of a supersized python defending its nest. The sound is so shrill that, along with everyone else, I reflexively cover my ears, squeezing them to the point where they hurt. A pair of Marines not quick enough to block out the noise collapse in front of me, crumpling to the ground when the high-frequency screech reaches its brief, burning crescendo. At that moment, I feel the armor covering my hands vibrate as the soundwaves try to physically burrow through the layers of plating and fabric to reach my ears.

Seconds after the shriek stops, a Delta Squad member and I kneel down to feel the pulses of the two fallen men. They've gone stone-cold, their heart rates just a bump above flatlining. It seems the snake-bot's battle cry is a sonic attack—one that's just taken these two out of the game.

"They're out cold!" the Delta tells his sergeant. Surprised the rest of us aren't, honestly—I can't be the only one with a hell of a surprise headache from the hiss, can I? Even if I blocked out the worst of it, that shit hurt.

"Grab their weapons and let's go," McGregor responds. "You too, Lieutenant Beecher." He's right—I'm in dire need of a rifle.

While the standard-issue firearms may not have the kick of my pulse rifle, I'm not sure it matters, considering what we're up against. The way I see it, any weapon is just a morale booster to make me feel a little less defenseless against scarlet scales over there. Now if only I had a pair of earplugs.

"Cover your ears when it attacks," Grimm barks before being interrupted by a barrage of rocket fire originating from a nearby tower.

All of us scramble to dodge, minus the pair of unconscious Deltas who have no choice but to take the blast head-on. Worse, the explosive splash damage snags a few of the able-bodied Deltas as well. The disorganized scuttle results in all twenty of us eating the ground, though not everyone gets up afterward.

By my count, we just lost five guys—if we don't get a plan together right now, we're all going to be robot snake food.

Grimm's way ahead of me.

"McGregor, put your second best in charge and have Delta provide a distraction. The rest of us need to handle those rockets." He gestures toward the roof of the neighboring tower where the rocket bots are.

"Captain—" McGregor protests, knowing he'd be sending Delta Squad on a suicide mission, especially without an ACA-suited leader to guide them.

Grimm recognizes the consequences of his order. He just doesn't care about them right now.

"We need every ACA handling the machines up top if we want a fighting chance," Grimm shouts, ordering McGregor to pass off command.

The Scotsman does as he's told, and within the next five seconds we're divided into two teams. The suicide squad will play snake-and-mouse while the all-star ACA team works on taking out multiple tanklike machines with a few weak guns and our bare hands. Honestly, I can't tell who's worse off.

"Go! Go! Go!" Grimm roars, kicking the plan into action.

At the sight of our division, the rooftop bots launch another volley of rockets toward those of us in ACAs. Their attack happens simultaneously with the basilisk's second screech, pausing Delta's advance and forcing the four of us with suits to handle two threats at once. I sheath my rifle and cover my ears as best I can, but my lack of a helmet puts me at a severe disadvantage. The enemy's sonic attack starts to chip away at my eardrums, and a sickening dizziness overtakes me. Thankfully, the noise dies down quickly, meaning I'm able to cling to consciousness and keep up the pace alongside my team. We skate past the rocket blasts untouched, circling the courtyard to reach the ambushing bots' perch.

Behind me, gunfire erupts, signaling that Delta's moving again and beginning its faceoff against the snake. More rockets slam directly behind our squad as we clear the Spire grounds and make it to the middle of the neighboring street. On the bright side, we're outside of rocket range for a few seconds. However, our new position opens us up to street-level threats, which happen to include hundreds of rifle bots converging on the Spire.

The moment they see us, their guns light up and both sides of the road become a yellow sea of muzzle flashes, spelling trouble for McGregor and me specifically since we're the only ones with anything exposed. Covering my head with my arms as best I can, I skate behind Grimm and company as they lead the way. With one rocket-powered leap, McGregor uses his fists to smash through our target tower's ground-floor lockdown barricades, getting us off the streets and inside the building.

Rampaging through tables and seats like four bulls in a china shop, we dash toward the elevators hiding behind the reception desk area. Not wanting to waste any time, McGregor smashes a hole in one of the elevator doors big enough for the four of us to climb through. Once inside, we have a second to look at the mess of a floor we've created before the box kicks to life and pulls us up the shaft. Luckily, the building's power is still online. We'll see how long that lasts.

"There are hundreds of those bots. Delta can't take them all!" McGregor moans as the exterior frames of floors pass by the gaping hole in our torn-open elevator.

"All of us combined can't take on that many!" Grimm replies. "Besides, they'll have to go through the Spire's fence chokepoints to get in—easy bottlenecks. As long as we clear the roof and get back down there ASAP, there'll still be a Delta to save."

McGregor's pissed, but he swallows the order whole. We continue our climb through the tower, the elevator whisking us straight up with no signs of stopping.

Of course, as soon as I dwell on the great time we're making, the box screeches to a halt and the lights die, trapping us halfway between the second highest floor and our target. McGregor, livid as all hell, wastes no time in getting us back on the move. Barging past the three of us to get to the front of the box, he reaches through the opening in the elevator, grips the exposed edge of our target floor, and pulls it down with all the force he and his suit can muster. If we can't come to it, it'll come to us. The metal framework bends downward as the sergeant tugs with all his might to create a slope. The floor boarding begins to break. Its surface tiles shatter and fall off, revealing a sort of makeshift girder ladder. Once McGregor's pulled said ladder down to where his waist is, he hoists himself up and climbs the improvised scaffolding. A few seconds later, he's standing on the top floor, waiting for us to join him. We each inch our way up and out of the elevator shaft, one by one, until the squad is reassembled. Now we just need to find a way onto the roof.

"Are we going to split up to locate the stairs—" I start, but

Grimm signals for me to shut up, pointing right above us at the fractures in the ceiling's boarding. New ones appear with every step taken by our enemies. Oh, shit. Right. Be quiet while we're underneath the big bad rocket robots.

McGregor gathers our attention with a hand, then makes a mini-pounce followed by a fisting motion. I understand we're pressed for time and finding the stairwell on such a big floor might not be the best idea, but really, punching a hole is our brilliant alternative plan? If his ACA can't penetrate the ceiling's reinforcements, we're going to have hell to pay from above. It doesn't look like we're voting on strategies, unfortunately. Grimm gives the sergeant the all-clear to breach, and Sierra Squad backs up, ready for the sky to fall.

Once we're all back a few yards, Grimm starts the countdown for McGregor's punch. Three . . . two . . . one. The sergeant kicks on his rocket boots and leaps up, motorized left fist extended and ready to rock. We watch in awe as his shining blue knuckles make contact with the ceiling and then pass through entirely, the sound of metal hitting metal echoing up above as dust and plaster pour over the four of us. A second later, his fist comes hurtling back down through the hole with a robot's leg in tow, creating cracks along the ceiling that warn us to get out of the way. The entire stretch collapses under the weight of fallen rocket bot number one, whose mechanical carcass comes slamming onto the tiles in front of us with a booming thud. Taking no chances, Grimm carves up the robot's skull with a round from his rifle before ordering us up. Now that the roof's exposed and we've lost the element of surprise, it's time to handle however many foes are up there waiting for us.

We boost through the massive opening in the ceiling and land topside, instantly diving into combat against the three remaining rocket bots, all of whom fix their attention solely on us and stop taking potshots at the Marines below. Given that I only have one functional ACA arm and no helmet, I decide my optimal role in the battle is to be the distraction while my squadmates handle the actual punchy-punchy stuff. First order of business: the bot standing precariously close to the edge of the roof facing the Spire. It shouldn't take much to nudge the machine over, as long as I can get it off balance.

"McGregor! On your right!" I shout, not waiting for him to keep up. Blasting toward the rocket baddie, I open fire on it with my dinky rifle, peppering its tummy with a little lead. That's all it takes to get its attention. Skating forward to bait it into swinging its mighty sword, I get my wish as the robot raises its bladed arm high in the air, prepping a killing blow that's sure to do me in—until, that is, McGregor's voice calls out behind me and I know we've caught the bot hook, line, and sinker.

"Duck!" he shouts. I crouch low as he soars overhead, punching the vulnerable rocket bot off the roof of the tower. Two down, two to go.

We turn around and see Gourd and Grimm tangoing with the other pair like pros. They're tricking the bots into swinging at each other by maneuvering between them, a tactic which inflicts far more damage in single blows than we ever could.

"We need one—" Captain shouts after a particularly close dodge, "alive!"

That'll be the tricky part, all right. How do we take one

down without accidentally handling the other? If we're not careful we could lose both, and then what?

As I ponder the conundrum, Gourd sweeps the leg of the back-facing bot, knocking it over so McGregor can knuckle-piston its face in while Grimm distracts the other machine. That works.

With only one enemy left, it's time to figure out how we bait the thing into firing on the big basilisk.

"Beecher, stand by the edge! Align with the Spire!"

Of course Grimm would make the worst part of his plan my job. As the one tasked with dodging missiles head-on, I back up toward the roof's Spire-facing border into the only position where I can hope a rocket will slide over the top instead of clipping the building and killing me. Meanwhile, the last big robot continues to square off against my three teammates, their combined efforts rendering its swings useless. The extended session of fruitless blade swipes eventually leads the bot's eyes to me, informing it there's another opponent to be dealt with. Since it's already engaged in close-range combat, the robot calculates its only option. It whips out its launcher and hopes for the best. *You and me both, big guy.*

Letting one loose on a path destined straight for my exposed skull, its first rocket fires directly at me with just enough of a warning that I'm able to dive out of the way in time. Moments later, I hear the rapturous hiss of the scarlet snake and know we landed a hit. Given that I'm all the way up here, with such a great distance between me and the robotic reptile, the thought to cover my ears doesn't even register until everything's already over. Thankfully, my senses remain relatively intact. As luck would have it, it seems the sonic attack has range limitations.

"Confirm!" Grimm orders.

Peeking my head over the side, I see the repercussions of our rocket as well as a whole lot more. The flood of bots that swarmed us on ground level are almost at the fence chokepoint across from the base of our building, completely filling the streets with nothing but yellow and silver. Also, Delta Squad's seen a slight reduction in size thanks to that last snake screech. And speaking of the snake, it's not happy. There's a deep scorch mark on the lowest coil of its body, as well as flames erupting from the stretch of tower immediately above it. The machine slowly unwraps itself from the Spire and slides its tail across the courtyard, toward the street—the one we're across from—as the head of the beast shifts its gaze in our direction.

"Another shot, fast!" I shout back.

"On it," Grimm replies.

My allies trick the robot into sending another rocket my way. It whips past me and, after an anxiety-inducing flight through the open air, connects with the snake's neck, slipping underneath its armor plates before bursting off a row of scales. Another deathly hiss erupts from the monster's mouth, though the Marines below are ready for it. Having not lost any Deltas to the latest sonic screech, it looks like we're finally making net-positive progress on taking down our enemy. The only problem is, its tail is a lot closer to our tower and it's still not dead.

"One more!" I order, hoping that's all it takes. That's all we have time for, in any case.

As the next rocket flies, I feel destiny take over. One last time, I dodge out of the way, leaving the flaming projectile with nowhere to go but toward the snake's big ugly face. Our enemy immediately realizes the threat is coming too fast to be avoided. Its eyes seethe with rage and its body braces for the shot to end all shots, until the explosive sticks the landing and—wait, there wasn't a detonation. Where could it—oh my God—are you fucking kidding me? The rocket is stuck in the snake's left nostril?!

"Did we get 'er?" McGregor shouts, sounding like he's dodging another swing from our rooftop opponent's blade.

"No, we did not—" I holler back, though I don't get to finish my sentence. Our building violently shakes, launching all five of us, rocket bot included, off our feet and onto our asses. None of us have a chance to stand up before the second tremor hits. The entire rooftop tilts in the direction of the Spire, and we begin to fall.

The snake's tail pummels away at support beams and destroys the foundation of the tower's lower levels. Our slight slope downward quickly turns into a steep drop-off as our roof collapses in on itself while the floors beneath it fall apart upon impact with each other. There's only one way I'll avoid getting eaten up by the concrete vortex beneath me: if I ride the fallen frame of one of our downed robots to the bottom of the avalanche like a damn lifeboat. Looks like the other guys have already thought of and executed my plan. Time to see if there's room for a fourth!

Pressing my hands against the cracking concrete, I push off and rocket-slide across the roof in a dash to reach the nearest robot's clawed foot, which I latch onto just before the tower really tears itself apart. The second I get a grip on the bot, a cloud of rubble bursts over me, blasting dust and debris against my exposed eyes. The collapse rate speeds up so much that the remaining stories compile on top of each other practically instantaneously, forming a plume of mile-high dust around us. We join the massive wreckage pool at the bottom, which the four of us come crashing down on top of thanks to our lifesaving arks. The impact is so rough I can hardly feel my body afterward. The only thing keeping me from passing out is the stirring beneath us as the tip of the snake's tail pulls itself out from the pile of wreckage it just created.

With my entire body covered in dust and my eyes all but blinded, I get to work on wiping off my peepers without getting more shit in them. By the time I have the left one cleared, McGregor and Grimm are already up on their feet, telling me to get my ass moving. Where's Gourd?

"Wait, where—"

Then I see it. His big, ogre-like hand sticking up stone-still from beneath one of the robot's shells. Somehow, during the fall, he got caught underneath.

"We don't have time!" Grimm says, roping an arm around me in an attempt to yank me away from the accident.

Too bad he tried to separate me from my best friend via my suit's working arm. After I give him one firm shove to the chest, the good captain abandons Sierra Squad in favor of joining McGregor and the rest of Delta in the final stand against the crimson basilisk. As for me, I have bigger priorities.

With all my strength, both muscular and mechanical, I lift the shoulders of the dead rocket bot. Gourd's chest armor is underneath. Shit, his head is buried under debris. Sliding into the small opening I've created, I rest the entire weight of the deceased bot's upper torso on my back as I dig hard and fast to reach my friend's helmet. A couple inches down, I hear a muffled noise.

"I'm coming for you!" I hope he can hear me under all that shit. Digging further, I discover his faceplate, cracked to all hell.

"P-please! Get me out!" he shouts, his helmet-muffled voice full of panic.

"Just hold on!" I reply now that his head's above the surface. I work diligently to pull his torso up and out of the wreckage. Not only does he happen to be the heaviest motherfucker in R Company, but he's so tightly packed into the rubble that it's like trying to split rocks with my bare hands; in other words, I'm not doing it without seriously hurting myself. And at the rate the machine's weighing down on my back, exoskeleton or otherwise, an injury seems imminent. Tugging with as much force as I can muster, both my hands wrapped under his shoulders, I desperately try to get him out from under the mess. Something's stopping me. I look down and spot the issue: he has a massive slab of cement directly on top of his legs, and there's not a chance in hell I'll be able to move it without letting the husk of the rocket bot collapse on top of us both. But he's alive in there; I can't let him just die inside a fucking suit—wait.

"Gourd, eject!"

"Can't . . . reach."

Shit, he's right. Using one of my arms to dig one of his out from under the rubble, I move just enough cement off for him to regain movement and help wriggle his left upper limb out of captivity. Once that's free, I move my feet so he can reach the ejection switch on his thigh, which is sensitive to each wearer's unique armor ID. Giving up my stable footing might come back to bite us in the ass, but at least we'll get to face that reality together.

The ACA's parts simultaneously unlatch, and Gourd pushes himself free, sliding his legs out of their trapped armor. Thin trickles of blood stem from all over his body, and there's an especially unsightly wound on his forehead, where his helmet must've been hit particularly hard. He quickly shimmies out of the remainder of his entrapped, destroyed suit and claws himself out of the wreckage, crawling to freedom underneath me.

"You out?" I ask, making sure he's cleared the space so I can drop the goddamn robot.

"Yes!" he rasps, encouraging me to get the hell out from underneath the metal carcass.

I boost as hard as my boots will allow and give the machine a small push upward with my back, buying myself just enough time to slip out from beneath it before it comes crashing back down onto the rubble. Finally, we're both free.

"You saved me," he gasps, his eyes wide.

I think that's as close as he's ever come to death. But being buried alive isn't enough to slow either of us down. Not here. Not now. I refocus, and Gourd instantly snaps back to proper form.

"You'd do it for me. You feeling okay?" I ask, not sure if we should recklessly dive back into the fight if he's going to bleed out on me halfway through it.

"Only flesh wounds. Let's go!" He's reduced to his day-old dragon skin armor, armed with nothing but his bare hands, yet still totally ready to take on the snake. Bravery and stupidity sure are a noble combo. Good thing the two of us have a surplus of both.

I follow him to the heart of the courtyard where Delta Squad has moved in on the writhing, hysterical snake. It's coiled itself back around the Spire. McGregor stands in its shadow, punching the base of its body to minimal effect while Grimm and the rest of the Deltas hammer its head with bullets, everyone aiming for the nose but failing to land a shot at such great range.

We reach our allies without much hassle since the lawn is still pretty clear. It looks like our tower collapsed on top of the nearest advance of rifle bots and blocked off the entire side's fencing, more or less. One less chokepoint to worry about.

"Nice of you to join us again." Grimm's words are sprinkled with contempt, his eyes trained on the enemy. "Gourd, grab a gun and form up. Beecher . . ." he starts, taking a quick glance at me and discovering I lost yet another rifle and am back to having zero firearms, ". . . help McGregor down there."

For the first time ever, Gourd doesn't take a superior officer's order as a mandate from heaven. Instead, he hesitates for a moment, seeming to toss the command around in his head. Still, he ultimately complies, shuffling off to pick up a rifle from a fallen ally. That's better than my response; I disobey Grimm's order entirely.

"Beecher, where the fuck do you think you're going? Lieutenant! Get back here! Now!" Grimm shouts as I take off, skating toward the robotic reptile's tail rather than joining

McGregor at its belly. Grimm's not thinking things out too well. Why tighten up a formation that's going to get us all killed? If he thinks *that's* a last stand, wait until he sees what I have in store.

Zeroing in on my target at top speed, I watch the snake's head to see if it will notice my one-man flanking attempt. It does.

The bot's tail moves in my direction and its tip lifts off the lawn. My enemy knows that in order to get any momentum going with its fat ass, it'll have to minimize resistance and cut through the air instead of the ground. There should be a gap tall enough for me to slip under during its attack—if I play my cards right.

Dropping to my knees, I slide into a rock-star kneel and lean my torso as far back as possible, kicking on the rocket boots just as the tip of the tail comes roaring past where my head would've been a moment ago. Without a helmet, the heat of the flames prickles against the back of my exposed cranium, but I don't mind it—if I'm feeling it, that means I'm still alive. My rocket-fueled power slide pushes me forward as the four hundred bajillion tons of mechanical snake whip by a few inches above my nose, my suit pouring on the speed until I'm out of the danger zone.

I clear the gap in the nick of time. The snake's tail, having stabbed out as far as it can, drops onto the ground and crashes behind me, momentarily hiding me from view. Ideally, the robot will think it got me and won't stop to notice what I have in store for it next.

The tail retracts, racing closer to where I'm hidden. Just gotta wait until it's close enough . . . there we go. The only

climbable point on the mechanical monster exposes itself:
the tail's flat, screwdriver-like tip, which whips around as the
snake attempts to coil up again. Hopefully it doesn't mind a
little water bug like me hitching a ride. Seeing my chance,
I dart out from my hiding spot and fire up a single perfect
rocket jump that launches me right onto the end of the tail.

Feeling my fiery boots, the snake writhes and wriggles its
bottom half, but that's not enough to shake me loose. The
bot's body is too tightly wound, and I'm too agile with these
rocket skates for it to beat me that easily. While the big baddie figures out a way to retaliate, I ascend its body like a spiral staircase, shooting up its spine in my rush to the dome. I
wanna pet the thing's nose, damn it.

Scale by scale, I blaze upward. All the while, the machine
aggressively ruffles its plating. The snake's movements slow
me down a bit, but I'm too fast and small for it to knock me
off, and by the time I reach the smoking gash from our second
rocket hit I know I'm in the clear. Leaping across its mechanical parietal bump, I burn a thin line right down its forehead
with my boots, my charge uninterrupted until a sudden shaking sensation breaks my flow—oh shit—oh *shit*—aaaand I'm
airborne!

The snake, in a last-ditch effort to throw me off, might've
just given me the biggest assist ever. It launches me into the
air with its snout as it stretches its mouth open for a defensive
hiss, inadvertently gifting me a fuck-ton more gravitational
force to deliver the big hit. I'm about to give the monster a
bloody nose it'll never forget.

I let out a ferocious yell, drowning out the sound of
its mechanical maw's buzzing pre-shrill wind-up. I kick

my boots on and surge through the air with the force of a bald-eagle-turned-ballistic-missile. Pulling my ACA-powered right arm back for the knockout punch of the millennium, I lock my vision onto the rocket stuffed into the snake's nasal cavity. With all the force I can muster, I propel my fist at the lodged rocket, striking it with so much power that it travels further down the snake's nostril before exploding from the inside, sending me flying once again. Flames erupt from the beast's nose, mouth, and eyes in the most glorious fashion, its implosion's blast launching me right back up toward the station's nonexistent sky. Now, however, I can't afford to come back down.

Flying through the air just a few feet from the Spire's exterior, I rocket myself a bit closer to the sparkling blue walls of the tower and plunge my ACA arm through the nearest pane of glass, clutching the edge before I can fall back down. I shove my other arm into the new opening to maintain my grip, swatting at stray glass shards overhead to make an entry point big enough for my whole body to fit through.

Once I've cleared enough space, I glance down at the collapsing crimson basilisk. Its massive body falls on top of itself, its coils slam into each other, and the beast finally loses its once-tight hold on the Spire. I still have a job to do, but I grant myself a single, self-indulgent moment of relief. At least one monster's been slain today.

Hauling my dangling, exhausted body up from the side of the tower, I grab a support beam on the other side of the glass and pull myself inside. I made it. I'm in the Spire.

CHAPTER 19

Gourd

"**D**amn it," Captain snarls.

I can't see him, since Delta Squad and I are too busy covering our exposed eyes from the cloud of debris the freshly crashed snake bot just created, but I hear him. He sounds pissed. As the dust settles around the courtyard, I stop shielding my face and peek over at Grimm. He's looking toward where Beecher's hanging, way up near the top of the Spire.

"What's the matter, Cap—"

"Nothing," he fires back, walking to the front of R Company's formation. He examines the corpse of the snake, part of which is blocking our only entrance to the building. Captain calls McGregor over, and the two have a quick discussion, one that's just a bit too far away for me to listen in on. Then, Grimm steps onto the sergeant's open ACA hands, and McGregor flings him to the top of the lowest coil of the enemy's carcass.

"R Company," Captain barks from atop the snake, "form up."

McGregor and Cap team up to lift each of us onto the robot's body. Once everyone's off the ground, Grimm gives the game plan.

"Delta Squad"—what's left of it, anyway—"half of you stay here and guard the perimeter. Enemy forces will be swarming the remaining chokepoints, so handle them. Fall back only once you're out of ammo." Captain then looks at McGregor. "Sergeant, you and the other half are coming with me."

After McGregor assigns units to the handful of Marines left in Delta Squad, those not designated posts along the giant snake barricade follow Grimm and me forward.

We slip over the inside edge of the big bot and land smack-dab in front of the tower's main entrance. McGregor punches a hole in the barricaded doors, then rips it apart until it's wide enough for us to filter through. As we enter the breach, some grunts from Delta mumble about Beecher, wondering what he's up to. I catch two whispering about whether the Lieutenant's gone rogue, pointing fingers at our scowling Captain Grimm. I bite my tongue hard and refrain from slapping the disrespect right out of those Marines' rosy red cheeks. The only reason we were able to climb over the snake and make it as far as we have is because said robot wasn't alive to squash our little meat sacks. But no one else seems to have a shred of gratitude for the guy who saved our hides. Even if my fellow soldiers are just frazzled and paranoid from all the bizarre traps and casualties we've suffered, that's no excuse for punk talk.

To maintain control of my slapping hand, I distract myself with the sight of the Spire's massive lobby, which I'm now deep inside of. It's huge, and pretty damn fancy. There's all the standard foyer stuff, like rows of big, comfy lounge chairs that I wish I could take a nap in right now, long desks, coffee tables with those dumb little vases filled with pebbles—nothing overtly communist. But just a bit beyond that is the room's main decor, and it reeks of the enemy's pride. Giant paintings of Russian presidents and oligarchs line the walls surrounding every stairwell, and holographic displays on the ceiling project looping footage of the Russian military right over our heads. Needless to say, it's not the footage I would use; my choices would include slow-motion replays of all the Russkies we've blown up on our way here. Actually, speaking of Russkies . . . where are they? I haven't seen a human enemy in a while.

With no immediate threats in sight, the fatigued R Company drops its guard a bit. Grimm circles the lobby's main seating area, teasing me with the sight of its soft, cushiony chairs, but pulls the rug out just as I'm about to sink into one and rest my tired, aching body.

"Stand, Lieutenant," he barks, still managing to make me jump a little even though my fatigued brain barely registers his order.

Everything in here is a cold, cruel shade of blue thanks to the light shining through the tower's glass walls, and Captain's eyes are giving off the exact same vibe. The long shadows eating up the room smack across his face, making that frown of his twice as pronounced. All right, Cap, I won't sit down for a damn second . . . yeesh.

"Delta Two." He turns his attention to McGregor's remaining troops. "You station here. Prep a blockade for when Delta One falls back." He looks each of the Marines in the eyes. "And let there be no doubt. Delta One will fall back."

He slides his visor down and turns away from the pack. With a hand gesture, he ushers me forward to join him. When I come up alongside him, he pauses.

"Sergeant," he says, looking over his shoulder at McGregor, "if you don't hear from me in an hour, abandon your post and come find us at the top of the tower. Bring Delta."

The sergeant nods, giving us the all-clear to abandon Delta Squad. As we march up the lobby's main staircase toward the second floor, Grimm lays out his plan.

"We have a little over sixty minutes left on the clock. I'm picking up broadcast frequencies on the floor above us," he says, analyzing his HUD from behind his visor's glowing eye lenses. "It looks like they originate from a communications terminal on the next floor. We'll check there first for anything useful and see if we can get word to Lieutenant Beecher, since he's ahead of us."

"And if we can't?"

"Then we take the first working elevator we find and stop the wipe ourselves."

"Can't you see his exothermic signature?" I ask, struggling to keep up with Grimm. God, my legs are fucking killing me. I hope nothing's broken.

"Negative, my outbound pings are jammed in here. We're on our own."

"Why aren't we bringing Delta for backup—"

"What?" The captain's voice is filled with annoyance; he's clearly preoccupied with tracking broadcast frequencies and guiding us through the second floor's maze of hallways. But busy or otherwise, I want answers.

"I mean, why did you only bring me?"

We arrive at a locked maintenance hatch. Grimm promptly busts the bolts off of it and rips it open, revealing a ladder.

"Because our mission is sensitive, and you—we, rather—may need to help Beecher," Grimm replies, climbing inside the opening.

"Help him with what?" I slide down the short ladder after Grimm, landing beside him in a hallway that looks pretty disconnected from the main route.

"Remembering the mission," Captain says, his tone unreadable.

We march down the path until we arrive at a locked door covered in yellow tape. I get the impression the Russian characters on the piss-colored warning label spell out something along the lines of "authorized commies only," but Captain doesn't care. He gives the door one good ACA-powered kick and sends it flying off its hinges.

As we step inside, Grimm gives the room a scan with his helmet. After a few sweeps, he spots something amidst a stack of computers and walks over to it. He tinkers with a few panels, revealing a touchpad.

"Found something good?" I ask, shuffling over to his position.

"Maybe. Hacking in now." He scans the pad until his helmet emits a low beep. Then he inputs a few codes, and presto, a speaker module affixed to a foam cube unfolds from one of the wire-covered cases in the wall facing us. It looks like exactly the kind of thing most modern office buildings use for PA systems. If I'm right, we should be able to reach Beecher easy-peasy.

But Grimm doesn't pay attention to it. Instead, he focuses

on the touchpad, inputting more codes until a little chip slides out of a neighboring computer tower.

"Want me to call Beecher?" I ask.

"No, hold in place." He pops the chip out of its slot and holds it against his helmet, downloading its info.

Man, I really wish I still had my ACA. I feel naked.

A few seconds later, Grimm finishes copying the chip's intel and slips it into a small storage compartment on his suit. He walks directly past the speaker module, heading in the direction of the maintenance hallway and ladder.

"Got a map file. We're close to a set of executive-level elevators that'll bring us straight to the top where the control center is. Closest way is to go two floors up then cut through the data archive hall; the elevators are on the far side of that room. Let's go."

I hold in place. "What about a transmission to Beecher?"

"No longer necessary," Grimm responds, beckoning for me to follow.

My mind tells me I should shut up and follow the leader, but my gut doesn't feel good about what's going on. "But Captain, he's ahead of us—what if he can do something right now? What if something goes wrong and we don't make it in time?"

He stops moving. Even with the captain's face hidden behind his visor, I sense his mood shift, and maybe I'm imagining it, but it feels like the room gets colder. Grimm doesn't say a word. He just tilts his head to the side a bit and looks at me for a good long second.

"Is James Beecher a good Marine, Lieutenant?" he asks after a beat.

I feel his gaze watching me—reading me.

"Best man I ever worked with, Captain."

"That's not what I asked," he replies, his tone souring as he looks me over one more time. "Change of plans."

He marches back over to where I'm standing and hits the speaker module's broadcast button. "Lieutenant Beecher, I know you're in here with us. I'm ordering you to return to the ground floor." He puts some extra emphasis on his next words. "It's urgent, and concerns Lieutenant Gourd." He stops broadcasting and marches back to the room's entrance.

What was that about? What concerns me?

I hustle after Grimm as fast as my legs will allow, trying to keep up as he makes his way down the hall toward the maintenance ladder.

"Cap, what on Earth-009 are you getting at? If I need to answer for something, I'll do it myself—"

"We don't have time," he says, beginning his climb back to the second floor.

"Excuse me, Captain, but you just used my name to—"

"I know what I did. Do I have your loyalty, Lieutenant?" He pauses to look down at me.

"That's not what I meant, Cap—"

"*I said*, do I have your loyalty?"

I lock up for a second.

". . . Yes, sir."

"Then you'll do your job by trusting me to do mine."

We climb the ladder in silence. When we reach the floor, Grimm turns to me, raising his visor so I can see his face. He's scowling, but I don't think his anger is meant for me. At least, I hope it's not.

"Lieutenant, James Beecher disobeyed a direct order, and I have no way of knowing where he is or what he's up to. I'm doing what must be done to uphold the mission."

Given how many years the guy has worked with him, I have a hard time believing Captain has so little trust in Beecher—probably the best lieutenant he's ever had. Besides me, of course. Anyway, it's not like Captain to be so . . . jumpy. Something's definitely off. But now isn't the time to question it.

"I understand." The lie tastes bitter. The last time I told a serious untruth to my commanding officer . . . well, I can't even remember it happening. Maybe it never has.

"Good. We're not far from the data archive hall, so let's move."

We hustle up the next two floors and the scenery changes. The higher we go, the more elaborate the architecture becomes and the bigger the rooms grow. The current area is so tall it's supported by columns, and I have to squint to see the ceiling. And while the first floors were loaded with office-typical overpriced-coffee-table bullshit, it looks like the dark matter's influence is what dominates the style choices of the current turf. Take, for example, the shit I'm walking past right now. Gone are the tacky, probably counterfeit paintings from ground level; up here, my flanks are lined with towering sculptures of naked men and women, and something does *not* feel right about them. It looks like they're made of black marble or some other kind of rock, but . . . I wonder . . .

I reach for the foot of one of the statues and instantly realize it's not made out of anything I've ever seen before. It goes from frozen statue to animated automaton the second my hand gets close. The other sculptures come to life as well, leaping up and around the columns, defying gravity as they jump toward the ceiling like zero-G ballet dancers, repeating little performances for us. Though I'm too confused to do anything, Grimm's still sharp as ever and draws his rifle, aiming down its sights at the statues bouncing around overhead, waiting for them to spring a surprise attack.

The attack never comes, and eventually both Cap and I calm down enough to keep moving forward once it's clear we're not being ambushed. No time to fret over distractions, after all; especially since living mannequin-things aren't the only decorations on display here. There are also more of those weird flowers we saw an hour or two ago, the ones that change shape and color. No doubt they're synthetic . . . but, even so, maybe I could give one of them a sniff. I lean in, hoping the Reds programmed these things to smell like lilacs—

Oof, Jesus, that's awful. Is . . . is that what the fuel smells like when it's turned into mulch?

"Quit fucking around," Grimm says a few yards up ahead.

I do as I'm told and get a move on, but just as I'm about to catch up to him, I pause again, spooked by the living sculptures scurrying down their columns and plucking petals from our overdesigned walkway's decorative flowers. Then, perfectly synchronized, they run up to the ceiling. They smear the petals above Grimm and me, painting the image of a flag— surprise, the Russian flag. Then all the sculptures, standing upside down on the ceiling, look down at us and start singing some creepy rendition of the Russian national anthem. At least, I think that's what it is. Just as I start to really listen to the melody, the voices stop. I blink, and all the dark matter flowers have regrown their plucked petals, the flag painting has dissolved into the ceiling, and the animated sculptures have started their whole routine from scratch.

I really don't like it here. I don't know if it's the eerie lighting or ultra-creepy decorations or a mixture of the two; I just know that everything here looks, smells, and sounds like a nightmare I once had. It gives me the heebie-fuckin'-jeebies, and I want out.

"How close are we, Captain?" I ask, silently praying to God we're almost out of the hall from hell.

"We're standing on the entrance walkway to the data archives; we're close."

He's right. Just a few short flights of stairs later we find ourselves in front of a door too tall and important-looking to not be what Grimm's been leading us to. As we get close, the door slides open automatically, revealing the archives within.

The room is so huge that it stretches from one side of the tower to the other. On one side, we're backlit by the black light coming from the front of the station. On the other, I see the rest of the Red Peril, including all the areas we've made it through. What a great view of bad shit.

"I need a minute," Grimm says, walking to the rows of holo-book racks beside us.

There are dozens of them, each stretching up toward a ceiling so high and drenched in darkness I can't even see what it looks like—it's just a speck somewhere hundreds of feet above me, up near where Beecher must be.

Fuckin' Beecher. I peer out the Spire's wall at the colony and all the hell he and I have endured to get here . . .

A day ago, he dug me out of a ditch I didn't think anyone

would help me out of, let alone could. And just a few hours ago, he did it again, hauling my sorry ass out of a grave I thought I'd be buried alive in. Hell, from where I'm standing right now, I can see the very ruins where he put his life on the line to save me. Every inch of the way through our journey he's been by my side, kicking ass and taking names. And now, at the eleventh hour, he's ditched me and everyone else.

Back in the shuttle, he made a big deal of saying that sometimes, in order to see the bigger picture, I have to see the smaller one. And I think I see it now: our military is only as good as the people who are a part of it, and it's the ones like Beecher who help make the universe a safer place.

So no matter what the guys below say, or even what Grimm thinks, I trust Beecher. I trust him more than anyone else in R Company. I just hope he knows what the hell he's doing up there, because time's running out.

I turn away from the window, from all the fires and smoke rising across the miles of land we traveled to get here, and return my focus to Grimm. Is he ready to go yet? Does he just wanna stand around in the archive all day reading data, or does he want to get a move on and actually save it?

I move to approach him, but stop dead in my tracks as he finally lifts his head from a holo-book screen and speaks for the first time in minutes.

"Damn it!" Grimm shouts, throwing his holo-book's palm-sized text projector onto the floor before tapping the shelf for another book. A new one slides down into his palm and he starts reading, until he freaks out and throws that one away, too. The hell is his problem?

Grimm yanks a third off the shelf and scrolls through its

digital pages, all of them loaded with random numbers, letters, and a whole slew of other shit I can't make heads or tails of. I don't understand what he's reading, but it's clear that the results of Captain's little literary detour don't make him a happy camper. He tosses the latest tiny projector over his shoulder, and it slides across the floor toward me. As it inches closer, its text disappears. By the time it reaches my feet, not a word is left inside the digital frame. Oh no.

Grimm keeps ripping holo-books off the shelves, scrolling through them as fast as he can, recording the texts with his helmet's scanner as he goes. But the words disappear too fast for him to keep up. He throws another holo-book in rage, and then another, and another.

"They're still wiping!"

He slams an armored fist into the rack in front of him. It dents the structure, bending its metals and knocking projectors off the shelves. The rack starts to curve in response to the hit, slowly but visibly caving in on itself.

"He's letting it happen." Grimm's tone is a bit too venomous for my liking. I know who he's talking about, and he's wrong. He has to be.

"You don't know what's happening to him up there," I fire back, cutting myself off the second I realize my reflexive blabbing just put me on the wrong side of Captain's mood.

"And you do, Lieutenant? Are you in on it?" he demands, raising his visor and stepping toward me.

"I ain't in on anything, Cap!" I protest, fighting every safety instinct in my body in order to stand my ground against the pissed-off CO in power armor. "You said the elevators are on the other side of the hall; let's stop arguing and get going!"

Grimm freezes. His eyes stay glued to my face.

"Why'd we even hang around here? Why didn't we just keep moving?" I ask, desperate to understand where the hell Grimm's coming from.

"I . . . wanted to be proven wrong." He turns away from me. "I'll go on ahead. You stay here."

"But—"

"That's an order."

He starts walking again, aiming for the elevators. Against my better judgment, I step forward to follow him.

"Don't move an inch, Lieutenant."

I can't stop them, though; my legs keep moving no matter what my brain tells them to do. My mouth also goes haywire, spouting shit I cannot control.

"What are you going to do up there if you find him?"

"Nothing."

I've almost caught up with Grimm, just as he's within sight of the elevators linked to the top of the Spire.

"That's a lie." I put a hand on his shoulder to stop his march. Big mistake.

His helmet's visor whips down, and he swings around faster than I can process, smacking my hand off with a force that sends my whole body spinning backward. I crash to the floor. For a few seconds, my aching body refuses to move. When I finally look up, Grimm is approaching me.

"The argument ends here, Lieutenant," he warns, getting closer as I struggle to lift my upper body off the floor. "Do not stand. As your commanding officer, I order you to stay down."

For the brief moment I'm able to hold my head up, I look at Grimm, right past his faceplate and into his eyes.

"No," I declare.

I tense, straining to lift myself with every last bit of energy I have left. I manage to get in a push-up position and start to stand up. Then a big, bulky metal boot presses down on my shoulder.

"Yes," he says, looking down at me. He applies more pressure, crushing me beneath him. But he doesn't stop pressing with his boot, even after he flattens me.

"You chose wrong," he hisses. "I know what you're up to. I know what you're all up to."

I don't know what the fuck he's talking about, and more importantly, I don't *care.*

"I don't know shit," I say, tensing my body one last time, "except you left me to die, and now you're threatening your best Marine."

I lift myself up again, overpowering Cap's boot. Grimm slackens for the briefest moment, caught off guard by the force of my resistance.

"And I ain't talking about Beecher."

I push up with all my strength and knock the captain's leg off me, putting him off balance just long enough for me to spring to my feet. The second I'm upright, Cap's already regained his footing and has his rifle pointed at my face.

I expect he's going to give some angry final warning or say a finisher line or something, but he doesn't. Before I can react, he pulls the trigger.

At the exact same moment, as my captain fires his rifle with every intention of finishing me off for good, an explosion knocks both of us off our feet. Cap's bullet barely misses my skull, grazing the hair above my ear. A spritz of blood blasts across the side of my head as the bullet wound opens itself, though I'm distracted from the stinging pain when Cap and I fall flat on our asses. What the hell just rocked our floor? Missile fire? I hear something rumbling in the distance, just beyond the Spire. The noise is growing louder very, very quickly.

Behind us, the glass wall that made up the south side of the data archive hall shatters, blasting icicle-sized shards across the room with lethal force. Where Cap and I are, protected behind rows of holo-book racks, none of the incoming debris hits us—but that's just phase one of the surprise.

An American fighter smashes through the window, coated in glass shards as it continues through the wall it's just destroyed and smashes through the shelves behind us. Grimm and I dive in opposite directions. The fighter barrels forward, ramming through the remaining racks until it's leveled the entire center of the room, leaving a thick wall of fire where its thrusters set the floor ablaze. It slows to a crawl on the other side of the room and then stops moving. At the same time, the trail of flames that's erupted between Grimm and me starts to die down. He's on the other side, staring in my direction. His visor's covering his face, but I don't need to see it to know that there's blood on his mind.

Thanks to our little shakeup, I'm now closer to the elevator than the captain is. He doesn't have his rifle anymore; he likely dropped it somewhere in the pool of fire that's probably melting the thing to scrap right now. If I make a run for it while the flames are still high, maybe I can beat him to—

I make a dash for the elevator, getting a good yard's worth of a head start before another surprise comes my way.

A burst of bullets whip past my face, just an inch away from tearing off my damn nose. That ain't the sort of aim that happens by accident. Those were warning shots. And they weren't from Grimm.

I turn to see who the owns the silhouette on my right, the one stowing their rifle and climbing out of the fighter's cockpit. The person is just a shadow at the current distance, surrounded by the flames of their busted, smoldering ship and hidden under the darkness of a network of smashed shelves twisting and warping above our heads, each one threatening to fall at any moment.

I glance over and see Grimm has his eyes laser-focused on the newcomer. I don't dare step toward the elevator again, since I know that's just gonna buy me a face full of bullets. Instead, I join Grimm in waiting for the new guy to step out of the shadows. I also keep an eye on the dissipating fire separating my captain and me. Warm blood drips down the back of my neck. Between the bruises, aches, and gashes scattered across my body, whatever vitality I have left better be enough to get me out of here.

Our mystery guest walks toward us at a leisurely pace, clearly in no rush now that they have our attention. As precious seconds tick by, I can't help but look back at the elevator, still just a few yards away.

"I wouldn't do that if I were you."

Why does that voice sound so familiar—

Our third wheel finally steps out of the shadows, and I make the connection. But it's not possible—it can't be him. There's no way he could've made it here; there's no way any friendly forces could've made it here. Unless . . .

"You traitorous piece of shit," Grimm growls, clenching his fists and adopting a fighting stance.

Looks like our new guest may not be so friendly after all.

CHAPTER 20

Gourd

Clad in shimmering blue ACA, complete with custom highlights, plating, and two iconic, wrist-bound retractable metal lassos, is the infamous leader of Virginia's 2nd Battalion, Colonel Bertram Artemis.

"Howdy there, boys," he says, his face hidden behind his voice-modulating visor. "What are the odds of seeing you here?" He laughs at his own joke.

Grimm and I don't move a muscle.

"Pretty high, I'd think," Captain responds dryly. "Anti-aircraft turrets aren't going to shoot down one of their own, after all."

Either Grimm's gone off his fucking rocker and is just pointing the finger at everyone, or he's been hiding something from me for way too long.

"So you think it's me, eh?" the colonel asks.

"I smelled treachery the second you landed on the station," Grimm answers, choosing to skip the banter and get right to the punching. He runs at Artemis full speed ahead, kicking his boots on to deliver a rocket-powered punch.

Artemis puts him down like a stray dog. With a lightning-fast flick of his wrist, the colonel extends one of his lassos and yanks back at just the right moment, catching Captain's legs. Grimm misses his punch and goes swirling across the floor as Artemis keeps him tied up, only releasing once the captain's boots are pointed in the direction of the Virginian's flaming fighter. With too much momentum to stop, Grimm flies at the burning ship, racing toward it like a giant blue bullet. The last glimpse I get of him is his armored body smashing through the craft, disappearing behind a shower of sparks and flames, eliciting another round of combustion.

My captain is gone. It's just Artemis and me. And something tells me my dragon skin armor isn't going to hold up against those lassos as well as Captain's ACA did.

"You wanna find out how tight these bad boys really are," Artemis challenges, reading my mind as he flicks the metal cables out of his suit's wrists, "or you wanna stay where you are and not end up like the sack of shit roasting to death inside my firepit over there?"

I glance down at my body armor, then back at his lassos. Then I lift up my hands.

"Good boy."

He keeps his distance, eyeballing me to make sure I don't have any tricks up my sleeve. Once he's convinced I'm just a battered, bruised warfighter who's completely out of options, he relaxes a bit.

"Now, you wanna tell me your name, Marine?"

I don't reply.

"Any day now," he says, sauntering around, though never straying more than a whip's length away from my position.

After a few seconds, he looks at me. "You know what? Take your time. By my count, we've got twenty minutes to kill, anyway."

My eyes go wide. "You . . . you know? You want to let it happen?"

"Did you ever think, Marine, that maybe your captain was playing tricks on you? I've known Grimm a long, long time, and the last time I trusted him . . ." As the colonel speaks, he raises his visor, giving me a clean look at his face. "I got this."

A scar stretches down the length of his face, all the way from the right tip of his forehead to the edge of his bushy silver mustache.

"He puts on a good show, sure, but when the chips are down, he'd leave you to rot," he posits, reading my face.

I try not to show what I'm thinking, but the second my lip twitches, he sees it.

"Ah, so you already know," he continues. "Well, then I can be frank. I care about the people I share my meals, beds, and days with. I do. Do you know how many men I've lost on to-day's mission?"

"How many . . ." I'm still not sure if I'm allowed to lower my arms. For a guy who claims to care about his fellow Marines so much, he sure likes flicking around those metal ropes of his.

"Zero. Not one. When the fight is over, every man in my battalion is going to go home to his wife and kids in a nice uniform. Not a body bag." He narrows his eyes at me. "Could Grimm say the same?"

Again, I try not to show any emotion, but my stupid fuck-ing face betrays me.

"So when I tell you we need to let that data wipe happen upstairs," he says, waving a hand to tell me I can lower my arms, "understand I'm saying it from a place of good intentions. That tech ain't gonna do nobody any good if it gets out of here."

"Okay . . ." I inch forward, now that Colonel Mustache thinks he's disarmed me. "But that still leaves me with a question."

"Shoot," he replies, letting me close the gap as I pour on the "dumb giant" act real thick.

I scratch my head, getting within arm's reach of him. "I'm just wondering . . . how did you know the data wipe is upstairs?"

His expression flips upside down. He realizes I'm still onto him, and before he can slip his visor back down, I land the biggest, hardest fucking punch of all time right on his nose. I pull my hand away and see it's splattered with blood.

Artemis stumbles backward a bit, his helmet immediately sealing and trapping those bloody, gushing holes of his inside with him. I don't know if someone can drown inside their own ACA, but I'd love to find out with the colonel. Just not right now.

While he's still reeling from the punch, I charge toward the elevator—also known as my ticket out of the shitshow—as fast as my feet will take me. Seconds pass, and it gets closer and closer until I'm an arm's length away, at which point I smash the touchpad with my hand, requesting that the doors please open right fucking now. Just to be safe, I hit the pad again, and again, and again, until the doors start to open, revealing the magic box that can take me to the top. I'm one step from freedom.

Something whistles through the air behind me, and a metal cord wraps around my ankle. It tugs at me, and before I know it I'm on my chest, being pulled across the ground, sliding over the all-but-dead flames still simmering in the center of the room.

The cord drags me until I'm about to slam into the wall on the opposite side of the room, at which point it releases me. I crash hard, and my right arm goes numb while the rest of my body screams in pain.

"Now why the hell would you go and do that?" Artemis asks with that damn acid tongue of his. My eyes are too watery to see him clearly. "I was gonna let you live!"

"Bullshit!" I shout back, still reeling from the hit. "You're an undercover agent for the Russians. I know whose lives you really care about!"

"Well, if you guessed my own and my family's, then I admit, you're on the money." He steps directly in front of me as I finally manage to open my eyes and see him for the traitor that he is. "But I really do hate unnecessary casualties."

He pulls out his rifle from the sheath on his back.

"Guess it's a good thing the next one's no longer unnecessary."

For the second time in five minutes, a superior officer points his gun at me, promising that I'm about to meet my maker. But then Grimm bursts out of the wreckage of the fighter behind us, and I know, for the second time, that I'm not ending here.

Artemis doesn't even have time to twist around before Grimm leaps into the air for a supercharged right hook, flames still rippling off his armor. He descends upon the colonel with all the fire and fury of an avenging angel. I roll out of the way and watch Cap clock Artemis in the face with such force that the traitor goes down in a single hit, smashing to the floor and dropping his rifle. A second after losing it, the colonel tries to grab it back, but Grimm's one step ahead of him and puts a rocket boot over the gun. He activates his thrusters and heats the firearm to dangerous temperatures, slagging the metal just enough to ruin functionality while using the rest of his body to pin down his opponent.

"You're done," Grimm hisses, hammering Artemis with a brutal punch to the back of the head. Then another. And another. At the rate he's coming down on the guy, even with the ACA, I'd wager the Virginian has another couple of seconds left before his head's too banged up to work anymore.

Since Grimm's busy giving the colonel his just desserts, now seems like a perfect time for me to get the fuck out of here and try to get a hold of Beecher—

"Halt, Lieutenant," the captain barks, spotting me across the room.

In that moment of distraction, Artemis sees his window and flings Grimm off of him. He hops to his feet and, before I can react, swings a lasso at me, catching me by the chest. He pulls me forward with enough force that my feet leave the ground. I hurl through the air until I'm within range of him, at which point he smashes me with a gut punch so strong that I crumple over, paralyzed. The lasso unwraps and slips back around Artemis's wrist as he goes to block an incoming blow from Grimm, who's back in action just a few feet away from my winded, floored body.

I stay down, unable to move a muscle as the two men

square off. Since I'm cut off from the other side of the room, the best thing I can do is watch as Grimm and Artemis give each other hell, and wait for an opening—if not from them, then from my body telling me it's willing to get going again.

As I work on relearning how to breathe, Artemis lands a hit on Grimm. Shit, that fire he was cooking in probably toasted his nanogel; now every blow is going to land ten times harder. With the way Grimm reacts to the hit, it looks like he's realizing the same thing. Recovering remarkably quickly for someone who just got ACA-socked, he gets over the pain and starts slamming the colonel before he can whip out the lassos. Grimm's arms move faster than I can keep up with, whaling on Artemis as though killing him will single-handedly save the country. Pretty sure Cap thinks it actually will, given how relentlessly he's going at it. For every punch Artemis blocks, he eats two more, and even in his damaged state, Grimm starts to overpower his opponent, boxing him into a bad position between his fists and one of the crumpling holo-book racks.

Grimm keeps up his flurry of attacks, rocking and socking the colonel at a rate so aggressive it looks like even Artemis's nanogel is having a hard time blocking the full force of the impacts. One gut-punch in particular sends the Virginian smashing into the shelf Captain has cornered him against, and before either of them know it, the whole thing starts to fall.

Hundreds of pounds of twisting and folding metal groan as the nearly ceiling-high rack tilts downward. Its foundation, already warm and soft from the fires that've been blazing for the past few minutes, melts apart like butter on a hot knife. Then the top of the rack breaks free and hurtles toward all three of us below.

I close my eyes, fully prepared for it to smash onto the ground and grind me to dust beneath it. But after a few seconds of ear-splitting noise, I realize none of the incoming debris is on track to hit me. Instead, it's going to bury Artemis and Grimm alive.

My captain sees the incoming hazard and drags the fallen colonel off the floor, tossing him right beneath the rapidly growing shadow of the largest pile of airborne scraps. Like clockwork, Grimm slips out of the way and earns the pleasure of watching Artemis get crushed by pound after pound of hard metal crashing out of the sky, raining down directly onto the man's ACA with a force I shudder to imagine.

The biggest piece fails to hit the ground. Instead, it gets wedged between a pair of still-standing shelves. It hangs over the pile that's buried Artemis, unwilling to drop. Grimm looks at it for a moment, unsure if he should try to shake the nearby racks to make it fall, but then, seeming to realize how much time the whole scuffle has already wasted, decides against it.

Instead, he dashes toward me. Without the nanogel swirling around his suit, I can just barely make out his eyes through his visor. They look angry . . . confused . . . tired . . . but also—God, I hope I'm reading him right—concerned.

"Lieutenant, can you move?"

I simply let out a groan, still not sure I want to voluntarily move any part of my body.

"Come on," he barks, hand outstretched. "You need to get up."

Why, why now? Does he . . . he . . . care? . . . I can't move my chest, or my legs, or arms, or anything else I should normally be able to move, and I can't feel much of anything . . . but deep down, I do feel one singular thing: a pang of gratitude. And in that moment, I start to regain control over the rest of my body.

Though it hurts like a bitch, I find the strength to raise my arm, feebly reaching for his hand. He grabs it and slowly, gently starts to pull me up.

"You just saw it; we've been infiltrated. We need to stop Beecher before he cripples our entire military."

Instantly, I let go of his hand and fall back to the floor.

"Lieutenant!" he shouts as I crash against the ground, having lost whatever magical sliver of strength I had a second ago.

"He's not . . ."

"He's not what? Betraying our nation? Not spitting on everything we've worked for? Not aiding an enemy hellbent on destroying you, me, and everyone we care about?"

Grimm yanks his hand back and stares at me with disgust.

"You sicken me, Lieutenant." His voice is cold and foreign in a way I've never heard it before. "Your punishment for insubordination will be severe. For now, enjoy your rest while I handle Beecher and make the choice you never could."

As he turns away from me, I hear a familiar whistle in the air. I don't have time to get a word out to warn Grimm before it's too late. The lasso shoots from beneath a shuffling pile of scrap, which displaces to reveal a seriously banged-up Artemis crawling out and regaining his footing. The metal cord wraps around Grimm's waist, tugging him toward the colonel with a degree of speed and strength he can't fight. On the other side of the room, Artemis shoots his other lasso over the wedged metal beam dangling a few feet above him, lowering the looped side over the edge to form a noose.

The second Grimm is pulled back far enough, Artemis flicks his wrist and the dangling noose slides around my captain's neck. The colonel tugs on it, yanking Grimm into the air by his throat. Before Captain can use his rocket boots to escape, Artemis releases the lasso around his waist and relocates it a few feet south, right around his shins. That doesn't stop Grimm from trying to kick the boots on and break free, but the little bursts he manages are easily countered by some smart counter-pulls from Artemis.

The ACA's neck brace is thick, but I have no clue how long it can hold up against the kind of metal the colonel's lassos are made of. If they manage to chafe through the brace . . .

And as if that weren't enough, now I'm in the worst position of all; the elevator is blocked by the fucking psycho trying to lynch my commanding officer. God, come on, body, work again . . . damn it, *work*.

"Can't say I imagined it going down like it's about to," Artemis announces, sounding supremely self-satisfied, "but I won't lie, I'm loving every second of it."

"Tell me . . ." Grimm coughs, struggling to gather enough air to speak, "how long has your double-dealing been going on?"

It's not a question, it's a request—a request for some closure as he prepares to die. I hear it in his voice.

"Grimm, I'm disappointed. I know we've had our differences over the years, but really, you let that petty anger of yours blind you the whole time? Who do you think leaked the research to the Russkies in the first place?"

But . . . no, the president said . . .

"Bertram . . ." Captain starts, straining to gulp down more air before asking his question. "Do the Russians have the research backed up somewhere?"

Artemis laughs.

"That's above my pay grade, Gerard," he says with a warmth that makes it sound like he's talking to an old friend. "All I know is, I can't let you stop that data wipe."

With his closing statement spoken, Artemis gives the noose another tug.

C'mon, Lieutenant, pick yourself up. *Pick your damn self up!*

Once again, I feel the tingle, the spark in my fingertips and toes that tells me something's happening.

I haven't come so far just to let a filthy fucking turncoat hiding in power armor get the best of Sierra Squad or, more importantly, get the best of me. And in a few seconds, that fucker is going to know it.

Artemis pivots to counter another one of Grimm's rocket boot flare-ups, forcing him to shuffle to the side and put his back to me. It's as clear an opening as I'm going to get, so I take it. I ball my fists and push against the floor, forcing my upper body to rise one last time. Foot by foot, I get myself standing, the light noise I create muffled by that of the crackling fires, screeching metals, and other chaos surrounding me. The colonel's not gonna hear a thing until it's too late.

I take one step forward to make sure I can move without collapsing. I can. So I take another step forward. And another. Within seconds, I've regained the ability to run, and I don't hold back. I charge like a rhinoceros at the Bolshevik bitch in blue, and just as he senses something's coming for him, I slam into the fucker like a damn boulder, knocking him to the ground.

Immediately after I gift Artemis's face a one-way ticket to the floor, both lassos loosen to the point where Grimm falls through them, leaving him to hurtle downward and crash beside me. He doesn't land on his feet, though; the half-suffocated captain lands on his back and coughs up a storm from inside his helmet. Thankfully, Artemis isn't doing much better—after all the traumatic head injuries that fucker's suffered since he stepped foot in the data archive, my last knock to the ground seems to have an impact, sending his dumb little noggin bouncing around one time too many. Good fucking riddance. But I can't do any more damage; my bare fists won't impact his armor in the slightest, and he's not why I'm up and about, anyway. I have bigger priorities—I have a squadmate to find.

I make one more dogged attempt to reach that damn elevator. I shuffle past the piles of scrap and destroyed racks littering the floor, navigate around the thin streams of remaining fire, get past all the bullshit, and finally, *finally* make it back to the elevator. Pressing a weary hand against its touchpad, I nearly faint when the doors open. Somehow, I manage to stay strong and make it inside the damn thing.

Before the elevator doors close, I see the captain climb on top of Artemis and start to pummel him once more. Though the scraps on the ground block my view of the colonel's body, I can only imagine that savage blows like the ones he's receiving mark the end of his run as an undercover commie. It's scary seeing Grimm go berserk. But what scares me more is the look he gives me when he stops breaking the body he's on top of and spots me in the elevator.

That look is the last thing I see before the doors close and I'm whisked off to the top of the Spire.

CHAPTER 21

Beecher

Eight minutes.

Only eight minutes left on the timer. We were that close to losing all the marbles for good. Now I just have to babysit the wipe for the final stretch and make sure it happens.

A nervous jitter runs through my body as I look out the glass walls of the command center, toward the dark matter storm raging just beyond the Spire. With every passing second, thousands of petabytes of the most valuable military research in the history of man are being wiped from existence, their purge monitored by none other than myself. The two technicians who were stationed here lie in the eastern corner of the unlit room, slumped behind a desk next to the elevator shaft, concealed in shadows so no one can see their bloody, beaten faces. That leaves the rest of the sweeping, panoramic overlook untainted by the ugly face of death. I've seen enough of that today.

If I make it out of here alive, no doubt I'll be held for high treason, sentenced to a military execution, and put down like any other war criminal—the whole nine yards. If that's the price of preserving the universe's freedom for a bit longer, I'm game. I'll take a meaningful death over a regretful life any day of the goddamn week.

Can I be sure what I'm doing is right? No, not at all. The only thing I *can* be sure of, the only thing I know without a doubt, is that power corrupts, and absolute power like the kind being dealt with here in the colony would corrupt absolutely. I can't let a stain like that spread onto the red, white, and blue flag I've dedicated my life to protecting. I hope Gourd forgives me when he finds out what happened here.

I drum my fingers against the master control monitor, watching the remaining data percentage dwindle. It almost hurts, seeing it all flushed down the drain, the collective work of humanity's best scientific minds scrubbed from the tower's servers and subsequently from history itself. If Faust was telling the truth when she said the colony was the sole home in the universe to Russia's variant of the fuel, then only those of us who fought here today will have ever had to experience a world where it was successfully militarized.

I hover over the monitor, hoping sheer desire will make the data erase faster, fast enough that it'll all be over before—

"Beecher!" Gourd stumbles out of the elevator behind me, his breath quick and voice concerned.

Why? Why did he have to come here?

"Man, you're not safe. Cap's gunning for you. He thinks . . ."

"That I'm an obstacle?" I turn around to face him. He looks awful; his condition's way worse than it was back in the courtyard.

"That you're an undercover Russian operative," Gourd

replies, flailing his arms, closing the gap between us. "Because you disobeyed an order, and we just found out Colonel Artemis was working with the Russians."

My whole body freezes. "That explains it . . ."

"Spit it out!" Gourd says, shaking my shoulders.

"He's been suspicious of me ever since we left Wesley behind. I heard him try to bait me over the PA system. He's sure I want to sabotage the mission."

I know what Gourd's going to say before the words are spoken. I can't even bring myself to look him in the eyes.

"Well, that's bullshit," he says, spotting the big flashing monitor behind me, obviously not stopping to wonder why I've positioned myself so carefully in front of it. He marches past me to see with his own eyes that I've stopped the data wipe, per my orders, like a good Marine.

"But that's the thing, Gourd . . ."

He leans over to examine the panel, his eyes growing wide as he sees the wipe's status.

"I do."

Seven minutes.

"Why?" he shouts, extending a hand to commandeer the control panel.

Before he can reach it, I catch him with my functioning ACA arm and hold him in place, the two of us a near equal match of force. Gourd without any armor at his current strength versus a reluctant me in a half-functioning suit would be too close of a fight to call in advance, and we can't let it come to that. *I* can't let it come to that.

"You saw what it did: the planet, the machines, Alpha Squad. All of it! It's too dangerous as a weapon!" I shoot back.

"That's the same bullshit Artemis said," Gourd roars. "You're one of them?"

He dives for the panel, but I whip around and hook my arms under his shoulders, restraining him.

"I don't care what Artemis said; I've never met him. And I'm not one of them. Got it?"

"You're lying!"

With his upper body still trapped by my arms, he lifts his legs and kicks off against the control panel, knocking us both backward. We fall to the floor, landing within a few inches of each other. Not giving Gourd a chance to sit up, I roll over and climb on top of him, again restraining his arms as best I can.

"Stop it! I don't know what the fuck you saw or heard, but I don't care! I'm not doing what I'm doing because of anyone else!"

His face flashes with confusion before getting angry again. He finds a reserve of strength I'm not expecting and knocks me off, proceeding to reverse our roles and get on top of me, trapping my weary frame against the floor.

"You're betraying our military!" He raises a fist, gearing up to knock my lights out.

"I'm saving it!" I yell. "You want the blood of billions on your hands when an officer tells you to wipe out a planet with dark matter? Huh?"

He pauses.

Seeing my opening, I don't let up. "Wes saw the problem. I saw the problem. Why can't you? Sure, the fuel will help us beat the Russians. But then what? We make every other nation and our own goddamn citizens scared of us when we whip out dark matter every time there's a conflict?"

"The military wouldn't use it like that!" His voice is raw, but his resolve is starting to crack.

Behind him, I spot the monitor's reflection on an adjacent glass panel.

Six minutes.

"No, *you* wouldn't use it like that. You really think everyone cares as much as us? Up until a few minutes ago, we thought guys like Artemis were on our side! Do you get it?" As I continue, he eases some of his weight off me. "All it takes is one bad apple for what we found here to kill everyone and everything we love."

Gourd's fist remains balled up as he looks at me for the longest second of my life. It'd almost feel invasive if I wasn't staring at him the same way. Does he understand? Is he following?

He smashes his fist down.

I flinch.

It hits the floor next to me.

"You don't know it'd turn out like that," he says, still seething, his breathing heavy and ragged.

"You're damn right I don't. And I don't want to find out. Do you want to see the US turn into one nation under fear, not God?"

He slackens his hold and looks away to avoid my gaze, probably half pondering what I'm saying and half ashamed he didn't think everything through on his own already.

"Look, Gourd," I say, desperately wanting to get off the floor, "I'm not going to fight you. So smash my head in and finish the mission, or get off me."

He stares at me again, clenches his jaw, then makes his decision and rolls off. With a bit of effort, I get my tired body standing and glance over at the control panel's flashing monitor.

Five minutes.

"But," Gourd says, forcing himself to stand as well, "we don't know if the Reds have the data backed up somewhere else. It might be for nothing." He moves toward the panel, extending an uncertain, shaking hand toward it. Just as he's about to undo my efforts to make the universe a safer place, he pauses.

"It might. But I'm choosing to believe our president's dying words," I tell him.

He looks straight at me, searching for something. "Either way," he says, "it's only a matter of time until they replicate the lost research and cook up another batch of fuel. And if our side doesn't have it by then, how can we fight them?"

I hear the skepticism in his voice. But I've talked him down so far; I'm not stopping now.

"Like we did today. We don't need to sink to their level to win."

We keep staring, each unsure if the other is really willing to go through with either version of what comes next. After all, is it worth letting the research go? If we secure the station, the US government's going to swoop in and immediately start reverse engineering every bit of tech from the robots to the cannon. Given the preliminary research our side already has, it'll likely be just months before they figure out the small stuff and definitely no more than a decade before they crack whatever scientific secrets are behind the big shit here. At best, we'd be sacrificing our careers . . . our lives . . . just to buy mankind another few years.

On the other hand, if we pause the data wipe, the US will be unstoppable almost instantaneously. And if Russia refuses to bend its knee, it'll cease to exist. Just like any other nation that kicks up a fuss.

No matter which way things go, we lose. But at least with the first option, we buy the rest of humanity time to win. After all, a lot can happen in a few years—years the rest of the universe won't have if the research here ends up in the hands of remorseless bureaucrats and soldiers thanks to our inability to act.

Something changes on Gourd's face as I watch him digest the reality of the situation. I see the glimmer of hope in his eyes—the one clinging to the idea that there can still be a happy ending for us—disappear.

"I think you're wrong . . ." he mumbles. "But I'd hate to live to see the day that you're right."

Against all odds, the ogre-sized bald eagle removes his hand from the control panel and shuffles beside me, signing on to help make sure the biggest military advancement in history slips through our fingertips.

"Thank you," I say. It's all I can muster.

Four minutes.

"Don't thank me yet. Cap's gonna be here any minute now, and he won't be looking to play games."

We share a tense moment of silence.

"Maybe we can try to explain to him—" Gourd starts, but it's wasted breath.

"He's been ready to leave us for dead based on a bullshit hunch," I remind my squadmate. "You really think now that he has hard evidence for his theory he's going to listen to a word we have to say?" Gourd and I look at each other once more as we let the thought of what's coming next sink in. "He has a mission to complete and just a few minutes to do it; you know what his plan is."

"He's not going to go down easy," Gourd warns.

"Neither are we. You need to hide. Behind that desk." I point to where I've stored the technicians in the corner by the elevator. It's the only cover in the room; the rest of the floor consists of nothing but open space lined with a row of control panels.

"He knows I came up here, man. He'll be looking—"

"Let's bank on him being distracted by what I have behind me," I say, patting the monitor. No way in hell Captain will care about Gourd's whereabouts if he sees I'm busy dicking around with the most important hard drive in the universe.

Gourd plays along and dashes behind cover, hunkering beside the bodies while we await our captain's arrival. Leaning back against the monitor with both hands, I get comfy and make it clear I have something to hide. When those elevator doors open, all Grimm will care about is the forbidden fruit.

Right on schedule, just as I've relaxed my body in anticipation of the hardest confrontation of my life, the elevator slides into place inside the metal shaft on the opposite end of the room.

Three minutes.

The doors slowly part, revealing the outline of my captain's battle-tarnished armor, its appearance every bit as worn down as my own. The man inside the suit walks toward me, displaying no signs of overt hostility. Yet.

"Stellar move back there," he says. "Really, Lieutenant. You've done our country a great service today."

He keeps inching closer.

"Thank you, Captain," I respond, my tone guarded. The man could nail me to a cross right now if he wanted to. Hell, who's to say that's not coming up.

"Now step aside."

I don't move.

"That's an order, Lieutenant."

"I know, Captain."

"*Move*," he yells, his already intimidating voice amplified by his helmet's speech modifier as he gets within arm's reach of me.

Out of the corner of my eye, I see Gourd slowly creep out from his hiding spot, beginning his silent approach toward Grimm. It's a good move on his part, since we're on the clock and it's clear that time is running out . . . for me.

"I'm not with the enemy; that's not why I'm doing what I'm doing."

"I don't care." He thrusts his arms forward to shove me out of the way.

"You're not stopping that wipe, Captain."

I move to counter his attack, but just as the *ain* in *captain* leaves my lips, Grimm locks me in a position where I'm crushed beside the control panel, unable to move a muscle. His left hand traps my neck against the monitor's edge as his right tries to turn my head into mush. The only thing that stops his punch from landing is my best friend. Captain's reflexes are too good for either of us individually, but maybe not for both of us together.

Gourd tries to get his arms underneath Captain's shoulders to lock him up, but my ally's strike isn't swift enough. Grimm spirals around and backhands him with what sounds like just one notch less than the ACA's full force, though that's still easily enough power to knock some teeth out. His retaliation against the sneak attack opens him up for me. While Grimm's back is turned, I go for a headlock, reaching my remaining exoskeleton-powered arm right around his neck. From there, I kick my suit's saw blade on so it starts slicing against his helmet's chin guard with enough force to create some sparks and blind him, the momentary distraction I need to get my other arm around the armor and yank the thing off his head entirely. I rip upward with all the force my biceps can muster, snapping the neck brace's lock in half and sending the helmet flying off.

That evens the playing field a little, though not enough to stop Grimm from landing an elbow jab right in my gut. The hit locks me up for the fraction of a second he needs to swing around and go for a punch that'll take my head off, one that I dodge by the length of the stubble on my upper lip. As he recovers from the swing, I rocket-boost my right knee into his contorted chest. My attack sends him into the ceiling, his hefty frame and exposed head slamming into it with knockout-level force before he collapses onto the ground.

Looking at his unmoving body, I'd say I've bought myself enough time for a peek over my shoulder.

Two minutes.

I swear, if Grimm will just stay down, the day's ugliness can finally end—

No time for finishing that thought. He kicks his boots to

life and rockets toward my shins, knocking me off my feet and onto the floor behind him. I can't even roll over before Grimm has my right leg in a lock, my boot's thruster held above his head so he can dodge my attempts at melting his face off.

Using the combined force of his exoskeleton's arms, he prepares to put me out of the game. With one hand underneath my thigh and the other squeezing my shin, he forces my right leg backward, pushing it into the air until—SNAP—it's perfectly straight at a ninety-degree angle against my flat-on-the-ground chest. My thigh muscle splits in half. Connective tissue pulls from the bone inside my whining suit's sparking, battered shell. I let out an animalistic scream.

The only thing that stops Grimm from ripping the entire limb off is my other leg's rocket kicking to life just in time for me to spin out of his grip and blast across the floor. I clear the area, and Gourd's massive fist fills the void where my almost-detached leg just was, landing a blow right across our enemy's face. He slams the captain's mug with perfect knuckle-to-nose contact, smashing Grimm through a deactivated monitor and onto the floor with a thud. But as I just found out the hard way, even repeated head trauma won't do the guy in.

Gourd's one step ahead of me. Just as Grimm weakly tilts his head back up, my ally drags him out from underneath the shattered monitor and delivers another punch. And another. And *another*. I know the captain's out cold for sure by now, but that doesn't stop Gourd. With each smash, the lieutenant's knuckles, then arms, then face become more splattered with blood, the red juice doing little to mask my friend's fury.

It's only when I hear the crunch of a skull shattering that Gourd's animalistic rage subsides and I know it's over. Unwilling to even have the man's body in our vicinity, Gourd slides him across the room like an oversized curling stone into the corner with the Russians. At least the pile of bodies is consistent—no one in it knew where to draw the line.

Now that the captain's out of commission, Gourd rushes over to help me, which we quickly realize means simply propping me up against the countdown monitor like a bulky rag doll, since my right leg's not going to be lending me support anytime soon. Sitting against the monitor, still panting and recovering from the pain of Gourd readjusting my position, I manage to eke out a question.

"How much . . . time?" I ask, barely able to resist the blackness edging into the corners of my vision.

"One minute."

He slumps down beside me. His cheek, in the whole sixty seconds or so it's had to flare up since he got smacked, is puffy as hell. No doubt a few teeth are missing, too. Blood trickles down his forehead where he slammed into the ground and reopened his wound from earlier, and the miscellaneous bruises all over his body from the past few days' worth of suffering haven't added up nicely. If it weren't for my own condition, I'd say I've never seen someone who's still breathing look worse.

Neither of us manages a word as we sit next to each other, waiting out the last sixty seconds of our mission. My heavy breaths and constant gasps of pain alternate with Gourd's grunts, the only bouts of silence between us being those brief few seconds when I'm close to passing out and have to force myself to stay conscious.

Our quietness persists even as the ominous glow emanating from the front of the station disappears and the dark matter's shadow fades from view, replaced by faint rays of artificial light coming from farther down the colony. In the distance, enemy fighters fall from the sky, their silver jet streams dissolving into thin air as their fuel writes itself out of existence. The robots in the streets below us cease activity as well, becoming lifeless scrap.

The deletion protocol has done its duty to ensure all traces of the station's greatest experiment are scrubbed from reality in an instant, with every drop of concentrated dark matter heeding the call of the remote dissolution order beckoned by the Spire.

No words need be exchanged. We've received the only indications we need to know the wipe has finished.

Even if Gourd and I have only postponed the inevitable, I'm confident it was worth it. That's the last thought I have in me as my body starts to shut down, but Gourd keeps me awake just a smidgen longer.

"You know . . . you know they'll be coming for us up here," he says.

"You're right . . . and they'll get us. But . . . but it's okay, 'cause . . ." I sputter, unable to finish my thought as the world goes black. One last time, my best friend has me covered.

". . . I'm with you 'til the bitter end."

If you enjoyed this novel, please consider leaving a review at your favorite book retailer's website. Reviews from enthusiastic readers are vital to authors everywhere. Your support is greatly appreciated!

———

ABOUT THE AUTHOR

Robert Carnevale lives in New York due to his unflinching, patriotic love of high taxes. He is an author, not a Cosmo Marine, and as such, has taken artistic liberties with depictions of the latter's activities. He thanks you for going on this journey with him and hopes this story has encouraged some thought regarding the nature of war, loyalty, and propaganda. To learn more about Robert and his literary endeavors, including upcoming science fiction novels, visit www.rcarnevale.com.

CPSIA information can be obtained
at www.ICGtesting.com
Printed in the USA
LVHW052158180922
728694LV00002B/213

9 781948 374439